GREAT RIVER

GREAT RIVER

By Glen Pitre and Michelle Benoit

PELICAN PUBLISHING COMPANY
GRETNA 1993

The word "Pelican" and the depiction of a pelican are trademarks of Pelican Publishing Company, Inc., and are registered in the U.S. Patent and Trademark Office.

Library of Congress Cataloging-in-Publication Data

Pitre, Glen, 1955-
  Great River : a novel / Glen Pitre and Michelle Benoit.
    p. cm.
  ISBN 0-88289-783-7
  1. La Salle, Robert Cavelier, sieur de, 1643-1687—Fiction.
2. Mississippi River Valley—Discovery and exploration—
French—Fiction.   3. Indians of North America—Mississippi
River Valley—Fiction.   4. Explorers—America—Fiction.
I. Benoit, Michelle.   II. Title.
PS3566.I845G74   1993
813'.54—dc20   93-22333
                                                              CIP

Manufactured in the United States of America

Published by Pelican Publishing Company, Inc.
1101 Monroe Street, Gretna, Louisiana 70053

For Margaret, Emelia, and Loulan

ACKNOWLEDGMENTS

Thanks to Newton Renfro, for his research, inspiration, and a dedication as profound as La Salle's own. To Annick Smith and Eddie Kurtz, for paddling along with us around every bend in the voyage. To Katie Callais and the Louisiana Catalog crew, for protecting us so we could write. To Peter Turner, for always believing. To Nina Kooij, for her sharp blue pencil. And special thanks to the many research libraries and librarians in Louisiana, Quebec, and California who made this book possible.

CHAPTER ONE

THE ALARM BELL CLANGED LOUDER than the frantic yelling of the tenants, louder even than the fretful cries of their livestock.

A bitter wind chased the sounds along the St. Lawrence River, rippling the rust hues mirrored from its bank. Leaves rode on the current, eddying around a large branch that months earlier had formed part of a beaver's dam far to the north.

For years the dam had housed the fat animals and created the pond in which they lived and mated and fed. Then a party of Algonkian Indians set snares around the dam. The beaver were trapped, bludgeoned and skinned, their furs carefully prepared. A fair-skinned stranger of an unknown nation wintered in a nearby village. For beaver skins he traded colorful cloth and ribbons, even precious beads each Algonkian was anxious to add to his buckskins.

With no beaver to maintain it, the dam fell apart. The pond reverted to a stream, and the beavers' absence was soon forgotten as other trapping grounds were found.

The branch glided past a rocky clearing where a young man watched the river warily. Here the bank had been shaved into an easy landing for canoe and longboat. The young man, La Salle, did not pause to consider the origin of

9

the branch gliding by. Even on a normal day he would have been too hurried for such idle speculation. Today, all he had worked for was at stake.

Back from the river, above the flood line, a tall stockade marked a trading post. Scattered beyond it several small cabins breathed trails of gray smoke—empty cabins now, for the women, men, and children who lived inside them were herding their livestock through the stockade gates. Chill winds flattened the billowing whites and browns of their clothes against their work-hardened bodies. Seeking shelter behind the manor's walls was instinct for generations of French, but this was the New World, with new dangers and new, frightfully unfamiliar enemies. The manor was nothing more than a few cabins within a rough palisade of sharpened logs, after the fashion of the Indians.

At river's edge, La Salle braced himself against the wind as he drew a brass spyglass from its dark leather casing. Deep furrows across his face showed where wrinkles would someday form, but today the creases were temporary, born of intense concentration. He tucked the spyglass case into the waist of his britches and extended the instrument to its shiny length. Strands of brown hair whipped loose from the tie at the nape of his neck, stinging his clean-shaven face. Grimacing, he fixed his sights on the horizon, but he saw nothing amiss, not yet.

Behind him La Salle heard running footsteps, and someone puffing from exertion. He turned, ready to fight, but it was only Henri, his personal servant, lugging a matchlock musket. Beyond Henri, up the shore, La Salle watched anxious homesteaders hurrying into the stockade.

"They've all been warned," Henri panted.

"Distribute extra arms. From the cabinet in my chambers."

Henri gaped at La Salle. Unknown tribes had appeared near La Chine before but never had its proprietor unlocked the munitions cabinet.

"The key," La Salle said as he offered it to Henri, but instead of taking it, his servant began to strike flint against metal to spark a flame onto his musket. The matchlock's hammer held a wick that when released lit a reservoir of powder that exploded a shot from the gun. Unlit, the weapon was useless, but the intermittent breeze frustrated Henri's efforts.

"I'll do that, Henri. You go. . . ."

"Didn't the Algonkians tell us the Seneca were coming? The Seneca, Monsieur La Salle! I'll not leave you here undefended!"

Henri's audacity was uncharacteristic. Any other time, even while inwardly admiring his loyalty, La Salle would have reprimanded him for disobeying orders, but today La Salle understood Henri's fear.

Almost every man at the post had been called up at some point to beat off Iroquois raiding homesteads on the edge of Montreal. Justly or not, the Seneca were reputed to be the cruelest Iroquois tribe. A bitter flavor rose in La Salle's mouth, recalling the taste after he'd been sick, physically sick, at seeing what the Seneca had done to some settlers the Frenchmen had reached a half-hour too late. He had tried hard not to show such weakness in front of the others, but the sight had overcome him. He had not been the only one.

Why were the Seneca coming? They were the only remaining member of the Iroquois Confederacy not to acknowledge New France's call for peace. La Salle himself had been among the first to persuade the governing bodies that a peace treaty had to be reached with all five Iroquois tribes. Without it New France's horizons could never expand. The Iroquois had the most abundant source of furs, and the Seneca, the most western tribe, controlled all trade from the west and the south. Acting on behalf of England, they had countered French expansion by refusing trade, and massacring any voyagers who attempted to go beyond Iroquois territory . . . territory that Europeans, French or English, had yet to survey.

Unnamed, unknown lands with riches I can only imagine, La Salle thought. If I can convince them to trade . . . he wondered about the families cringing inside the stockade, and Henri at his side frantically trying to ready the musket. He sighed as he turned to pry the unlit musket from Henri's hands.

"Go back to the post, Henri. Reassure the others."

"They'll slaughter you!" Henri cried.

La Salle's throat flushed red. The danger was real, but needlessly losing any member of his trading post was an unwarranted price. Henri would be safer in the stockade. La Salle alone would meet the natives.

"I'm certain," he lied, "they've come to trade."

"Seneca trade with the English!" Henri shouted. "We French, they scalp!"

"From godless land, we've pulled a good life," La Salle responded calmly. "In the name of King Louis and the new treaty, I will implore them to rest here."

His jaw slack, eyes wide with fright, Henri could not make himself move.

"Go," La Salle commanded. "Now!"

In a flash of panic, Henri sped up the shore. Only when shortness of breath began to slow him did he start to wonder how he would explain to the others. Never before today had he questioned La Salle's authority. Like everyone else he had heard the warnings when he accepted the position of manservant to the young trader homesteading on the farthest western edge of New France. It had been a perilous venture. Henri counted the times like today, when he was prepared to believe he and his master would not live to see nightfall.

But within a year, La Salle had proven an able diplomat with the local Indians. With hard work and more families joining the post, they had all prospered. La Salle's reputation as a foolhardy pioneer had been replaced by one of a successful adventurer constantly blazing new trails into the wilderness interior.

"From godless land, we have pulled a good life," Henri practiced telling the others, trying to muster the eloquence Monsieur La Salle commanded so easily.

Henri made it through the gates just before the nervous homesteaders closed them. He was confident now he could convince them of La Salle's plan. Instead, they nearly broke his limbs venting their frustration over the calamity paddling toward them.

"Monsieur La Salle will discover their intent," Henri blurted at the belligerent tenants. "But we must arm ourselves, and provide him cover." Fear swept their anxious faces.

La Salle tried to ignore the harried rise of voices from the post. He turned his attention to scan the horizon for signs of the Seneca.

Do they really come to trade, he worried. La Salle looked back at the stockade, measuring the length of time it would take to gain its safety. How much of the local trade jargon do they understand, he wondered as he nervously pulled out a kerchief to wipe the lens of his spyglass. If I concentrate on replacing the more French terms with Algonkian words . . . no, they could take offense at Algonkian. My knowledge of Cayuga and Mohawk is too shaky to help. Confound it, I've become too complacent, relying on the local jargon.

The kerchief tucked away, La Salle lifted his spyglass to the horizon. His grip tightened. In his sight, four canoes drifted on the current. Deft dips of paddles kept them facing him. A gust caught the Frenchman broadside. His heart in the pit of his stomach, La Salle fumbled at refocusing the spyglass.

The wind tugged at the white and gray feathers wound into a Seneca warrior's scalp lock, the long hank of hair hanging over his right ear that dared his enemy to grasp hold of it to better take his scalp. La Salle could not see if the feathers were blood-tipped, a war signal for some tribes. Perhaps other signs declared murderous intent, signs of which he knew nothing. Swallowing hard, he searched for some clue. He had heard they painted their chins yellow or black to signal attack. Red would mean bravery. If he could only control his trembling, which he wanted to attribute to the brisk wind, and focus better . . .

A warrior abruptly tensed and locked his eyes on La Salle, then thrust his arm in the same direction with a shout to the others. A shock of fear jumped up La Salle's neck. His hand instinctively went to the silver crucifix hanging there.

"I'll be the first Frenchman to trade with them," he muttered, shoving his spyglass back into its case. "If they don't kill me."

Son of a merchant from Rouen, René-Robert Cavelier La Salle was twenty-two when he first trod up the stone steps to the heights of Quebec, wobbly after months aboard a pitching ship.

His departure from France had not been easy. After years of studying for the Jesuit priesthood, anticipating his order's commission to station him in New France where his older brother, Jean, had already been sent by his Sulpician order, La Salle had been called in by his Abbé and assigned a teaching position at home instead.

Jesuit training had taught him discipline and dedication but both those virtues had been sorely tested as reports continued from the New World, where Jesuit missions grew without him. They described a rich land unscathed by centuries of war, civil feuds, and economic problems, a land where an energetic, intense, and able man, such as himself, could make his mark.

For weeks he troubled over the dilemma. Yes, he had forever given up everything, all his worldly possessions including his future family inheritance, to join the priesthood. Yet, if he stayed with the order, he could not be true to his real calling. What his real calling was, he was not exactly sure, but since boyhood he had suspected the future held adventure, and that destiny intended him for greatness. Greatness, La Salle knew, was the child of audacity. Greatness would not likely find a homebound teacher of Jesuit novices.

La Salle knew he must go to the New World. What lay ahead for him there, he could not imagine. But the challenge of the unknown consumed his every moment, asleep or awake.

Late one afternoon, in the dank confines of the seminary, La Salle decided he could wait no longer.

"Monsieur l'Abbé," he said softly as he entered the seminary leader's cramped study. The low glow of the hearth barely offset the damp chill settling in over the stone enclave.

The Abbé frowned up from his task. He'd no affection for the young man before him. La Salle's lack of obedience to God's word, as put forth by the order, was a thorn. Impatiently, the old priest gestured for La Salle to speak his mind so he might return to his duties.

"Monsieur," La Salle began, "I request I be transferred to a post in the New World."

"And again I deny it. The order has need of your . . . intelligence, as a teacher of novices." La Salle's numerous requests had not gone unremarked. To the Abbé and his counselors they indicated a headstrong individual whose selfish ambitions went counter to the authority of the order. Many years of countless hours in service would have to be spent before such a request would even be considered.

"Obedience," was the Abbé's only explanation.

Obedience, yes, La Salle thought, but to my own calling.

"Then I must quit the order," La Salle stammered. He was too overwrought to notice the small victory that might have made him glad. It had been years since anyone or anything had surprised the Abbé, but La Salle had succeeded in doing so.

"What you have given up will not be returned," the Abbé responded with a glare, referring to La Salle's now forever lost inheritance, before accepting the formal withdrawal from the seminary.

"That's as it should be," La Salle replied, allowing himself a measure of pride.

Without the shelter of the order, La Salle would have nothing but the infrequent handouts he could garner from relatives. But he had already decided his forfeiture of money and inheritance served him best. With nothing, he could only serve himself. With nothing, he was forced to make his own way. Alone.

"I'll be too busy building a future to bother with the past," La Salle announced.

The Abbé's eyes widened at the determination that consumed the young man. As La Salle strode to the door, the old priest wondered at the abrupt transformation from a trembling novice making an unreasonable request to a volcano about to erupt.

With open arms La Salle's sister had welcomed him, but in the following days she came to find her restless younger brother an unsettling presence among her growing family. Her estate had benefitted when first Jean, then René, relinquished their inheritance to join the priesthood, but gratitude was not always enough to help her endure La Salle's intense silences. She would almost prefer him to return as a freeloading knave, with laughter to lace his larceny, instead of as a hungry stoic.

One morning after prayers La Salle caught her alone in an upstairs hall. She was fresh from scolding a deserving handmaid, and La Salle sensed her good mood.

"A woman of your station needs more room for her family," he suggested.

"You are not in the way here, René," she lied. "You are my brother, and you are welcome to remain as long as you like."

"That's not what I meant. You should have a wing added to the manor. And the gardens extended all the way down to the river." He measured her surprise before continuing. "When guests visit from the capital, you'll need a new stable to house their horses. A larger carriage house for their coaches. A better class of servants. Fine wines and fowl to feed those who will plead for invitations here."

Catherine straightened her shoulders to make a better impression on the imaginary guests her brother had her almost seeing.

"But how do I pay for all that?"

"With the fortune in New World products I will make for you if you and your husband invest in my transportation there."

She nearly burst out laughing at his grandiosity.

"If you were half as charming as you are clever, you'd be taking a wife with you to this New World."

"Someday I'll return to let you help me find a wife," La Salle replied to his sister's oft-mentioned advice. "But I can hardly consider marriage before I establish myself in New France."

"Then I've no choice but to fund you," Catherine happily agreed. She had long known her younger brother was not cut out for the priesthood and was glad her marriage to a wealthy landowner permitted such an easy act of generosity. If the refined guests and enlarged carriage house would once more become idle daydreams, at least René would be out from underfoot.

In New France, La Salle was instantly separated from the majority of newcomers from the Old World who immigrated under the auspices of government, church, or royal patent. The Abbé de Queylus, head of the Sulpician seminary at Montreal where La Salle's older brother, Jean, was a prominent member of the order, was particularly anxious to meet La Salle. Never had Queylus seen the usually dispassionate Jean react to any news the way he had to that of his brother's arrival. A fount of sibling antagonism about "always trying to best me," and "self-righteous ambition," had welled up. That in itself whetted Queylus's curiosity.

Besides, the Sulpician order needed someone to manage its lands to the farthest western area of the island of Montreal. Queylus had been at a loss to find someone brazen enough to take that exposed post until he saw the fervor in La Salle's eyes.

"It's an enormous responsibility to take on the proprietorship of our lands. They are farther west than the farthest settlement, and above the rapids that block longboats from traveling upriver," Queylus warned. "The Indians there have not yet completely warmed to the French embrace."

"I will have much to learn from the natives," La Salle declared. Then his face relaxed, and he concluded with a rare smile, "And they as much to learn and gain from a trading post so close to their villages."

Queylus liked that attitude. It could take a man far in a wide-open frontier unwilling to be defined by the laws and limitations imposed on crowded Europe. With the Sulpician order to help him through establishing trade, and exacting its tithe, an association with La Salle could be well worth the effort. Besides, La Salle had left the Jesuit order, a mark in his favor since the Abbé despised Jesuit ambitions, which directly conflicted with the Sulpician's own in New France.

With the challenge of developing the land grant before him, La Salle set to work. The distance from Montreal to his new post was not great when measured in leagues, but it involved a long, difficult, and dangerous portage around rapids. Iroquois warriors and even French bandits preferred such a spot, where the unwary could be ambushed as they carried their heavily laden canoes over a steep, rocky trail.

At his grant, La Salle found nothing but primeval forest. In a day and a half, he put up a lean-to. Immediately he ventured into the villages of nearby Indians. With help from one of the intrepid trapper-traders known as *coureurs de bois,* or woods runners, La Salle traded the glass beads the Indians coveted for a few furs. By signs and the simple words needed to explain "more trade goods" he drew maps to his post. Within a year his simple lean-to was transformed into a palisade with several buildings as word spread of La Salle's accessibility and reputation for fair deals. Homesteaders were persuaded to occupy the land around the post. The herculean task of clearing stones in preparation of tilling the land wrenched an almost civilized appearance from the wilderness. By the end of his third year, the post reflected roughhewn prosperity.

La Salle's forays into allied Indian lands brought him news of better furs and inland waterways that linked a path across the unknown continent to the west. But beyond friendly nations lay the Iroquois Confederacy: the Seneca, the Mohawk, and others, allies to the English. With the tentative Iroquois treaty that had been reached by the governing bodies in

Quebec had come restraints on exploration. Fearing the opening of new land would further rob the struggling colony of young men as they rushed off in search of easy profits, the crown tightly controlled travel into western lands. The hunger La Salle had felt in the Jesuit seminary, instead of being satisfied, continued to grow.

One night at Bertaud's Inn in Montreal, La Salle boasted he would be the man to travel into western lands to find the passage to the Orient.

"The farthest west you'll ever get on the route to China is your own post," his cohorts and detractors both laughed.

So his post became known as La Chine, the French word for China. The nickname stuck, and mocked the suppressed explorer inside La Salle as season after season La Chine became his profitable prison.

Wind rippled the fur around Thaka's shoulders. His black eyes bore into the white man squatting across from him under the two-sided lean-to at the outer corner of the La Chine post. An array of trade goods lay spread between them. Behind the Seneca leader, other buckskin-clad tribesmen carefully guarded several bundles of fur. Thaka inventoried the samples Henri had noisily dropped to the ground: a pot, some needles, cloth and ribbon, a string of fat, white beads, and a small hatchet. Careful not to display too much, as La Salle had always instructed, Henri hurried off, stealing a fearful look back at the group of painted warriors.

They're no bigger than the Abnaki or Huron, La Salle considered, recalling how claims that the Seneca were giants had often been mixed in with the stories of their bloodthirsty ways. Their reputation for cruelty and bravery was as legendary among the French as among other native tribes. La Salle realized, if few others did, that as much as their warlike ways, it was geography that kept them in such a position of strength for so long, for the Seneca guarded the bottleneck between the seaboard colony of New France and the unknown interior, including perhaps a route that might provide easy passage to the fabled Orient.

This one's countenance is fierce, La Salle thought, with chin painted red and black stripes across his eyes, but no more so than our own native allies painted for battle or even Frenchmen, with red eyes and soured frowns, remembering their friends slaughtered and children stolen.

La Salle watched the Seneca's eyes follow Henri to a small trade warehouse. He saw him measuring its size, calculating what it contained. Is he just curious, La Salle worried, or does he plan to plunder it after slaughtering us all? La Salle's body was rigid with anticipation. Thaka's quick gesture to the others caused La Salle's heart to lurch. A warrior threw off the cover of a bundle, then knelt beside it. Brushing the layers of pelts with his ruddy fingers to show their lushness, he leered at the white trader.

La Salle breathed deeply to calm his pounding chest and reached down for a small roll of leather that lay before him. Slowly, he unfolded it to expose a calumet. It was a small pipe made of red stone that a local tribe had given him years ago in honor of the ritual smoke of peace they shared. Protests erupted from several warriors. With a single syllable, Thaka silenced them. His black eyes narrowed on the pipe La Salle held patiently in his hand. These were two adversaries, two cultures, and neither was sure of the other.

"English trade guns, powder, shot. Rum," Thaka stated in the trading language the northern tribes shared. None of those favored items appeared on the blanket between them.

"The English are in Albany. You and I are here," La Salle replied, relieved the Seneca's trade jargon almost mirrored his own. With thumb and forefinger he packed tobacco into the pipe bowl.

The Seneca leader almost imperceptibly brushed his right hand across his left arm. The warrior crouched at the bundles extracted a single pelt. La Salle mentally replayed the gesture, incorporating it into Indian signs already familiar to him. Thaka spread the fur over the trade goods.

La Salle resisted his trader's instinct to take up the pelt and examine its quality. But even without fingering it he could see it had been trapped at the height of the season when the beaver's coat was thickest. Restraining his desire to count the bundles still guarded by the other men, he estimated how many furs they had brought as he bit the stem of the calumet, struck a spark, and inhaled a long draught of smoke.

Trade would not begin without establishing a smoke of peace between them. If the treaty was to work it could only happen one step, one man, at a time. La Salle resolved to begin it here between these wary Seneca and himself, and eventually those homesteaders waiting inside for word of his transactions with their most feared threat in the New World. La Salle was already the most successful trader in Montreal, perhaps. If he aspired to become more, he must be bold, but not hasty.

La Salle raised the calumet, its small bowl trailing smoke, to the sky and to the earth. Then he gestured to the four directions: north, south, east, west, as his Indian allies had shown him. Smoke had magical qualities. It purified and bonded all things. He took another puff and extended the calumet to the Seneca leader. Again, voices erupted in protest. Thaka raised his hand for silence.

"We will make good trade," La Salle said, the calumet still extended. "And friends."

Thaka hesitated. Other tribes had reported that this Frenchman was powerful, knew Indian ways, could speak the trade languages. The Iroquois Confederacy had sided with the English long enough. It was time to show that the Seneca were loyal to no one except their own people. His village to the southwest had managed to fend off the encroaching white men. But now, with the other nations of the Iroquois Confederacy weakened by years of warring with the French and pressed out of their eastern lands by the growing English colonies, it was time to reevaluate the situation, time to measure the worth of friendship with the Frenchmen. Thaka reached for the calumet.

With the exchange of smoke reluctantly completed among the remaining warriors, trading began. La Salle stepped over to a bale of furs and crouched to dig at the thick pelts of beaver. This was the merchandise his English competitors had monopolized. He had seen enough. The furs were of the finest quality. Each bale would bring at least six louis in Montreal. From the corner of his eye he saw the Seneca leader watching. La Salle pretended to find a flaw and harrumphed his feigned disapproval.

"Very fine furs," Thaka responded, then added in emphasis of their worth, "from far west. Near Meche Sebe."

At the Seneca's words, La Salle looked up. His mouth pursed to form an eager question but he checked himself. Averting his eyes, he once more examined the furs, but his mind raced with the words he had just heard. Meche Sebe meant Great River, the Father of the Waters. He had heard tales of it among the surrounding tribes. Which Great River, he wondered. Could it flow far enough west to be the passage to China?

"You travel far if you come from Meche Sebe," La Salle suggested.

"No, from near Meche Sebe. These furs from river Oyo."

He stared at the Seneca, trying to analyze every nuance. This Oyo was not something he had heard about. But the warrior's face was a mask. Don't be too curious, he warned himself. If they travel this Oyo, and Meche Sebe really exists, it will be valuable information, well worth the wait. Don't make them reticent by being enthusiastic.

"You must rest here the winter. Regain your strength, share our food."

Thaka explained the proposition to his fellow warriors. The surprised Seneca looked warily at each other. The white man was different from others they had encountered—not just the way he dressed, but also the way he had not rushed trade, insisted on smoking the calumet first, made the Indian gesture of the world before, and now invited them to stay the winter as any Indian tribe might. The English had only offered smelly quarters that the Seneca had shunned in favor of returning to the shelter of close-by tribes. Thaka decided they would consider the offer.

La Salle beckoned Henri from the trade warehouse where he'd been hiding. As his servant approached, La Salle wondered just how he could explain this strange new situation to the homesteaders huddling within the post's walls. But he resolved to keep peace long enough to convince the Seneca to take confidence in him, and long enough to discover all they knew about the Oyo, and Great River.

La Salle's excitement astonished the hesitant Henri.

CHAPTER TWO

At the bluff of Quebec city, hand-pulled and ox-drawn carts weighted with merchandise squeezed through narrow cobbled streets. Residents of the principal settlement of New France darted in and out amongst them, stopping occasionally at small stands to purchase daily necessities, wheat flour for the well-to-do, ground Indian corn for the less fortunate. The recent thaw had sparked new life in the capital. The roof of the Parish Church glistened beyond the Jesuit College, where black-robed clerics educated the noisy youth of the prospering colony.

La Salle moved past the few closed gates and paved courtyards of larger residences before he turned into a short street that led toward the garrison. Its high stone parapet blocked the end of the street but for a narrow passageway. Along the garrison wall strode men in curly wigs and stockinged legs, reflecting King Louis XIV's reign over fashion that even reached the governmental echelons of distant Quebec. La Salle smoothed the sides of his blue dress coat, trailing a finger over its frayed edge. Glancing around to make sure he was unseen, he tightened the ribbon that tied his dark hair at the nape of his neck.

I should have purchased a wig, he reprimanded himself.

His had grown so old that when he pulled it from his armoire at La Chine many of its curly locks had fallen out. He imagined that his sister in her manor near Rouen would be shamed at his appearance. She would say I belonged with the stable hands, he thought, and that a brave adventurer intent on expanding the horizons of New France should make a more dashing presentation.

"Monsieur La Salle?"

La Salle looked up. As he neared the office that he sought, a young clerk indicated the path to follow with an outstretched hand.

"That way, monsieur, please!"

La Salle stepped through a large, wooden door and moved to stand before a document-covered desk, watching the well-dressed man seated behind it gingerly dip a quill into a heavy brass inkwell. A just used blotter rocked silently atop some papers. The intendant Talon, financial and business administrator of the colony, signaled La Salle to sit, then concentrated on writing a few last lines.

La Salle turned instead to the wall map of New France. To the east was the Gaspé Peninsula, just south was Acadie and the settlement at Port Royal. To the northwest lay Quebec and southwest of it, up the St. Lawrence, was the island of Montreal, at the western tip of which lay La Chine. Farther west lay the Great Lakes so long blocked by the Seneca and other Iroquois. But west from there were undiscovered lands yet unmarked on the map until the Pacific coast was sketchily outlined.

"News of your Seneca visitors reached us before your request for an audience," Talon said as he handed several documents to the clerk, who sped away.

"I request permission to travel into their lands."

Talon raised an eyebrow at La Salle's frankness. The blue velvet coat and knee breeches over grayed stockings betrayed a rugged trader and dauntless businessman. Though he had never met La Salle face to face, they had been in contact. La Chine and its clever manager had by no means gone unnoticed by the colonial government. Abruptly Talon stood and indicated the chair in front of his desk.

"It's good to finally meet you, Monsieur La Salle." He watched the young man move into the chair, then added as he regained his seat, "And put a face to all those stories."

La Salle suppressed a smile. Between reports from the Sulpicians, the Jesuits, the tradesmen, and the Indians, La Salle knew he seemed an enigma, an image he cultivated for the freedom of movement it allowed. The Sulpicians valued immensely his energy and perspicacity; the Jesuits reviled him for the same reasons. Tradesmen despised his business acumen that usually won him the best furs and prices. But New France's rivaling factions were the least of La Salle's concerns. His eyes were turned west, not east.

"In brief, the Seneca wintered at La Chine. They offer to guide me and a few men of my choice to their village on the western shore of the Iroquois lake."

Talon pursed his lips in a frown. The Seneca had been the last holdout of the treaty. Everyone knew they controlled all the trade coming from lands to the west and south of their territory. To grant La Salle governmental permission into those lands might give him undue advantage. Eventually Governor Courcelle and he would have to grant permission to someone to go to the Seneca, but he had been leaning towards sending missionaries, who wouldn't be so anxious to control the trade.

Talon wavered, weighing the possible repercussions of granting the request, La Salle saw. He decided to risk revealing a bit more, knowing full well anything shared here would spread to every trader's house in Quebec by nightfall.

"They speak of a chain of rivers." La Salle leaned forward conspiratorially, stifling the pleasure of watching the intendant do the same. Of all the men in government, Talon was the most farseeing, the most likely to approve such a venture because it would benefit the colony he was working so hard to populate and cultivate.

"They speak of the Oyo River, how its waters mix with the Meche Sebe. That Meche Sebe, Great River, flows into a warm, red sea, very likely the Vermilion Sea off California. The northwest passage. The trade route France needs to strengthen her empire in the New World."

Talon raised his eyebrows. Could La Salle really be that ambitious? Or was he just like so many of the merchants of Quebec and Montreal, willing to do or say anything to get a jump on his competitors?

"The colonial treasury cannot afford further exploration after the drain of the Iroquois wars, Monsieur La Salle," came a voice from the doorway.

"But expansion should not be suppressed by financial woes," La Salle retorted, turning quickly toward the gentleman entering the office.

"Ah, Your Excellency," greeted Talon. "Monsieur La Salle, I hope you don't object to Governor Courcelle joining us. He too is interested in your Seneca visitors."

The elderly dandy bent slightly to greet the prosperous fur trader standing before him, then moved to take the seat behind the desk, which the intendant had vacated to offer him. As the governor eased his bulk down, La Salle eased himself down with a watchful eye on Talon.

Everyone knew Governor Courcelle was not the real decision maker in the colony. That's why La Salle had decided first to meet with Talon. If he could garner support from the most respected administrator in Quebec, the governor would be hard pressed to refuse his commission. But now he feared he might have offended the governor by having asked to see Talon first.

"Talon, I'm surprised you'd even consider such a venture. Our coffers are all but empty," Courcelle whined.

La Salle clenched his teeth. He had prepared for this obstacle. "I'll finance the journey," he submitted.

Courcelle and Talon shared a brief look of surprise.

"Might you take along a map maker?" Courcelle wondered aloud.

"I'm a quite capable map maker myself, Your Excellency. Thank you all the same . . . ," La Salle said, then watched dismay tinge the governor's face. Obviously Courcelle was promoting some unspoken agenda. La Salle decided he must flush out what it was.

"If you like, I can show you maps I have made of the area around La Chine. You will find . . ."

"Yes, but," Governor Courcelle began, with a quick look at Talon, "there's a small group of priests that could accompany you. And they've an excellent map maker."

La Salle sat up. So that was it. He had said he would pay for his expedition but not someone else's too.

"Explain to the boy, Talon," Courcelle mewed.

"You understand, of course," Talon began, "it is impossible for the crown to ignore the expansion of Christianity. Now that the treaty has been signed, it is our obligation to send the cross. . . ."

"Make no doubt, sirs, I understand the task at hand," La Salle declared as he slammed his hands onto the arms of his chair. Abruptly he began to pace, chiding himself to hold his temper. If he had to agree to take along a few priests, and pay for their supplies, what matter when he got into Seneca lands and began to establish trade alliances? Besides, if the Oyo and the Meche Sebe were so near to their lands . . . he sighed. This was growing into more of an undertaking than he had planned. But he could not proceed without governmental sanction.

"If I agree to support the extra men, will you honor my petition for this voyage? And what concessions will I have on the trade I find?"

La Salle positioned himself on the edge of his chair and turned his flushed face to negotiate what approval of travel into Seneca lands would entail.

Stepping across the portal of the government offices into the narrow street La Salle looked up at the king's standard. Gold fleurs-de-lis shone against a glimmering white field. A dark flutter in the corner of his eye moved La Salle's gaze to the somber figure turning into the street, head bent low, a lean frame briskly moving nearer with each deliberate step. La Salle glowered and turned again to study the insignia. He could see it flapping against the background of the vast wilderness he was soon to cross. Mysterious frontiers no white man had seen would soon be confronted, and in the corner of each charted mile of waterways and routes into the continent would be the king's standard beside his own name.

"Always dreaming, René."

La Salle swung from his revery to look at the immaculate gray robes of his brother's Sulpician order, and he sighed. Jean had not approved his leaving the Jesuits. He had resented La Salle's coming to New France, where he had already firmly established himself. He had doubted La Salle's ability to manage the Sulpician land grant. La Salle could just imagine the sharp words with which his jealous sibling would greet his new plans.

"I heard you took in the Seneca. Typically rash," Jean stated, before La Salle could even step away from the offices.

"And in Montreal," La Salle countered, "I heard you had intercepted my request for an audience with Talon, and that you would not have sent it on but for . . ."

"I knew you were onto another speculative plan that could risk everything I have helped you build here. I'm not wrong about that, am I?"

"*You* helped me to build? You fought my every step!"

"René, your schemes risk ruining more than your own soul."

"My ventures bring honor to those I serve, Jean. If you've come to interfere . . . ," La Salle paused, knowing his older brother would have no appreciation of the monumental task he was about to undertake. Nevertheless, he would find out eventually. "The governor granted my request to travel southwest into Seneca lands."

The missionary swallowed his surprise. He had long worried that the quick position of wealth La Salle had managed to obtain in the last few years had gone to his head, and would be his undoing. This new scheme seemed to confirm his fear that La Salle's ambition would endanger both his life and soul.

"Is it greed that drives my little brother to voyage into such savage grounds?"

La Salle stared. Didn't Jean see how La Salle's journeys did the Lord's work? Hadn't La Salle just agreed to take along an entire mission of priests?

La Salle gave his brother a terse explanation of his plans as the two headed toward the steep path from the bluff to the foot of the colonial capital. La Salle moved briskly, passing the slow crowds, trying to keep his brother's inevitable harangue at bay.

The streets nearer the water's edge contrasted with the provincial elegance the two men had just left. Small groups bartered in front of warehouses and open shops. Carts jostled bewigged and great-coated Europeans against smelly woods runners' worn buckskins.

"When you failed at the priesthood, even as a Jesuit, I put it off to youth and weak will."

La Salle bit his tongue and continued walking. Jean moved quickly to stay apace.

"But now if you forsake your responsibilities here by speeding off into untold dangers . . ."

"I'm not forsaking any responsibilities, and I didn't fail as a Jesuit. I left voluntarily to make my way, alone. Without you, without anyone." La Salle stopped and faced his brother. "I'm the first French trader the Seneca came to. You cannot deny that. I swore I'd become the greatest trader in Montreal, and haven't I succeeded?"

"But at La Chine you had the Sulpicians to guide you," Jean countered. Didn't his little brother see what perils he was entering into?

"Well, I'll have Sulpicians along this time, too. And I'll have to sell everything I own just to pay their keep!"

La Salle realized too late he had divulged what had been weighing on his mind since he had left the intendant's office. Jean's dark visage turn colder.

"You plan to sell the land grant? You're going to abandon the concession I worked so hard to get the order to grant you?"

La Salle hadn't acknowledged it until the moment it was said but indeed he would have to sell everything, including La Chine, to finance the journey he had agreed too. But he was certain now it would be worth it. Not only would he be the first to trade in Seneca country, but he would be the first white man to travel the waterways they had so long dominated. If what he had convinced Talon and Courcelle of were true, that the northwest passage existed in that territory, he would be repaid a hundredfold what La Chine was worth.

Henri rose from his resting place as La Salle stepped onto the quay. He waved to catch his eye then recognized the somber robed priest behind him. Henri swallowed hard. Every time his master met up with his older brother he came back in the foulest humor. The trip back to Montreal would not be pleasant.

At La Salle's harried signal Henri rushed to a longboat. He stooped to pick up a few pebbles, then tossed them onto the nodding hat of the owner, who would ferry them home. The man lumbered awake to call his rowers to ready the craft. Henri watched them anxiously, not wanting to turn and face the scene he knew was taking place.

All his life Jean had tried to protect his little brother from his follies. Now not only did René risk losing his own life but he was also endangering the solid fortune he had established, a chance for security in a changing world.

"You could land in debtor's prison!"

La Salle was sick of having his abilities always doubted. Couldn't Jean see he had finally discovered what he was good at? And this trip would test all his skills.

"I will bring our family and our country glory, Jean. You'll soon boast that I'm your brother."

"Boast that you've become a common woods runner?"

"Not common." La Salle gripped Jean's shoulders to confess, "I have been chosen for great things."

Jean shook him off. Had he heard right? Had La Salle taken the sin of pride so deeply into his bosom? "The Lord may strike you down for your blasphemy."

"What blasphemy? Because it is me and not you?" La Salle climbed into the readied longboat. "Shove off!" he commanded to the rowers watching the dispute.

"René! Drive out the devils that push you to such folly," Jean implored from shore.

La Salle stared ahead across the St. Lawrence. He wanted to call back, defend himself, but he had tried all that before.

"Your scalp will adorn some savage's longhouse," cautioned the priest, hands cupped to hurl his message across the water.

But La Salle had closed his ears to his brother's protests. He struggled to regain composure with each stroke of the rowers' oars.

CHAPTER THREE

ABBÉ QUEYLUS STROLLED through the seminary toward his meeting with La Salle. His thoughts were heavy from his encounter the day before with Jean. The older brother had warned that La Salle would be forced to sell his land, the very grant the seminary had given him, in order to pay for a vainglorious mission which he feared would end in failure. The Abbé shook his head wondering at the animosity between the two brothers.

Yet, La Salle's lack of funds does jeopardize my own mission, the Abbé reflected as he opened once more the lengthy letter from Governor Courcelle. It refused him help with the seminary's northwestern mission, and suggested he take advantage of La Salle's southwestern journey by sending a group to accompany him. Rumor had recently been confirmed too that the Jesuit Joliet had been financed to journey southwest. All the political juggling, the many schemes to be aware of and egos to satisfy, made the Abbé quite tired.

"Ah, dear," the Abbé moaned as he pushed open the door to his office. He brightened at the sight of the younger La Salle standing near the hearth. At least here was someone whose forthright view of the colony he could count on.

Over La Salle's objections the cleric poured them each a

short glass of wine, but paused with his halfway to his lips when La Salle confirmed Jean's prediction of wanting to sell La Chine.

"Funding my own expedition and yours," La Salle emphasized, "leaves me no other choice."

The Abbé nodded several times, accepting that the Sulpicians would have to pay for their own mission directly if La Salle could not finance the entire trek. Regretfully he raised his glass to the young adventurer before him. Yes, he thought, La Salle's clever. I can hardly refuse to help him when his expedition includes my own priests, now can I?

"La Chine will soon be enveloped by the expansion of Montreal," La Salle continued with a smile. He knew the Abbé well and that too much subterfuge would only confuse the old priest. "The land will be fought over for living and business quarters in ten year's time. . . ."

The Abbé pretended to grab his chest at such a pointed attack. Not only should the seminary consider buying back the land, but at a substantial price. The old priest tut-tut-tutted with his tongue as he set down his glass. There was much to consider. Oh, how he rued losing such a clever ally on the wild edge of Montreal.

La Salle leaned back in his chair, content that the Abbé fathomed the inextricable link between his monetary needs and the seminary's mission. When Courcelle had suggested he take St. Sulpice's priests with him he had felt coerced, but it was baggage he could contend with in order to travel into Seneca lands. It wasn't until after arguing with Jean that he realized how St. Sulpice could be obliged to help him in his land sale or lose their own mission into new territory. La Salle relaxed. Let the Abbé consider the situation a bit, he thought, and have another glass, then we'll barter.

The morning grew late as back and forth they went, assessing a fair amount for the property. The bargaining tired the Abbé and more glasses heightened what he felt was the loss of a brave young colonist.

"Monsieur l'Abbé, I can do much more than get rich and fat here," La Salle reiterated.

"Many would not find that so unpleasant, René. Such a large expedition, and into unknown lands. It is quite an undertaking."

La Salle's desire to be surrounded by wilderness always impressed the Abbé. Though he himself had also grown up in the midst of world expansion, he was not half so daring, nor could the Abbé imagine enduring the harsh climes of untold regions and the fear of less known tribes of savage Indians. Montreal itself seemed often too foreign and uncivilized to him in spite of its constantly improving amenities.

Yes, growth, expansion, he thought, is what propels La Salle. To venture into something not knowing what risks or fortunes can be found. Ah, to have some of that energy and strong will, the Abbé lamented. Then his face brightened with an idea to help La Salle fund the mission, yet keep him tied to the seminary.

"René, the order will acquire a third of La Chine."

La Salle rubbed his eyebrow. "Its value is greater kept whole."

Exactly, the Abbé thought as he wiped his lips and rested his glass on the table. Whole again it shall be when you return with the new fortune you will undoubtedly find, and buy back St. Sulpice's portion of La Chine. The Abbé dared not suggest to La Salle that one day he would be a settled merchant living on the tamed outskirts of Montreal. The Abbé was certain La Salle's savings could cover the remaining needs of the expedition. After all, his young friend was one of the wealthiest traders in New France.

La Salle frowned. He had hoped all his money woes would be solved in this one visit. It had taken years of backbreaking labor to bring La Chine to its present value. Thanks to him the Indians surrounding the grant had welcomed the Sulpician missionaries. He had carved a successful post from their useless parcel of land, and now the Abbé would only take part of it back. La Salle had sunk every sou he had into the post. Indeed the Seneca's tempting news had not arrived at a good time. It could take six months to a year to build back his savings. But there was no time to waste. The race was on to discover what lay in Seneca lands. He would have to make the best of the Abbé's offer.

La Salle stipulated that St. Sulpice pay in equipment and trade merchandise instead of money. The Abbé breathed a sigh of relief and poured himself another glass. He watched La Salle quickly draft up the agreement, not a little surprised La Salle had been willing to trade equipment worth even less than the third of La Chine.

The Abbé congratulated himself on such a clever business proposition as he embraced his friend farewell. For the first time ever in his dealings with La Salle he felt he had bested him in a transaction, but the Abbé didn't know what La Salle did. The supply ships from France were running late this year and remaining stocks of trade goods, powder, shot, and other necessities for the expedition were selling at a premium. The Abbé's bargain would cost him dearly.

Leaving behind the morning's fatiguing round with the Abbé, La Salle strode into the muddy streets of Montreal. His thoughts focused on one thing. Who was the best prospect to buy the remaining land at La Chine?

"In total, Monsieur l'Abbé, we should need three canoes. One for each of us," Casson estimated with a nod to Galinée, "and one for our Sacraments." The Abbé motioned to Galinée to make note of their needs.

"And six or seven men for our crew," Casson concluded.

The Abbé was surprised Casson felt the need for such a large number of men. The priest watched his superior, anxiously hoping he would not try to persuade him to take fewer men, but that is exactly what the Abbé felt he must do.

"When Monsieur La Salle agreed to finance our expedition along with his own, I believe he assumed you'd be traveling as a smaller party."

"My brother's single-mindedness makes him stingy," Jean apologized from the corner. Father Galinée lifted his eyes from his papers to check the reaction of his superiors, Father Casson and the Abbé. The former crossed his thick arms against his sturdy chest as he watched Jean stride across the room. The Abbé looked away to minimize Jean's interruption.

Young Father Galinée returned to his task, resting his quill briefly against the inkwell rim to let the excess run off before completing the map sketch he had hastily prepared while the Abbé had described their upcoming journey. He carefully blotted the thick paper and handed it to the Abbé, who reviewed it casually before passing it to Father Casson.

Jean grew ever more pensive. His little brother was a trader, not a woods runner, certainly not an explorer. He had never led more than himself and a few others to villages already trading with the French. If René failed, and Jean feared he would, it could only reflect badly on them all, including himself. The older La Salle hoped to become Abbé himself one day. Having his younger brother lead Casson and Galinée to their deaths would not help his cause.

"Of all the insolence," Jean blurted, "forcing you, Monsieur l'Abbé. Forcing your hand to buy back land you had granted him."

"Father Jean," the Abbé beseeched, "I requested your presence at this meeting because your standing in the seminary demands your assistance in planning. If you insist on attacking your brother instead of addressing the situation at hand . . ."

"Monsieur l'Abbé, it's a death march."

"Silence," the Abbé commanded.

Jean grew calm, but his quiet frustration seemed all the more lethal for not being vented.

"Do you doubt my abilities," Father Casson boomed from where he leaned over his fellow voyager's map, "to survive a simple missionary excursion, Father Jean?"

"I'm certain," the Abbé interceded, "Father Jean is aware of your prior life in the king's army, Father Casson. He cannot doubt your capabilities." The Abbé placed a calming hand on Casson's stout forearm.

Casson nodded and returned to studying the map. His jaw clenched and unclenched as he marked places where he could best force La Salle to head north. The Abbé had acknowledged little problem in the drastic change from a northwestern mission to a southwestern one. Even young Father Galinée, again consumed with detailing a piece of parchment, seemed untroubled by the change. Of course, Casson thought, all he cares for is surveying and map making, small matter where he goes as long as he can chart it. I'm the only one who fully realizes what an affront this is to St. Sulpice. Except for Father Jean, Casson noted, though his reasons seem overly personal.

Jean circled around to sit at the table. "René seeks self-glory from the savages, not the glory of God for them. Neither I nor even the Jesuits could ever teach my brother obedience. He's willful, and too proud."

The older La Salle's attacks against his brother had gone too far, the Abbé decided. "This meeting is concluded. Should any of you have further comment or requests about this expedition it will be addressed to me alone. It will not be discussed among the brethren."

The Abbé rose to dismiss them. Jean lingered behind the departing figures of the two other priests.

"Father Jean," the old priest said, holding up his hand. He watched Casson and Galinée glance back at them, then continue down the corridor before he again addressed Jean. "You will constrict your activities to study in solitude and prayers until the departure of the mission."

"But Monsieur l'Abbé . . ."

"You will not disparage them with your accusations!"

Jean's face darkened. He thought of how his brother was compromising the seminary's integrity. St. Sulpice already lagged well behind the Jesuits in establishing missions in native lands. Now more time would be wasted as La Salle misdirected them to the southwest where the Seneca ruled.

Blast René, Jean thought furiously, as he bent to kiss the ringed hand the Abbé offered in conclusion of their exchange. His whole body burned as he realized he had been cursing his baby brother when he should have been concentrating on an act of supplication.

Again, René, your faults pull at me. Blinking back hot tears, Jean retreated to the sanctuary.

La Salle shook hands with Milot, the ironmonger, as they stepped from the sweat-and-brandy reek of Bertaud's Inn. The day was moving into early evening, a time when shop owners, traders, and housewives of Montreal hastened to conclude their daily transactions along Rue St. Laurent. The setting sun burnished the stone foundations and wooden beams that had begun to rise above the rocky soil of the island. Trade spilled onto muddy streets from cabins half-finished in the hurry of commerce. Larger than most, the rugged facade behind them, Bertaud's Inn, was softened by a tentative row of boxed flowers along the front.

The proprietor stepped between the two men, unwilling for them to take their leave.

"I wish I were a young daredevil again. When Josephine and I left Quebec to come here, it was like La Chine before you came, La Salle. Business waiting like a ripe apple."

"Listen, Bertaud," Milot began with a laugh, "if you're trying to augment my esteem of La Salle's property you're too late."

"Well," Bertaud said with a bit of surprise that La Salle had concluded such a large transaction so quickly, "Monsieur La Salle's never been known to waste time. . . ."

"And soon I'll be passing from the St. Lawrence into the Iroquois lake," La Salle said with unusual joviality. He was happy to have garnered a good price for the rest of La Chine and anxious to begin preparations for the journey.

"Don't put ideas in Bertaud's head, La Salle," Milot joked. "Given half a chance he'd sign up with you!"

"Why, I could stand it!" Bertaud defended himself. "The first four months I was here, you couldn't even plant 'cause the ground was so hard. Thought for sure Josephine and I'd perish, but then I killed that bear . . ."

"Bare-handed," La Salle finished for him, with Milot joining in. Everyone in Montreal, possibly New France, had had their ears bent by Bertaud's story, La Salle thought. But Old

Bertaud could have been a good trader, even an explorer, if he hadn't decided to settle down and become apron tied.

"That bear grows bigger each time you tell the story. Soon, *mon vieux*, it will have grown big enough to feed all of Montreal," La Salle chortled.

The three men joined in laughter. La Salle hadn't felt so unfettered and elated since he had first boarded ship for New France. A new life stretched before him. His casual confidence drew the attention of passersby. Business acquaintances crossed the uneven street to tip their hats and exchange greetings.

From the doorway of the building opposite the inn a sandy-bearded man focused his pale blue eyes on the group. He fingered the end of a small twig clamped between his teeth and watched La Salle disentangle himself with a final nod to the ironmonger and proprietor of the inn. As the straight figure headed down the street, the man tossed the twig aside and hurried to follow.

"I'm bound for Iroquois lands myself," the man said as he came within earshot of his quarry.

La Salle turned to look at the frontiersman towering beside him. It never failed to astonish him how quickly news spread among the woods runners and trackers of Montreal.

"Normandin's my name. Be pleased to join your contingent."

Not the least taken aback by Normandin's bold offer, La Salle answered, "I don't believe I've heard of you."

"No matter, I know my way around," Normandin winked.

Studying the rugged man, La Salle surmised he probably traded with the English more often than the French.

"Have you gone to the Iroquois lakes?"

"Rich lands," Normandin offered. He saw La Salle's eyes narrow and knew the explorer was wary. At the brothel last night, he had heard that a man named La Salle, a very prosperous trader, was going to be the first Frenchman into Seneca lands. They said La Salle was a gambler, that he'd built the farthest post from Montreal and gotten rich doing so.

That he'd be offering substantial wages and perhaps a percentage of trade in return for making the trek.

Some of the men dismissed the journey as a pointless search for the route to China. Many said La Salle was a crazy man who'd end up dead and penniless if he didn't learn how to settle for what he had. But Normandin wasn't about to be left out of the best opportunity around to get into new trade lands, now that the government had restricted travel solely to those authorized. And if he'd figured right from the conflicting stories, this La Salle probably would've agreed to finding the trade route to anywhere so he could get the jump on better furs. Normandin decided to play his trump card.

"One night at a calumet ceremony, the Indians I was wintering with described a huge river, the Meschaseppi they called it."

La Salle reacted with a start, then shook his head. Here was confirmation that rumors had spread all over Montreal. Normandin's claims were only meant to show himself equal to the venture.

"And what exactly did they tell you?"

"Now that, sir, will take quite a long journey to share."

La Salle stopped walking to regard Normandin a long moment. He's strong, obviously clever, he thought. At least the stories at night will be interesting.

"I've no doubt, Monsieur Normandin, that your story may take more than a journey to unravel," La Salle said with a careful smile as he stretched out his hand. Normandin grasped it in acceptance as the first man to sign on for the trip.

The flat, continuous bunk raised a couple of feet off the ground almost filled the outermost shelter at St. Sulpice Seminary. Henri glanced up from where he and his master carefully double-checked the readiness of the compass, spyglass, and measuring equipment before the expedition set out the next morning. La Salle followed Henri's gaze to where Normandin stood on the bunk illustrating the lyrics to a bawdy song. The woods runners and watermen hired over the last few weeks egged him on from their bedrolls spread across the platform.

Normandin surveyed the group from his perch and fixed his sights on the young priest Galinée bent over his drawing case. Galinée blushed fiercely as Normandin included his name in the lyrics. The men roared with laughter.

Casson angrily looked for La Salle to silence the rude play but saw the expedition leader helping his valet move his pallet from the floor, where he had intended to sleep at his master's feet, up to a space made when La Salle requested some of the men to move down. Galinée looked sheepishly at his superior and saw he would intercede if La Salle would not.

"Cease that blasphemy now, Normandin!"

"Use Casson's name," the men shouted.

Normandin easily inserted the elder priest's name into his song as Casson shook his fist in the air.

La Salle jumped atop the platform and headed toward Normandin, whose song slowly subsided.

"Thank you, Normandin, for such an invigorating melody," La Salle said as he came aside the burly man. The men whooped approval. Normandin bowed and then acquiesced to the explorer's gesture that he take a seat.

"Tomorrow, we begin a long journey. Our path heralds a new time for France." La Salle studied the faces of the men. Each comes for his own reasons, he thought. Some strictly for the money, others for the possibility of establishing their own trade connections, and others because it is the only thing they know how to do.

And why do I do it? he wondered. La Salle admitted to himself that finding the northwest passage before the Jesuits did would taste of sweet vindication, but as he looked around at the men who would follow him on the morrow, the tools of his vision, he decided he was journeying west because he had to. It was his destiny. The explorations begun by the great Cartier and Champlain must be continued. La Salle knew he had been chosen to do it. He realized he would never be satisfied with just going into Seneca lands, but what a grand beginning it would be.

La Salle's gaze moved to Father Galinée's young face and the stiff stance of Father Casson.

"For our Savior," La Salle continued, "and for France we must be diligent and persevere against many hardships to succeed. Rest well tonight for the morrow brings untold adventures."

The men leaned in to one another to talk. La Salle jumped off the bunk and strolled back toward his sleeping space. He stopped here and there to respond to a variety of questions, to offer a word of encouragement. More than one inquired of the Seneca who would be traveling with them, or of the lands into which they ventured. La Salle understood their concern. Many had lost friends and family in Seneca raids. He tried his best to calm their fears, promising that the Seneca had complete trust in him, and that he would monitor their every move.

When La Salle reached Fathers Galinée and Casson he extended the wish that they would offer a special blessing before climbing into the canoes the next morning. With forced politeness Casson responded it would be his honor. La Salle bowed his head in appreciation.

Hanging lamps were extinguished as the men bedded down. La Salle took one still lit and stepped into the warm night air. Moths besieged the flame as he made his way to the low campfire where the Seneca prepared to sleep. Thaka and several warriors bid him welcome.

In the language they had improvised between them to supplement the trade jargon they shared, La Salle thanked the men for honoring him with the journey to their village. The Seneca accepted the formal words and told La Salle that, as promised, they would provide him with a guide to the Oyo River when he reached their village, a town no white man had visited before. With the exchange of respects they parted.

La Salle extinguished his lantern before re-entering the sleeping quarters. A chorus of snores played as he found his pallet. Many hours would pass before his excitement ebbed enough for sleep to overtake him.

CHAPTER FOUR

Rᵢᵥᵤₗₑₜₛ ᴏꜰ ꜱᴡᴇᴀᴛ streaked the bare torsos that were moving less spryly than three weeks ago at the journey's start. La Salle slapped mosquitoes as he planted a sharpened branch into the ground for the loose stockade being thrown together. He glanced at the sun. In only a few hours the insects would descend in full force to torment them.

"Henri," said La Salle as he wiped his neck with the cloth his servant had handed him, "have Normandin set Blackie and Bruno to building a large fire."

The small man wiped his brow at the thought of such additional heat on a sweltering day.

"Perhaps Patrice will deliver on his cooking stories," La Salle explained between gulps from the bowl of water Henri had put in his hands.

"Yes, monsieur," Henri almost drooled.

The expedition had been sustained on dried jerky and cornmeal, and the Frenchmen's complaints had grown. Although it filled the belly and allowed for them to keep a steady pace without slowing down to hunt and cook, La Salle saw he would have to make some allowances. He had steeled himself for the Seneca's pace of paddling sixteen or more hours a day, stopping only to sleep. He wished he had found a crew that could keep up.

Just a necessary delay, La Salle consoled himself as he moved to the shore where the Seneca propped up canoes to drain. What a luxury it would be to wake up under trees, instead of in rocking canoes as they had done several nights, and put one's feet into a dry craft even though it wouldn't long stay that way.

Thaka and the others paused in their work as La Salle approached. Patiently he waited for the Seneca to sit, as was the custom, before speaking.

"Fishing good here?" La Salle asked. Thaka nodded. "And fowl?" Again he nodded. "Will you honor us with your hunting and fishing skills before the sun sets?"

The day was late. Seneca preferred to spend a day fishing then another smoking and drying their catch. La Salle saw he was asking them to do something out of the usual routine.

"Tonight we will make a special ceremony to celebrate going into the great Iroquois lake tomorrow."

Thaka exchanged a few guttural words with the others that were beyond La Salle's Seneca vocabulary. Eventually the warriors agreed, and began their preparations.

Wind rustled through leafy branches. The acrid smell of wood smoke overtook the fresh green of the tall trees as the men stoked the fire. La Salle wouldn't bother suggesting that any of them join the Seneca hunting party. He knew they wouldn't go with the Indians but instead would split off and turn the attempt to have a good meal into full-blown competition. Relations had been strained between the two groups when forced to work together. For the most part La Salle had managed to keep them at a distance, and the Seneca had become more withdrawn because of it.

Patrice readily accepted the challenge to cook, and La Salle turned to seek the Sulpician priests, on his way directing the men to finish the low stockade that would give them some shelter from beast or man during the night. It was hard work but the change from the monotony of paddling and the spreading word that tonight they would eat a real meal livened their movements.

A couple of woods runners plunged into the water to cool themselves. Many would sleep half-naked, impervious to the stings of insistent bugs, while others would fully clothe themselves in hot buckskins for protection. La Salle and many of the more woods wise, like Normandin, simply slathered on the bear grease and herbs, the Indian's remedy, that repelled most bites.

A natural leader, Normandin had frequently stepped in to direct the other men. It was against La Salle's better judgment to share control, but this expedition was larger by far than any he had ever led. Grudgingly, he admitted to himself he could not personally oversee every detail, and portioned some authority to Normandin, who had already claimed as much as he could, short of obvious insubordination.

Lately Normandin had tried to coax La Salle into discussing details of his strategy. Assaulting La Salle with questions whenever the leader confirmed the lay of the land with the Seneca, Normandin often met with a sharp rebuke. Every bit as proud as La Salle himself, Normandin smarted from such treatment, but it did not curtail his confronting the expedition leader.

"You know, La Salle," Normandin grumbled, "me and Blackie could have shot several doe by now."

"I expect, Normandin, you will provide us with a venison feast soon," La Salle placated as he continued toward the priests. "Very soon."

When La Salle was out of earshot, Normandin declared with a scowl, "Never trust a man who sides with Indians." He spoke to no one in particular, although many overheard.

Father Galinée transferred the readings he had taken throughout the day into his journal. Next to him Father Casson let out a groan. Galinée looked up to see La Salle approaching them and knew Casson preparing for an argument.

For the past several nights, Casson had worried Galinée with his angry threats of forcing La Salle to change his course as soon as they reached the Iroquois lake. It would be the perfect moment to take a northwestern journey instead of a southwestern one since they would be obliged to follow the shoreline in one direction or another to reach the Seneca village at its western end. Galinée doubted Casson could persuade La Salle to change direction, but had not said as much to his superior.

A faint breeze played at the expedition leader's untied hair. The confident expression on La Salle's tanned face made Galinée reciprocate with a smile. It's no wonder people follow him, the young priest thought; his very carriage commands attention.

"Fathers," La Salle greeted them, "tonight will you grant us a special Mass? To replenish our spirits in preparation of entering the lake tomorrow . . ."

"Of course, monsieur," Casson answered with excessive civility. "A much better idea to celebrate a mark on the journey than to take time out for a holy day."

La Salle held back a retort. Casson had suggested several Masses before but La Salle had not wanted to detract from the freshness of the voyage. And the men hadn't evidenced any remorse at going for so long without Communion.

"In this summer heat, it'd be wise to follow the northern shoreline to the Seneca village." Casson watched La Salle. "I have been told it is much cooler and no longer distance than the southern shore."

"Your suggestion is greatly appreciated," La Salle replied with only the barest trace of sarcasm. "But since we will continue traveling south," La Salle stressed, "after our stay at the Seneca, it'd be wiser to establish knowledge of the southern shore."

Casson placed his fists on his hips and planted his feet apart as if he were once more in the army. In contrast La Salle relaxed his posture. Galinée caught back his laugh at the thought that La Salle was almost beckoning Casson to strike a blow, and wondered if this argument would be limited to verbal sparring.

"Your mind is so crowded with more important things, monsieur, that I am compelled to remind you of the Jesuit presence on the southern shore."

"One Jesuit in one village. I have not forgotten."

"No Jesuits and no Sulpicians in any northern villages."

"Nor at the Seneca village we journey to, nor with the southern tribes we'll meet en route to the Oyo River. The route," La Salle continued, "that our government, in the name of His Highness, has commissioned that we undertake."

He bowed slightly and started to leave but Casson would have the last word.

"And I foolishly thought," the stocky priest said with a forced chuckle, "that perhaps you'd forgotten our mission in this wilderness.

"Just for a moment," Casson continued, letting his chuckle die, "I thought your brother was right."

Barely able to control the enraged tremble surging through him, La Salle spun away. Casson eased himself down next to Galinée as they both watched La Salle head to where Henri prepared his master's bedroll.

"That, Galinée, was most enjoyable."

Galinée set down his journal. "But you didn't change the direction of the journey."

"Not this time," smirked Casson, confident he would soon push La Salle aside to send the expedition in its rightful direction.

Some islets crowding the entrance to the great lake were only gray rocks; others were small tufts of long green grass that stilt-legged birds circled like sentries. The shores were lined with fine chestnut, walnut, and elm broken by stretches of prairie where in the distance an occasional herd of elk or deer scurried away. La Salle declared he had never seen such beauty, but most of the woods runners ignored his enthusiasm.

That morning, with the milestone of gaining the lake finally passed, the men had let out a cheer. The full dinner of fish and heavy breakfast of fowl had made them all feel better. Even Father Casson had been pleased as the men had thanked him for Communion the night before. As much as anything the healthy change of scenery had lifted everyone's spirits.

But now at the height of the day, as the summer sun pounded down, the men griped. The broad water of the lake stretched past the horizon. Patrice and Bruno, along with other woods runners born in the colony, had never crossed the ocean and, nervous at such an expanse of open water, rushed to hug the land with their canoes. La Salle, Normandin, and the Seneca continuously had to call them back out to where paddling went more swiftly.

But farther out a stiff breeze fringed the waves with white foam and rocked the canoes. Soon bouts of seasickness overcame the less hardy. La Salle realized that instead of sleeping in the canoes to save time as he had hoped, they would be forced to go more often ashore.

As the days dragged on, La Salle changed his regimen. To put up a protective palisade each night would fatigue the men too much for the morrow's paddling, so he decided instead to post double guards. This was not a solution without shortcomings, as those on sentry were always less able the next day and more apt to be ill-tempered. The situation was further complicated by the Frenchmen's refusal to allow the Seneca to take their turn at watch. With murderous glances at the Indians, they whispered loudly among themselves that the bloody savages would slit their throats as soon as their eyes were shut.

Normandin and his small entourage of admirers usually escaped such duty by becoming providers of game. But the hunt with musket and shot was so easy that the pleasure in exhibiting this prowess soon wore off, especially in comparison to the Seneca's skill at spearing fish in shallows and sometimes catching them with bare hands.

Father Casson kept to himself as Galinée became more involved with La Salle in charting the southern shore. The day they passed the waterway leading from the huge falls the Seneca had spoken of was particularly exciting for Galinée and La Salle. Although tempted to follow the inlet, La Salle knew they would have plenty of time later when they returned this way with the guides that the Seneca had promised would be waiting at their village.

One morning, just after daybreak, a gray fog enveloped the flotilla as it headed from overnight shelter at the mouth of a small creek. As the group moved into the lake a stiff breeze rose that wiped clear the mist, and tugged at their hair and the fringe of their buckskins. The canoes veered into the wind. The fog whisked from the dancing water but the reflection of the slate-gray sky remained. The men paddled unevenly, unnerved by the darkening, rumbling clouds overhead.

With no sun to mark noon, La Salle judged the hour by his hunger. He waved the men ashore. The worsening waves were making them queasy and he doubted many would keep even cornmeal down if they ate in their rocking canoes. The brief meal finished, Normandin voiced his objection to setting out again.

"We'll only get drenched," he complained, and several woods runners muttered agreement. "Besides, how much closer can we get to your damn village in this wind?"

La Salle went to discuss the situation with the Seneca.

"See whose opinion the emperor of China prefers," Normandin criticized. Casson chuckled at the woods runner's remark.

The Seneca confirmed La Salle's suspicions. The wind would not slow them much and if the weather worsened they would need better shelter than this exposed spot. Up ahead, several creeks fed the lake, which could lead them away from the shore and lend protection.

La Salle helped shove off his reluctant flotilla into the rollicking surf. Away from shore the canoes fared better, rocking and pitching but seaworthy enough to keep passengers and cargo dry until the dark clouds finally cracked open. The windswept drizzle that had stung their faces grew into fat drops that splatted down harder and faster.

La Salle stopped every few strokes to peer at the shore through sheets of rain. He knew he could easily miss an inlet from such a distance, but the surf crashing against shore made travel closer in too dangerous. He wondered if he was wise to have consulted the Seneca. With the growing animosity between them and the woods runners, they might have ill advised him in order to test the group. La Salle dismissed his concerns. They were all in agreement of their mission, he was certain. The men are just weary, he told himself.

"If this is a summer storm," La Salle yelled back to Henri, "then winter travel must be impossible. We'll need bigger boats eventually, proper ships with sails to transport furs back east."

A loud moan in reply made him turn around. His paddle tossed aside, Henri clung to the sides of the surging canoe as his stomach heaved.

"Hold on, Henri," shouted La Salle. Again he searched the shore. There was little he could do to comfort his companion except find safe harbor. Double-checking the group, he assured himself they fared better than Henri. Normandin waved that everyone else was all right.

A break appeared in the tree line that probably marked a stream. La Salle couldn't be sure, but he had to be to risk sending the canoes in. Rain pummeled him. He moved a hand from his paddle to slick back his hair, then held his hand against his forehead to shield his eyes. A wave slammed into the canoe as a gust of wind struck them broadside. La Salle felt himself going overboard and clutched at the boat frantically. Water cascaded in. His first few words of prayer were cut short by the eerily calm realization that his brother had been right: they would all perish because of his dreams. He was a fool. He would die from his foolishness, and he would lead other good men to their deaths as well.

Then the bark canoe popped itself back up. Full of water and riding lower on the lake, the craft the Indians had been perfecting for a millennium proved its worth.

La Salle blessed his good fortune until he realized he had lost his paddle and with it his ability to help control the canoe. As he wrenched around to look for it he saw that Henri was gone. Why in blazes had no one shouted, La Salle

wondered. But every boat had been hit as hard by the freak-
ish wave.

"Count the men," La Salle frantically ordered Normandin
as he searched the water for Henri. Shouting and pointing,
the men directed his attention to where Henri bobbed, his
head above, now under, then again peeking over the churn-
ing water.

"Turn! Turn!" La Salle cried over the howling wind to
Bruno at the stern.

"I'm trying!" Bruno shouted, urgently wrestling the waves.

In desperation, La Salle leaned forward and paddled with
his hands to bring the vessel to where Henri struggled. The
canoe responded, fighting the waves as La Salle and Bruno
labored. Water lapped over the sides.

"Bail!" Bruno yelled over the crack of thunder and pounding rain. "Can't help him if we sink!"

But La Salle ignored him. Henri's head rose less often
above the water, and his arms no longer flailed.

"I'm going in after him." La Salle rose up on his knees to
hurl himself over the side.

"You'll drown!" Bruno yelled.

La Salle defied the warning and prepared to dive when another canoe, nearly forgotten in his fear for Henri's life, cut
through the waves toward the drowning man. Normandin,
his hair flat against his head, rivulets streaming into his
beard, scooped Henri's limp body toward him with a paddle,
then with a strong arm pulled him aboard.

"Bravo!" called La Salle. "Bravo!"

Normandin's canoe flew by. La Salle saw the other boats
heading toward the break in the trees. He turned to direct
Bruno to follow but the woods runner was already paddling
in the same direction with all his might.

Huddling under the hastily prepared shelter while the
storm blew for two days—going on three—exasperated the
men. Small irritations usually overlooked grew into squab-
bles. In such close quarters, La Salle knew he could not order
them to control themselves as he needed to when journeying.

Instead he tried to humor them, exchange stories, and speak freely about the trials of the trek. More often than not, his attempts at camaraderie were futile.

Although La Salle felt he had made the best possible decision to go back out on the lake, the men resented him for having risked their lives and almost losing one of their team, even if it was La Salle's valet. La Salle refused to defend himself against the veiled accusations that erupted, but such refusal only served to alienate him more. Stoically, he concentrated on his journals and maps.

Henri, fully recovered, spent every free moment showing Normandin his gratitude. The burly woods runner now received the first cut of meat or dish of stew previously reserved for La Salle. Normandin took the homage as his due and La Salle encouraged his valet's deference to the man who had saved his life, at least until Normandin grew slightly abusive of Henri's willingness to serve him by piling his own and his buddies' mending on the slight servant. La Salle suggested to Henri that he had shown Normandin his appreciation well enough.

"I'm certain there will be times you can help out Normandin in the future, Henri."

Normandin resented La Salle taking Henri away from him even though the leader assigned Henri to helping the Sulpicians, not back into service for himself. In hopes of calming the men's nerves, La Salle had approached the priests about spending more time among them. The tired priests could certainly use Henri's help more than he or Normandin.

"It would be our pleasure to console the men," Casson had said almost too politely. "And yourself as well, Monsieur La Salle, should you seek the comfort of confession."

Galinée had wanted to express his disapproval of Casson's barbs, but such a reprimand of his superior was not in Galinée's nature. Nevertheless, when La Salle had blushed in anger, he had done so too in sympathy.

Meanwhile, the men devised amusements to help them endure the misery of the ceaseless downpour. Several worked on embroidering their leggings, trying to outdo one another by adding designs to the already extravagant patterns each used as his signature.

Blackie had spent the first afternoon of the storm carving a pair of dice from willow and painstakingly marking each face. Soon the men became obsessed with who won or lost the fortunes they planned to make on the voyage, ignoring the priests' objections to such an idle vice. They kept the tallies in their heads and argued loudly when the losers' count did not keep pace with the winners'.

Soon they came to blows when Blackie was accused of having unfairly weighted his homemade dice. La Salle broke up the fight but was reluctant, when asked, to judge who was right.

"If gambling causes distrust, stop gambling. For all our sakes."

"But I was winning," Blackie argued.

"Only because you cheated," the other objected.

"Enough from both of you. Give me the dice." La Salle inspected them. Blackie had done a fair job of carving. They were almost perfectly square with the dots on each face nearly as evenly spaced as the proper dice imported from France that one could buy in Quebec's boutiques.

"Weigh them," implored Blackie. "They're as fair a pair of dice as a . . ."

"As a habitual crook like Blackie could come up with," Normandin interjected to the jeers of the others.

There would be no happy settlement to the argument, La Salle saw. He plunged into the pouring rain and with all his might hurled the dice into open water. With twin splashes they dropped into the creek, to the woods runners' dismay.

"No more gambling on this voyage," La Salle commanded, hoping the matter was over. He had solved the problem for the moment but the men, even the losers, resented him for it.

Soon they replaced their gambling with bartering and arguing over the colored threads they used for the emblems on their leggings.

The Seneca began to worry La Salle. He had come to know them over the winter at La Chine but now could not breach their distant expressions. Increasingly restricted to their area of the shelter, they became uneasy under the stares and occasional accusations of the men who had lost relatives to the Seneca and their Iroquois confederates. La Salle did his best to spend time with them, and reassure them that, like all animals, men grew crazed under such constraints. The Seneca understood but now regarded La Salle with as much coldness as they did the rest of the Frenchmen.

The wind changed and the skies cleared. The troop pulled on extra shirts and woolen stockings against the suddenly cooler mornings and evenings as they set out onto the lake once more.

Late one afternoon the Seneca directed the party to a tree-shrouded cove and indicated where the canoes should be stored for the journey to their village, which lay not far inland. La Salle refused to leave the canoes unattended and designated Galinée to stay behind with a little more than half the men until their return.

"What if we're attacked?" Father Casson reprimanded, yanking La Salle aside. "We'd be stronger as one unit, not two weak ones."

"There's no concern of attack," La Salle assured as he pried loose the priest's grip. "As a smaller party we'll move more quickly and be less threatening. Our biggest worry is to keep our canoes secure.

"I know what I'm doing, Father," La Salle insisted as doubt clouded Casson's face.

He had chosen Casson to come along, instead of the more amiable and, because of his map-making skills, useful Father Galinée, in hopes that a visit to a godless village would convince Casson the lake's southern shore was as much in need of his ministries as the northern route he had badgered La Salle to travel.

La Salle wondered if the priest questioned his commands not because he preferred a northern route, but because the former soldier wanted to be in charge once more, and deeply resented taking orders from a younger, nonmilitary man. But now La Salle almost regretted his choice.

La Salle forced a confident smile at his entourage as he watched Normandin, Henri, Casson, and a few more men head down the path behind the swift-moving Seneca. Not one of them could tell that La Salle, as much as they, was anxious about what awaited them. But unlike the others, La Salle looked forward to the uncertainty of what they would encounter.

He heard every sound of the forest; his nose tracked every scent. Never did he feel more alive than at moments like this, alert to the danger, but thrilled by the prospect that he'd soon visit an Indian town no white man had ever seen.

CHAPTER FIVE

THAKA AND HIS TRIBESMEN broke into a run. Between the weighted packs and the rutted trail, the Frenchmen could not keep pace.

"What is it?" puffed La Salle.

The Seneca warriors did not respond but made loud whooping cries punctuated only by the rhythm of their feet. The party burst from the woods into an expanse of fields. In the center rose a tall log palisade. La Salle signaled his men to stop running and continue more slowly down the path to the village gate through which the warriors had disappeared. All eyes fixed on the looming structure before them.

"Sacred heart of Jesus," Blackie said. "I've never seen anything so huge."

"A Seneca city thrives within these walls," La Salle marveled aloud. He saw Father Casson cross himself as they neared the open portal and himself reached up to touch the silver crucifix of the rosary tucked under his shirt.

Indians, men and women, crowded the parapet around the inner edge of the palisade, watching the group's approach. They pointed and shouted to one another, calling behind them to describe the men to those who could not see. The whooping cry the warriors had made echoed from within.

61

"Why are they making that noise?" Henri asked.

"It's a greeting," La Salle assumed. "Our friends have been gone a long time. Now everyone knows they're back."

"And that we're here," Normandin added.

The men glanced around nervously as they stepped across the threshold into the Seneca domain.

"When you lead me to the Oyo River," La Salle said in trade jargon with a smattering of broken Seneca, "my great and powerful father, the Sun King, will honor you."

The seated elders and warriors again asked Thaka to translate. Most had understood what the foreigner said, even with his strange accent. At least all of them sensed the importance of his meaning. But it would not pay to trifle with the nuance of his words. When Thaka concluded they looked to one another, exchanging brief comments. The eldest man, seated across from La Salle, spoke for them through Thaka's translation.

"We will bring you many furs from Oyo."

"When you take me to Oyo, my brothers and yours will become one strong tribe."

The Seneca shrugged. "We are already strong."

La Salle rested his hands on his crossed knees. They had smoked the calumet, they had exchanged pleasantries, but for the moment he seemed unable to negotiate passage to the Oyo.

"The river Oyo is so great that many tribes must know its riches," La Salle stated. Perhaps he could goad them into divulging something about the southwestern trade routes. He watched the befeathered old men lean toward each other and gesture at him. He ruefully sensed his audience was at an end even before Thaka told him so.

"Tomorrow," explained Thaka as he unfolded himself to stand, "they will talk with you again. The Oyo lands hold much . . . peril. There is much to consider."

La Salle stood up. The Oyo lands indeed hold much peril, he thought. Peril to whom? Most likely to the Seneca because of the excellent trade they're afraid to share. But I will discover those lands with or without your approval, he added to himself as he looked them over once again. Gracefully he bowed an exit to the council of elders.

"A ceremony has been arranged to welcome you and celebrate the success of our warriors on a Shawnee raid," Thaka explained as he led La Salle past curious villagers strolling the crisscross of well-trod paths connecting the elongated rounded buildings, covered in sheaves of bark, that each housed many families. Above each longhouse door hung an effigy carved of wood: a turtle, a fish, a man. Crossed poles topped with feathers and totems were propped outside. Horn tools, fired clay utensils, and baskets hung on them mingled with European iron pots and steel hatchets.

La Salle noticed that the Seneca clothing reflected years of trading with the English post at Albany. Mixed in with fur and buckskin were woven textiles, tunics cut from blankets, and colorful ribbons tied to buckskin fringe. An older Indian wore a faded British army coat and several had wide-brimmed hats.

A strident, bloodcurdling yell pierced the blue-black dusk as Thaka led La Salle to a clearing at one side of the dozen or so longhouses. It appeared most of the village was seated in a wide circle around a tall pole. La Salle spotted his men isolated in a small group amidst the crowd. He and Thaka moved to sit beside them.

A running warrior, his long feathered hair floating behind him, burst into the space around the pole outlined by the ring of expectant villagers, who cheered his arrival with whoops and shrill cries. He circled the pole, covering the space between it and the crowd in an energetic dance, all the while shouting at the top of his lungs.

"They celebrate bravery on a raid," Thaka explained and La Salle repeated to his men.

Suddenly a stream of shrieking young men flooded the circle. Perspiration glistened on the black, yellow, and red war paint of their faces and bodies. They waved heavy war clubs and feather-tipped bows above their heads. In the middle of them a closely guarded Indian tried to keep up. The warriors danced around the circle keeping him surrounded.

La Salle noticed that the Indian in the center did not dance. He looked strikingly different from the others because he wore a roach, a line of hair a few inches wide centered across his scalp from forehead to nape with the sides clean-shaven or plucked. To Thaka, who had stayed close by, La Salle indicated the difference between Seneca scalp locks and the man's roach.

"Shawnee," he explained. "Captured on the raid."

"What is it?" Henri asked when he noticed the sudden drain of blood from his master's face.

"We've been invited to a death ceremony," La Salle grimaced.

The small group of Frenchmen looked nervously from one to the other. Everyone had heard tales of how the Seneca tortured their captives to a lingering death. The stories were gruesome and, La Salle hoped, overly embellished.

The village elders moved to the front of the crowd and took their seats of honor. When the eldest called out, a middle-aged woman stood up. The crowd fell silent. The dancing stopped. Slowly she raised both hands, screamed out several words in Seneca, then fell to her knees wailing.

Two warriors yanked the Shawnee to the pole. With rawhide thongs they bound his hands and feet. He shouted out in a singsong voice as the Seneca pulled his bonds tighter.

"He is the one who will stand for her husband," Thaka told La Salle as he pointed to the Shawnee and the wailing woman. "Her husband was killed by a Shawnee in our raid, so a Shawnee will be killed," the Seneca concluded, with a smile at the perfect balance.

La Salle turned to his men wondering how much they had understood of the Seneca's words. Normandin whispered to them. He pointed to the prisoner and the woman, then caught his leader's eye. The two men shared an uneasy look.

The newly widowed squah was offered a spear. Its sharp point of chipped flint glinted in the light. Weeping and shouting she ran at the Shawnee, jabbing him in the thigh. The crowd shouted their approval.

"Mother of God," Casson prayed, "forgive their sins."

The Frenchmen listened to the victim's painful song grow louder as the embattled warriors circled him. Each taking a turn then stepping back for the next, they inflicted harsh blows and stabbed the helpless prisoner. Bruno could not stand it. His brother had disappeared near Iroquois lands. He could only imagine that the same had happened to him. He jumped to his feet to leave but Seneca rushed towards the group to prevent him. Several woods runners pulled him back down.

"Back in France in front of the cathedral at Reims, when I was five or six, I watched a man be flayed alive," Normandin boasted. "It took all day for him to die."

Bruno clamped his hands over his ears. The other woods runners watched the torture before them and listened to Normandin in abhorrent fascination. La Salle recalled that Christian heretics, like the Shawnee before him, were given the same horrific deaths.

"How long will this last?"

"If he is very brave, half a day," Thaka told La Salle. "Even now the Shawnee says the men do not strike hard enough. His heart is very brave. When he dies the warriors will share it and gain his strength."

La Salle understood. A celebration in our honor is not what they display, he thought. They show their cruelty and strength to deter us. They gloat over their savage bravery that allows them to eat another man's heart. But they cannot make me turn back.

La Salle studied his men, their fascinated, panicked faces. He knew they wondered if the Seneca would perform similar rituals on them. La Salle fought back his desire to insist that Thaka lead them away from the ceremony. It would only show weakness.

"You honor us," La Salle declared, "with your display of strength."

The Seneca did not acknowledge the compliment but watched in amused silence as La Salle forced his attention back to the ceremony.

La Salle was last to stretch out beside the fire on the low cots lining the inside wall of the rectangular shelter. He brushed his hand across the large, rough sheath of elm bark with which the Seneca constructed their dwellings. The vast empty expanse of the rest of the longhouse loomed beyond him. He repressed the desire to explore its every nook and cranny, to study every tool, basket, pot of unguents, and hanging herb. It seemed a shame not to take advantage of the absence of the Seneca who inhabited this dwelling. They had refused to stay with strangers but La Salle suspected it was the elders' idea to keep him apart from any more curious, and possibly more sympathetic, members of the tribe.

When the group had regained the relative safety of the longhouse, after the ceremony and a meal for which few of them had any appetite, some of the men had raged at having been obliged to witness the Shawnee's tortured death. Casson's anger had culminated in a frothing fury before La Salle had convinced him that whether it was a ceremony in their honor or a show to terrorize them, they had had to stay. There had been no choice but to match the Seneca at their own game.

Arguing in self-defense, La Salle had felt justified. Now, alone in the silence, watching his men restlessly toss on the hard beds, worried about what unpalatable experience the morrow would bring, he pressed back burning tears. More than any of the others, he had negotiated and lived among the natives. He acknowledged their extremely different perspective on justice, on man, on life. He did not approve of it, as Casson had accused, but understood that each waking moment of a warrior's life was a chance to prove his right to live, to prove his worthiness over his opponent. To conquer such a people, one had to best them on their own field. Tonight, though a small victory, was a test that La Salle had met.

A muffled chorus of male voices made him rise up on one elbow. As it grew louder, La Salle realized it was one lead song, repeated by many others. The men who had not drifted into sleep looked across the low fire to their leader. The sound was nearing and a rhythmic beat, of what sounded like sticks striking one another, joined it. La Salle sat up on his cot as the noise encircled their dwelling and stopped.

Slowly at first, then more rapidly, the sticks began beating on the outside walls. La Salle jumped up, colliding with the other men. They were terrified.

"Calm down," he ordered, "Calm! Father Casson, Normandin, see to the men. There is no strength in panic."

Half-dressed, La Salle raced from the longhouse. Seneca warriors swarmed around it, chanting and pounding the walls with their sticks. He grabbed the arm of one brave, who angrily wrenched away from him. Thaka intervened.

"What is this?" La Salle demanded of him.

"Evil spirits roam at night," he explained. "The elders sent us to frighten them away from our honored guests."

La Salle's eyes blazed. He dashed back inside to explain to his men.

"This is an outrage," Casson boomed. "They are expressly tormenting us."

"I know, Father," La Salle spat back, as he finished dressing. "I know and I'm going to resolve this with the elders at once. Stay inside. Show no fear." He looked directly at Normandin. "Don't even consider retaliation."

La Salle pushed his way back outside and stormed off in the direction of the elders' council hut as the warriors continued their staccato pounding. He would not protest the Seneca's "assistance" in keeping away evil spirits, although he knew it was just a ploy to strain the men's nerves and keep them at odds with each other tomorrow after a sleepless night.

Instead he would insist the elders allow him to use his own cure to ward off bad spirits. He fingered the rosary hanging around his neck until he came to the small silver crucifix at its end. Tucking it more securely into his shirt, he searched his mind for the rhythms of a hymn.

In the stark moonlight, longhouse shadows loomed up, confusing La Salle's path. He turned down several alleys until he came near the central plaza, where he could take his bearings. He saw the council hut across the clearing, where villagers still lingered. Several warriors intercepted him.

La Salle shook off their grasp. "I will see the elders now," he said in broken Seneca.

The warriors looked at one another. La Salle pointed at the council hut and began in that direction. The Seneca blocked his path again.

"Blast you," La Salle shouted. "You cannot cow me."

Weak laughter emerged from behind the small group of Seneca warriors. A Shawnee prisoner stood with his hands bound before him, tethered to one of the Seneca. La Salle flinched as a warrior grabbed the Shawnee's roach and yanked his head backward. In the moonlight, La Salle saw the rough welts and cuts on the captive's face and head. The Shawnee's eyes, veiled with pain, fixed on the white man.

The prisoner was hardly older than La Salle. He would die, La Salle knew, die horribly as his tribesman had. The Seneca were cruel. And cunning, La Salle thought as he suddenly realized he had been tricked. He had not convinced Thaka to bring him here, he had been lured. And he had taken the bait as quickly as any mindless carp.

The Seneca would never lead him to the Oyo. He was the biggest trader in Montreal. They knew that, and they had brought him here to refuse what he bargained for, to illustrate their power and ruthlessness so that he might return defeated and thus send the message to all other traders of the impenetrable Seneca wall that even La Salle could not breach.

La Salle chided himself for his stupidity in not perceiving their plan. Even if he could find and persuade a more self-ambitious Seneca to guide them, after what they'd seen, his woods runners would never follow.

Damn, damn, he thought, I've given up every hard-won

moment of my life in New France to finance this voyage. I can't turn back now. This cannot end in failure.

Drunk with pain, the young Shawnee captive laughed again. La Salle drew the stout knife from his waistband and lifted it so the blade glinted. The Seneca grinned and, chattering among themselves, motioned for him to go ahead and strike a blow to their captive.

"You're the same as the damn Seneca," the Shawnee mumbled in La Salle's French-Indian trade jargon.

Suppressing his surprise at the Indian's knowledge of French words, La Salle completed the motion he had begun. In a sharp downward move, he sliced the tether that bound the Shawnee, then shoved the Seneca jailer back. La Salle held tightly to the Shawnee, yanking him into protection behind him. Growling like a bobcat, La Salle brandished his blade.

The Seneca did not retreat but neither did any of them show a desire to advance on the white man. To insult them so brazenly, when they were armed with war clubs and he was alone with only a small knife, was surely an act of madness. Madness was part of the order of things. Madmen were often protected by spirits, and therefore not to be trifled with.

Loudly, the natives spoke to one another, then to the Shawnee. La Salle tried to follow their discourse, but only caught a word or two.

"They think you are either very brave or crazy," the Shawnee translated.

"Tell them I am both," La Salle responded, "and that I will take this worthless Shawnee."

"I am not worthless," the captive objected.

"Tell them!" La Salle directed the Indian behind him. "And tell them their elders will see me at daybreak tomorrow and answer my demands."

The Shawnee translated. The Seneca did not respond. La Salle released another growl before backing away from the Seneca braves. He half-expected to have his head clubbed in, but instead the warriors simply watched their stumbling prisoner be led away.

"How do you come to speak my language?" La Salle inquired as he cut loose the Indian's bound hands.

"I speak all trade languages. I am Shawnee."

La Salle had vaguely heard of the Shawnee tribe but could not recall if any had journeyed to New France. They moved along the path back to the men, guided by the rhythmic sound of sticks against the longhouse.

"Where do Shawnee come from?"

"Southwest."

The Shawnee abandoned his task of untangling the leather thongs that had lashed his wrists to face the light-skinned man who stopped abruptly in front of him.

"Do you know the river Oyo?" La Salle asked. With a gentle tug he pulled the remaining thongs from the Shawnee's hands.

The Indian studied the Frenchman as he rubbed his wrists. He had traded with white men before but this one was strange. Never had he seen a white man risk angering another tribe, especially the Seneca, on behalf of a single Indian.

"I know Oyo."

La Salle possessively put his hand on the Shawnee's shoulder. The Seneca are not going to help us journey south, La Salle said to himself. Tonight's events make it obvious they are determined to intimidate us. The Shawnee's shoulder moved in irritation under La Salle's hand.

La Salle gazed at the Indian. They were roughly the same age. One had journeyed from the northeast, the other from the southwest. Both were here together. For La Salle it seemed a fateful coincidence. Tomorrow he would tell the Seneca he had decided not to continue southwest. But when he and his men were far enough away, that would be the direction in which they would head, with this Shawnee as their guide. Elated, La Salle threw back his head in relieved laughter. Once more, the expedition had escaped disaster. It made him feel powerful, hungry to begin again.

"I am La Salle," he told the Shawnee. "You will travel with me southwest."

The Shawnee hesitated to speak. This white man was claiming him in a way he did not like. But at the same time the spirits, in the shape of this man, had prevented his journey to the higher world, the world to which his uncle had traveled that evening at the Seneca ceremony. The Shawnee knew he was in a period of transience, that he was not permanently in any world. It would be best to remain disinterested until the shape of the chosen world became distinct.

"I am Nika," he said somberly.

Aware that the Shawnee was withdrawing for some reason, La Salle dropped his hand. He inclined his head in acknowledgment of the Shawnee's name and, with an outstretched hand, invited him in the direction of the longhouse. They continued on as La Salle glanced occasionally at the silent Shawnee beside him, who stared unwaveringly ahead.

CHAPTER SIX

"You told the Seneca we weren't going to the Oyo. You lied to them before God," Father Casson quarreled.

On the autumn-dappled path leading from the Seneca village back to the shore where the rest of the expedition still waited, the group of men hesitated. Fatigue from their frightful stay at the Seneca town mingled with relief from having somehow survived it. Now irritation overcame them as outrage grew on the priest's face. They knew the trek back to the rest of the group would be peppered with objections from the soldierly cleric.

"So what if he lied to them? Who the hell cares? As long as we're away from there," Normandin growled, pointing back up the path. The others nodded agreement as they hoisted their packs to their shoulders and began to trudge forward.

"I said no such thing, Father," La Salle insisted as Casson marched on several paces ahead. La Salle checked to see if Nika, the Shawnee, was keeping apace with the group.

This morning the Shawnee had helped him explain to the Seneca elders that the expedition no longer wanted to travel southwest with their guides. It had been a great asset for La Salle to have fluent translation of his trade jargon. It had allowed for careful concealment of his real intentions. Now he could continue to the southwest without Seneca help but with Nika as their guide instead. The Shawnee was intelligent La Salle saw, and clearly realized that La Salle was stretching the truth here, lying outright there.

La Salle had hoped the Shawnee's gratitude at being saved would make him as faithful a guide as he had been a translator that morning, yet the Indian had remained eerily silent since then. Even now, as La Salle watched him amidst the woods runners, the Shawnee held himself aloof, staring ahead as if in a trance.

La Salle remembered the homage Henri had paid Normandin after the woods runner had pulled him from the frothy lake. Certainly Nika was not so transparently grateful as Henri had been, but then La Salle reminded himself the Shawnee were a nation with which he was unacquainted.

La Salle studied the others. As they walked, the men cast dulled eyes back at him and Casson, listening for the debate to continue. Normandin especially tried to overhear, but glanced away when La Salle caught his eyes. La Salle swallowed his frustration at having his mission questioned, looking to Henri for a vote of confidence. But the servant refused to meet his gaze. A storm was brewing just like the ones between La Salle and his brother, but Henri was simply too weary to sympathize with his master's turmoil.

"The Seneca were informed we no longer needed their assistance in traveling to the southwest," La Salle summarized for the priest.

"Do you hear? You said you weren't going southwest. They believed you. We . . . I believed you," Casson hissed. "The Seneca's lying ways have infected you."

"To convert a heathen you must preach in the heathen's language," La Salle retorted. "As diplomatically as possible I," he emphasized with a hand on his chest, "extricated our expedition from a threatening situation. And gave no ground. Nothing has changed. We travel to the Oyo River."

"Seems to me much has changed, and will change further."

"Father, do you sincerely wish to give up all we have suffered for thus far?" He riveted his gaze on Casson and anyone else who made eye contact.

"Think how blessed we are to live in an age when we can walk into the woods," La Salle continued, encompassing their surroundings with an arm, "and unearth treasures, rich lands to claim as our own? You really would give up such an opportunity?"

"You've made yourself rich and hope to get richer. And you don't care whom you rob of salvation, just so you can be the richest trader in Montreal."

"I *was* the richest trader in Montreal. I'm going to be the richest trader in all the New World. That's the path I've set upon and I'm not going to trod it begrudgingly. I'm going to run along it, leap the streams and fallen logs that might block other men."

La Salle made sure his words registered with everyone, then turned his attention back to the angry priest.

"Glory seeker," Casson muttered.

"Yes, I seek glory," La Salle retorted, "glory for France and for our Lord. Behind me I'll leave men like these." He indicated the woods runners, all of them attentive even as they tramped on. "Each with a position to fill his pockets, a job to perform in a grand design to improve his lot and others'. And the natives too will have their place, each nation baptized in turn, each providing French merchants with the harvest of their lands and receiving in turn the fruits of French ingenuity."

"All that," Casson jeered in a voice destined to reach each woods runner, "you intend to accomplish with a surly Shawnee slave as a guide."

"Yes!" La Salle jumped at the chance to elaborate on Nika's value. "He speaks many tongues and knows Oyo lands." He noticed Normandin's suspicion at the Shawnee's role and continued in defense, "Don't you see that fate has intervened to send us a better guide . . . ?"

"And you begin this grand empire by running from the Seneca, deceiving them, offering them not a single word of gospel nor a single drop of holy water."

Irritation at having to defend again what he saw so clearly inflamed La Salle. He grabbed Casson's shoulders and, eyeing the sun for direction, turned the sputtering priest to face west. The small group came to a straggling halt, anticipating blows between their leader and priest.

"What do you see?" La Salle demanded.

"Trees," Casson answered defensively, shaking off La Salle's hands as he tried to discern the explorer's trick. Normandin and a few others snickered.

"How far do you see?"

"I'll not play your games."

"How far?"

"Forty, maybe fifty paces."

"There is your answer, Casson. You can see fifty paces ahead. I look west and I see the Vermilion Sea, the island of California, and beyond to China."

With each phrase La Salle gestured west until every man, even Nika, looked in that direction. Having made his point, he turned to lead the group back down the path, leaving the priest behind.

"This is absurd, La Salle," Casson shouted. "When we join the rest of the party, we are heading north. North!"

"You forget who pays for this expedition," La Salle reminded him without so much as a pause in his stride.

"I've forgotten nothing, least of all that north was St. Sulpice's original mission until you intervened," Casson rebutted. Angrily he looked once more to the west then gathered his robes about him to catch up with the others just as Nika stepped past.

The Shawnee shot a surreptitious look at the red-faced priest. He hadn't understood all that had been said but knew that the man, La Salle, expected him to lead the way to the Oyo and that the gray robe was determined to take over as head of the strange group. This was clearly not a hunting party, nor it seemed was it a trading party in any sense that he knew. The men carried heavy packs of goods that had scarcely been opened the whole time at the Seneca.

Nika reflected back to earlier that morning. He had enjoyed the sudden change on the Seneca's faces, from clever grinning to worried frown, when the white man had told them, very politely and in hidden terms, that he no longer needed them. The white man understood much of Indian ways but something about the gray robe made him react badly. Yet just now when he had said something about me and the Oyo, Nika remembered, the white leader's whole body had changed—as if he had shaken off the dark the gray robe had cast upon him and taken on all the sunlight. The outcome of these white men's battle might be interesting, Nika decided.

At the head La Salle picked his way around tree roots and occasional branches extended into the neatly defined path. He rubbed his hand across the fire of his forehead. Casson's accusations were just like his brother's or any Jesuit detractor's. La Salle pressed his eyes closed, then opened them, willing away the echo of Casson's words. Inhaling deeply the crisp air, he watched golden streaks filter down through no longer green trees. Every single thing I have, La Salle reminded himself, has been forfeited for this journey. To travel as far past Seneca lands and along the river Oyo as I can, that is my mission. And it has been blessed with a new guide, a better guide.

He glimpsed back to where Nika strode. The Shawnee met his eyes but did not return any sign of acknowledgment.

As the reunited expedition settled in around a row of campfires, La Salle carefully watched Father Casson speaking with Louis Joliet. The well-known explorer had a certain bonvivant competency about him. His buckskins looked like any other woods runner's but his headgear had caught everyone's attention as they had entered camp. Unlike the voyagers who preferred long caps often ending in a tassel, decorated in much the same manner as their leggings, or wide brimmed leather hats, Joliet wore an enormous beaver hat with several huge plumes extending behind. A thick silver cord around the crown completed the striking headgear.

La Salle considered his own outfit, half-Indian, half-French, and wished he had had the foresight to purchase some item to distinguish him among the natives and woods runners. That was why Joliet wore such a hat. It was a notable sign, available only to him, that announced his arrival and that made memorable his departure. Unfurling his bedroll, La Salle decided he would search all the shops of New France for the brightest crimson great coat. It would be an emblem for everyone to recognize, and it was a color the natives admired. Red signified power, strength. It would make them pause much longer than that absurd-looking beaver hat.

His sleeping place arranged, La Salle wove his way toward Joliet and Father Casson. Joliet made no secret of being an agent of the Jesuits, and La Salle knew the trader was even now returning from a brief journey into Iroquois lands under the auspices of Quebec. Joliet had only stumbled upon the group at the shore a day before La Salle and the party had returned from the Seneca village. La Salle wished now he had made the expedition camp some distance inland; then Joliet would have paddled right past none the wiser. La Salle worried what Joliet might have told the men, in the interest of besting him and the Sulpicians on behalf of his Jesuit masters.

"Did you visit many tribes, Joliet?" La Salle inquired. His fellow explorer and competitor glanced at Father Casson and stretched his legs towards the glowing fire.

"A few," Joliet yawned, "and skirted around many others who weren't so happy to see Frenchmen." He leaned comfortably against his packs. "Not all the Iroquois nations interpret the treaty the same way."

"The Seneca stayed at La Chine this winter past to trade," La Salle stated. "At first, we weren't sure they meant to be peaceful. Henri can tell you."

"Monsieur La Salle just stood there, fearless as a hungry wolf. He wouldn't even let us light a matchlock," Henri imparted dutifully from where he poured the three men a finger of brandy.

"Must have been just after I met up with them and convinced them to smoke the calumet and make peace," Joliet goaded. "Good furs, eh?"

La Salle's chuckle at Joliet's assumptions died slowly under the ugly, frowning gaze of Casson.

"How far south did you go?"

"Not much past Niagara after I verified that the reports of silver mines were false."

"The natives love to lead us on with grandiose stories of mines and miraculous routes to riches," Casson interjected.

Joliet snorted at the priest's obvious warning to La Salle. "Father Casson says you're thinking of heading north."

"The worthy Father is mistaken."

"Monsieur Joliet tells of heathen tribes to the north, only but a few days' journey. Father Galinée," with his chin Casson pointed to where the young priest was bent over his papers near the fire, "is copying Joliet's map now."

"The forests are full of heathens, Father," La Salle insisted as he watched the young priest's rounded shoulders. "You will find a ready supply just as godless on our prescribed route."

"Tomorrow, this expedition goes north," Casson proclaimed loudly.

"You forget what we discussed on the trek back here," La Salle reasoned with a glance toward the resting men to gauge their reaction. Everyone had quit their task, set aside mending and bragging, to listen.

"We go north," Casson reiterated. La Salle's plan had failed as far as he was concerned. It was up to him to decide what the Sulpician order would best have him do. Weren't the religious duties of this mission of greater importance than any grand scheme La Salle might have?

La Salle groaned and rubbed his eyes. "What a damn pain."

"What did you say? Repeat it!"

La Salle glared at the angry priest, then with a stiff smile clutched his chest.

"What a pain overtakes me that you are deserting the expedition," La Salle concluded coldly as he stood.

A low rumble of curiosity coursed across the camp.

"Deserting!"

"Yes, Father Casson. Desertion," La Salle said loudly, spinning around to make sure that everyone heard. "If you decide to leave this expedition and head in the opposite direction of the governor's commission then you, and the men who follow you, will be deserting."

Father Casson sputtered, unable to gain enough composure to offer an argument.

All eyes were on the two men. Joliet could barely control his amusement as the priest's eyes bulged at the accusation. But the rest of the Frenchmen were seriously drawn into the argument. Some bet on who would win, some decided with which man to side. From his solitary spot, comfortably away from the rest, Nika raised himself up to watch.

Only a word here or there could he make out, but that was not what drew him to the scene. The white man La Salle moved around the campfire; he gestured to the seated men and circled back to point at the gray robe. To Nika, it was a dance. A powerful dance that focused energy from one source, transforming and moving it to another. He remembered most recently his tribal shaman doing a similar dance before a ceremonial hunt. It was as if he took long, flashing arcs of the men's energies and sent them whirling in a direction of his own, wrestling them up into one or spinning them off. It was a powerful, angry dance.

Nika walked slowly to the outer edge of the circle. He saw the gray robe's furious looks and the strange white man who seemed not a part of the expedition grinning mischievously. Nika watched the almost imperceptible shifting of the men from one side to the other. He saw the entire circle that La Salle was trying to form suddenly break into two.

La Salle's eyes came to rest on Nika as his angry argument dissipated into the night. Nika felt the unspoken exchange between them as the rest of the circle fell into darkness. He knew then that he would assist the white man on his journey.

Rising to his knees in the bow of the lead canoe, Nika directed the three craft through the narrowing passage between the lakes. The rush of the nearby falls muffled the men's shouts as they pulled to shore.

"Camp here," La Salle yelled, "and portage fresh tomorrow."

The men grumbled as they unloaded their boats, and continued to grumble while preparing camp. La Salle weathered their sullen resentment as he insisted they build a better lean-to. With the smaller party, attack by animal or unfriendly natives was much more likely. The men realized that; La Salle did not see why they should complain.

Nevertheless, he thought, the disadvantages of a smaller expedition could never outweigh the advantages. Thankfully, he was back to his original plan of taking a small party through Seneca lands to the Oyo River. Now, without the priests and their contingent, and their arguments, La Salle and his nine remaining men moved much faster. With luck and good weather, they would gain the Oyo before winter had fully set in.

For a somber moment, La Salle remembered the morning when more than half the men had announced they would follow Father Casson and Joliet's scrap of a map to the northwest. Casson had kindled dissension well, and Joliet had been more than happy to fuel it further with half-truths and propaganda. La Salle had resolved not to try to sway the men. He doubted he could have won over very many, and he had refused to make an even greater fool of himself in front of the Jesuit agent Joliet.

The three groups had parted: Joliet back to Montreal, undoubtedly with news of the expedition's split; Casson and most of the men to the northwest without a guide; La Salle and the rest to the southwest with Nika.

The men relashed the lean-to and settled about camp. A few moved in close to the fire to take up the endless task of mending. A few leaned in to start up the swap of stories. Normandin pulled out his coveted foot balm to swathe his cracked, sore feet. He had stayed with La Salle strictly for the potential money. The others either followed his lead because they felt the same or because they had some attachment to the sandy-headed woods runner. Henri, stepping back to Normandin's side as the refueled fire caught, dropped his gaze to the ground.

Poor fellow, La Salle thought, he has certainly gotten more than he bargained for—almost drowning, being made to serve so many masters. . . . Who would Henri have followed, La Salle wondered, if Normandin had chosen to go with Father Casson? La Salle reminded himself to be less demanding of his servant.

And Nika. Mysteriously, after that unpleasant night when he and Casson had almost come to blows, Nika had contributed to drawing and redrawing maps, pointed out edible tubers, shown how to vary slightly their paddling so as not to fatigue as easily; in short, he had become invaluable to La Salle. Yet he remained distant, unwilling to participate in hunts or talk around the glow of the fire.

He vexes me, La Salle thought. After all, some sign of friendship might be shown for my preventing his death at the Seneca village.

Unrolling the latest map from its leather tube, La Salle headed over to the Shawnee, now finished draining the canoes, to consult on how long it would take to pass around the great falls, and to try again to breach his reticence.

Early the next morning the men strapped on as many packs as they could and wedged the rest into the canoes, which they hefted horizontally, shoulder high between them. Nika veered from water's edge to lead them onto the well-trod trail into the woods. The crash of water grew, masking their footfalls and the slap of branches against canoes. The woods runners nervously exchanged looks. None had ever heard such continuous thunder before.

"Blessed Mary, he's sending us off the edge of the earth," Normandin protested.

A sudden sweep steered them into a partial clearing. Cascading water thundered before them. With shouts in awe and fright, the expedition staggered to a halt.

La Salle stood silent. The water plummeted in sheets of frothing white. A deep laugh filled his chest. Like the others, he could not help but be astonished at the sight.

Nika remembered the stories his people told of this curtain of water, and how he himself had sung to Nature when first he had seen the falls of Niagara. Thrusting a hand around to dig in his pack, Nika pulled out some parched corn.

Normandin saw the Shawnee and angrily reached to prevent him, but La Salle stayed the burly woods runner.

"If he eats whenever he wants, he'll be asking for our rations soon," Normandin objected.

La Salle stifled his amusement at Normandin's miscalculation and reached an open palm to Nika, requesting a bit of the corn. Nika halved his small handful. Together they stepped near the precipice. While Nika muttered a prayer of thanks to Nature in Shawnee, La Salle did the same in French.

"God, continue to protect and guide us, and bless us with the majesty of Your work."

In reflex, Normandin and the others intoned a quick amen, then crossed themselves as La Salle and Nika cast the corn out in offering to the waters. Before turning back to the path the Shawnee briefly met the eyes of the white leader, wondering how he had come to appreciate Indian ways.

Within a week of clearing the portage and launching their canoes into Lake Erie, La Salle called for careful rationing of each meal. By the time they gained the southern shore, extra woolens were no longer sufficient against the chill. Furs were distributed amongst them at night but soon became standard wear during the day as well.

Normandin insistently pointed out a distant trail of smoke or the remains of a fish trap as they followed the shore, even though La Salle repeatedly ignored his suggestions that they go inland to scout the villages and trade. It was difficult to deny his own curiosity, but La Salle worried that the onset of winter would soon delay their progress. Each day Nika indicated on the maps how much closer they were, but La Salle could not decipher over what kind of terrain they might have to carry the canoes. His imperative was to reach the Oyo as soon as possible.

Normandin grew more exasperated at each refusal to seek out native tribes. Wasn't that what he had signed on for? To travel beyond Iroquois lands and find out the true source of the abundant trade in which the Seneca trafficked?

On a clear afternoon Nika pointed out an inlet that marked a river flowing into the lake from the south. The days of upstream paddling as they followed the river were difficult, but nowhere near as trying as the days after they reached its headwaters, when the men struggled to portage the canoes and their packs over rugged land plagued with ravines and shallow streams plunging into short waterfalls. They trudged through drifts of sodden red and yellow leaves patched with slick, crusted ice. Thankfully they shot a deer and had at least one meal where everyone could eat his fill.

But the brief feast ended and the trek through snowflakes drifting down from somber clouds began anew. The snow doubled, then tripled. La Salle directed the men to take shelter under the canoes near a cluster of trees. Within hours everything was encased in white.

Slowly they dug themselves out from drifts piled against their makeshift shelters. Again the group trudged on. Men faltered, finding it impossible to keep their footing in the loose snow. Continually circling back to help one another, the woods runners shared their misgivings.

"If winter here is as bad as in Montreal we'd better settle in with some tribe soon," Normandin griped. The forlorn men agreed. Only La Salle and Nika seemed impervious to misery.

A week later, toward noon, Nika led them to a stream, larger than the others. By early evening they had reached the Oyo River. Along its course the indigo sky gave rise to a huge moon. The river flowed west. La Salle's high spirits spread as the men settled in close to the evening's campfire, their chatter dying as they fell into exhausted, relieved sleep.

La Salle checked the dryness of his maps, then rolled them into their tube. He knew the men considered the journey over, and in truth they had made the planned destination. But La Salle had long before secretly decided that when they reached the river Oyo the journey would have just begun.

Unlike Normandin, who was satisfied that he had acquired all the knowledge he needed on how to get to the Oyo so he could return again and again to trade, La Salle yearned to go farther. Here was an easy-flowing river, a direct route that led farther inland than any European had gone. How could he turn back now? If the Oyo connected with the western passage that had been sought after since the time of Cartier, then La Salle had to discover how far across the continent it traveled. As far as they could go before winter and lack of food forced them either to turn back or to settle in with local natives, that was what he was going to do—what he must do. The only way he could return to New France to face the rumors Joliet and possibly Casson had undoubtedly spread was to arrive with the glory of having pushed farther than anticipated.

La Salle watched the Shawnee cocoon into his bedroll. He looked around at the sleeping men. Except for Patrice, on sentry, and Henri, who twitched in some dream, they were motionless. Sapped. He stretched out and wondered how tomorrow he would convince them to travel the Oyo River.

"What do you mean?" Normandin unshouldered his backpack and let it fall to the ground. He and his cohorts glanced around in shared disbelief at what La Salle had just announced. They wouldn't be scouting tribes to trade with after all, but instead would continue down the freezing river.

"We're here and so is winter," Normandin went on, trying to break La Salle's determination. "This is the agreed-upon end of the trek. Today we scout tribes and trade. Those tree markings," he pointed to a large oak with bark cut from it to signal Indian territory, "mean there's a tribe near here. Let's find out what they've got and trade."

"It isn't enough just to have reached the Oyo," La Salle explained again. "We must learn about it. Track which way it flows. Find out if it will indeed give up a route to the western seas. We must continue on."

"We're tired, La Salle, and frozen," Normandin argued.

The other Frenchmen resoundingly concurred. Even the usually hesitant Henri sided with Normandin. Only Nika remained silent.

"You've gone mad. What they said back in Montreal was true. You're so obsessed with finding a route to China, you'll stop at nothing," Normandin spat. If he could not dissuade La Salle, at least he could deepen the other men's doubts about his competence.

"If such a route does exist, Normandin, will you be content to settle for trade along the Oyo?"

"Damn the saints, man! And damn your blasted China!" Normandin shouted as he leapt to confront La Salle. "Don't you ever get tired?"

"Yes! Yes, Normandin," La Salle grabbed the burly man's shoulders. "Yes, I'm tired. As tired as you. And I curse my body for its weakness and hunger. I curse it that it makes me stop to let it sleep.

"The English and the Spaniards and even our own Jesuits race to claim the continent before we do! We cannot stop!" La Salle swept up Normandin's pack and added it to his own slung across his back. Without a second of hesitance he marched toward shore, refusing to continue the argument. This was his expedition, he had come to a difficult decision, and the men would have to do as he directed without further discussion.

The sandy-headed man shrugged in irritation as the others looked to his lead. Under his breath, just loud enough for them to hear, he muttered, "He's gone mad. We'll never see Montreal again if we don't do something soon."

The Frenchmen angrily assented, asking among themselves how they were going to get out of this predicament. Normandin hushed them with a jerk of his head toward Nika, and the others fell silently in behind him to head down the path, staring back in distrust at the Shawnee.

"I've got a plan," Normandin whispered. He shook off their anxious inquiries, knowing that whatever he decided to do, the rest of the group, even Henri, would go along now. They were half-starved and past exhaustion. Any inspiration they might have taken from La Salle's fortitude was gone.

The white leader is very brave to ignore the fury of these men, Nika thought as he trailed behind them to the shore. Up ahead he could make out La Salle intent upon loading the canoes single-handedly. Why do the spirits make him risk so much? And why, Nika worried, was I prevented from leaving this world to stay with him?

The expedition spilled onto the chilly width of the Oyo following closely the treelined banks as they continued west farther than Nika had ever traveled. Now they were without a guide, at the mercy of nature and La Salle's obstinate refusal to hunt out local villages. The men, Henri too, had withdrawn into fretful, suspicious silence. Constantly, they glanced toward Normandin, as once they had La Salle, waiting for some signal.

Rocks jutted from the shoreline ahead into the lane of water. A low froth of white billowed.

"Rapids," La Salle shouted. "Gain the shore!"

The canoes bounced perilously along. Frigid water slapped men and supplies. Boulders hidden in spring loomed up during the early-winter low. Struggling, the men lurched to shore and climbed from their canoes wet and chilled.

"Water's too low to run them," La Salle hollered over the rush of water. "Head in to a clearing and make camp. Tomorrow we portage."

Normandin eyed the snow-locked woods. La Salle ignored his furious looks as he began yanking the canoes away from shore, tucking the trade packs securely beneath them. Nika observed Normandin carefully move from man to man, helping one to reposition his pack, bending to feign retrieving something another could have dropped. Keeping a watchful eye on La Salle, Normandin spoke briefly to each, and each gave a brusque nod in return. Normandin spotted the

Shawnee watching and glared threateningly. Quickly, he finished with the men, taking extra time with Henri, who regretfully hung on the big man's sleeve. Finally Normandin moved to assist La Salle, ready to intervene should the watchful Shawnee mention he had seen anything suspicious.

Soon the party was stretched out on the frozen ground around a brilliant fire. Normandin readjusted his hat and scanned the camp from his volunteered post on guard duty. Only his face and the barrel of his musket protruded from the blankets and furs he had wrapped around himself. All was quiet. He rubbed his aching feet to warm them against the wet chill, and studied La Salle's steady, deep breathing.

Silently, he rose. Blackie sat up as his friend stood. With a foot he nudged Patrice, who in turn tapped the next man, until all except La Salle had been signaled. Many were already awake. They gathered their things, obviously prepared, and quietly slipped away from the fire down to the shore. La Salle slept on.

Henri stared at his master's sleeping form, hesitating to pick up his pack. Normandin put his arm around the shoulders of the servant whose life he had saved and pushed him to follow the others. With a scowl at Nika, who had seen the proceedings, Normandin gestured for the Shawnee to leave, not inviting him along, but pointing into the woods. Then Normandin followed the others to the boats.

Nika watched them go, then looked over at La Salle, still asleep. Minutes passed before the Shawnee pulled the furs back over himself, and hours more before he gave up wondering what would happen in the days ahead and drifted into sleep.

CHAPTER SEVEN

NIKA HAD OBSERVED LA SALLE'S awakening to his men's abandonment. The Frenchman had grabbed the musket kept by his side through the night, then had bolted to the shore, flinging up clods of snow and leaves. He had lumbered back, kicking everything in his path before dropping to the ground to mechanically rest elbows on knees, forehead in hands.

Nika stood to roll his pallet and tie his pack. La Salle flinched. Their eyes met for the first time that morning.

"Didn't you hear them?" La Salle bellowed, jabbing his finger at where the men had taken not only the canoes but all the trade goods and extra food rations.

"I heard them," Nika responded without interrupting his task.

"Why didn't you stop them? Or at least sound an alarm?"

Nika offered no answer. La Salle clenched his hands and growled. Curses steamed the air. None of them, he thought, not a one, not even Henri, understand the importance of my journey. Haven't I suffered it for them as much as for myself? For the prosperity, even survival, of all New France? His anger turned to a derisive snigger as he once more faced the Shawnee. Of the entire troop only the Indian could see far enough ahead to follow me, he thought.

"Alone, Nika, alone you stayed to serve me."

Nika cocked his head. When the others had left last night, he had considered leaving, heading east to his own tribe. But he had wondered what the white man would do, if he would follow the deserters to ambush them, or retreat to the hills to fast and purge his shame. Perhaps the spirits who guided the white man were abandoning him, Nika had considered. Or was this another passage they had put before him, a portage on the journey through the living world? Perhaps Nika had remained simply to see what the Frenchman would do. But he was certain he had not stayed to be a slave.

"Maybe I stayed to kill you," he said.

"I prevented your being eaten by the Seneca!"

"You prevented an honorable death," Nika retorted at the implication he owed this man something. "I showed them no fear. I laughed at their blows. I had begun my Death Chant. The spirits were waiting for me. I would have died a warrior."

La Salle checked his surprise, then nodded in silent comprehension. Though the fierce hero Nika described did not match the frightened young man he remembered, La Salle had indeed yanked the Shawnee from a tradition-worn sacrifice that would have assured his passage as a brave warrior. La Salle was ashamed he hadn't realized that before.

"Then why have you helped me thus far?"

"Understand, La Salle," Nika answered, for the first time using his name after their many weeks together, "the night the gray robe left I saw the spirits that lead you. They, I follow, not you."

"Magnificent," La Salle muttered. "You've stayed because you think I'm a crazy man driven by some queer visions."

Then he snorted at the realization that many people in New France would agree with such a description, and that the woods runners, and even perhaps Henri, had deserted for the same reason. La Salle sank under the weight of his dilemma. He had come so far. He watched the sullen Shawnee gather his pack and sling it across his shoulder.

"Where are you going?"

approval of the tree's limberness, La Salle struck a few hatchet blows, then cleared it of branches, before continuing the search for others.

At the campsite Nika lifted the pot of boiling water from the fire, and showed La Salle how to mark a section of the bark of a large tree, then loosen it with steam and hot water. These were not the thin strips of birch the Indians near Montreal used, but thick, rough elm such as the Seneca used.

Nika bid La Salle to try it himself. La Salle grinned as he peeled off a large section without tearing it. Later, they sewed two wide strips onto the sapling-ribbed frame. Nika wrinkled his brow and demonstrated how to get it tighter, surprised that La Salle, who seemed so powerful at times, could be so inept at others.

A *V*-shaped notch cut into the bark of a gum tree oozed a tiny trickle of thick sap. Nika knew in spring the sap would flow freely, but they needed a canoe now and could not wait. Careful not to waste any, Nika and La Salle applied the pasty sap over the canoe seams. The final step was done. Weary and satisfied, they settled into camp.

When the canoe sailed into the freezing waters of the Oyo, it rode easily. La Salle burst into the silly refrain of a sailor's shanty recalled from his youth. Nika tried to pick up the tune but settled for shouting out the rhythms.

"A fine canoe," declared La Salle.

"It will take us far," Nika replied. "To China."

"To China," La Salle laughed, then took up the song again.

They traveled the Oyo for many days. Low water and ice-crusted banks forced them to paddle nearer the middle than La Salle would have preferred. He and Nika fell into a routine that would have wasted the ablest woods runner. Paddling all day, without a stop, they became extremely adept at reading the river, avoiding stalling in eddies, and catching the safest streams of current to propel them onward.

One day the muted honk of a late flock of southbound geese made them pause briefly from their paddling. The huge *V* filled the cold sky. One long-winged fellow trailed behind. La Salle pointed him out to Nika and was about to comment on his struggle when a swift current hit the canoe broadside. Sideways they slid, slamming their paddles into the water to regain control. Shouting at each other to gain the shore, they narrowly avoided collision with winter's debris caught in the rocks. They careened to water's edge and clambered out, yanking the canoe up the snowy bank.

La Salle watched the mangled mass of flotsam drift past. Relieved, he looked at Nika panting beside him and followed the Shawnee's gaze to deer tracks clearly outlined in crisp snow.

La Salle and Nika crept along. On previous journeys La Salle had hired Indians as hunters, but he had never accompanied them. Next to the white man's musket, the bow and arrow were feeble weapons, but using them taught stealth, the stealth that made the Iroquois such formidable adversaries to the French.

A deer pawed at the ground in search of leaves. Moving his mouth in a silent Shawnee incantation of thanks, Nika let the arrow fly. The doe took off but the arrow held.

Hours later, La Salle and Nika found the spot where the animal had fallen. La Salle started to rush forward to where her warm red blood melted the snow, and her death throes had kicked wide a wallow, but Nika held him back. Many times he had seen dead animals frightened back to life. He whispered another Shawnee prayer. Impatiently La Salle listened.

"I will teach you Christian prayers. More pleasing to the ears of the Lord."

"I pray to the deer, who gives her life to feed us. Shawnee prayers are more pleasing to the deer."

Nika shot another arrow. As he had suspected, the now twice wounded animal found its feet to run again, but a few steps were all it could manage. With a last, weak kick, it died.

Nika began carefully skinning the deer, a job he refused La Salle because he didn't trust the white man's skill at keeping the needed hide in one piece. Waiting until he could help with the butchering, La Salle ambled just past the edge of trees and froze. Noticing, Nika quit his task to join him.

Before them loomed a treeless hill. Its high sides and flat top continued for a hundred yards. The smooth snow covering it revealed no signs of life except an occasional animal track. Its symmetry prevented its passing for any natural phenomenon. With a cautious look, the two men scaled the slippery incline to stand at the crest. The formation continued in either direction in a sinuous design.

"Mound Builders."

La Salle responded with a questioning look.

"All of them gone," Nika continued.

"Wiped out by unfriendly neighbors?"

Nika shook his head at La Salle's easy explanation. "Many tales my great-grandfather heard and told us about strong tribes that lived atop hills to be closer to the sun. Their power grew too great, they reached too near the sun, and were extinguished."

Nika surveyed the strange formation, then with a quick glance at La Salle, indicated he would return to the deer. With a step he slid towards the bare trees.

La Salle walked the wide top a few yards more. What was this nation that was so powerful it could have engineered this mound, he wondered. It would have taken many people, much work and organization to erect such a structure. Its grace and strength was frightening. They reached too near the sun, La Salle repeated to himself, and were extinguished. It reminded him of his brother preaching to him about being too ambitious. These Mound Builders may have disappeared, La Salle thought, but look at the glory they left behind.

La Salle remembered studying at the seminary illustrations of the decaying Egyptian pyramids. He recalled sketches of the Spaniards' conquests far to the south, with stone pyramids less refined than Egypt but more sophisticated than these.

A civilization at its apex can seldom sustain itself, he recited from his history books. The Egyptians, the Romans . . . I wonder how much farther France has to journey before it collapses. At least the length of Great River, he hoped, and smiled in admiration of the mound's majesty.

Miami children scampered past the small group sitting around the strange men. La Salle watched them from the corner of his eye as Nika spoke. The children played hard, tossing a stick then running after it. Whoever got there first threw the stick and the chase began again. The snow crunched beneath their feet. Shouts of glee fogged the air.

La Salle shifted his gaze to Nika, waiting for him to finish speaking this language that was so alien to La Salle. With numb fingers, he took the calumet a Miami offered him.

Late that morning they had followed a trail of smoke to these four lean-tos built hastily against the worsening winter. It had been good to share a bellyful of stew before settling into the relaxed calumet ceremony.

A tawny Miami shook his head in answer to Nika's questions. A dark gap in the right side of his lower front teeth appeared then disappeared as he formed the incomprehensible words.

"Missi Sipi," the Miami repeated. A brisk, chilled wind made them readjust the furs wrapped at their necks.

Missi Sipi, La Salle rolled the sounds over in his mind. Missi Sipi, Meche Sebe. Yes, it had to be the same river. The Father of the Waters, Great River.

"How far, Nika?" La Salle interrupted.

Nika nodded, and addressed the Miami. The man pointed west.

"What does he say?" La Salle demanded before the Miami had finished speaking.

Nika glowered at La Salle's impatience. "Eight, ten days on foot. Less by canoe."

"So close!" La Salle's face broke into excited relief. "In which direction does it flow? Ask them."

"South, La Salle," the Shawnee said slowly. La Salle stared, unwilling to understand the words.

"Great River flows . . . ," La Salle began slowly.

"South," Nika finished.

La Salle squinted into the cold wind and wrapped the blanket tighter around his shoulders as the Indians talked. His fears rose to consume him again. A south-flowing river could not be the northwest passage, could not lead to China. He would have to go back in failure, having given up his fortune and having faced two desertions. La Salle grabbed up handfuls of freshly fallen snow and pressed them to his hot face.

"La Salle," came Nika's familiar voice. La Salle flinched. When he looked up, he saw the Miami retiring to the relative warmth of their lean-tos.

Nika squatted beside La Salle. The man before him had grown stronger since the day he had awakened from his retreat, but at this moment the guiding spirits were abandoning him. It was apparent in his empty eyes. Nika watched him pick up a stick and sketch a map in the snow. Finished, he idly fingered the twig.

It was very cold. Nika huddled into his wraps to think. The news that Meche Sebe flowed south changed much. Although he had never been sure what China meant, he understood it had represented much to La Salle when it lay west. And the Father of the Waters of Indian lands flowed south.

"China is not at the end of Meche Sebe?" Nika asked.

La Salle snorted at the question, snapping the twig in two. Watching Nika's wait for a reply, La Salle rubbed his eyebrow.

"No, Nika," he began but was unable to contain his anger. He leapt up and pounded his fist into his hand. "The blasted river flows right into Spanish lands!"

Several Miami quit their tasks to watch the crazy white man. Nika watched too, remembering the night he had first seen La Salle's angry dance, when he had decided to lead the Frenchman to the Oyo.

Then La Salle stopped. He swung around to stare at Nika, standing motionless for a long moment as an idea came to him.

"Look!" La Salle raced to Nika's side. In a fresh patch of snow, he quickly stomped out the shapes of the great lakes, then grabbed another twig. La Salle resketched New France and the Oyo, adding Great River, guessing where it might begin.

"With the English here and the Spanish here," La Salle continued, pointing to the eastern coast and the southern gulf, "a stronghold on Great River can curtail the expansion of both. If New France can establish forts along it . . ." He clapped Nika on the shoulder.

"The furs these Miami have are good, and they say there are many more, right?"

"They said the lands along Meche Sebe are very rich."

"Then I'll be able to finance construction of fortified posts with speculation on trade." La Salle calculated the wealth along Great River. He wondered at the possible extent of the Spanish knowledge of Meche Sebe, if they had ventured to establish any forts near its mouth.

La Salle rubbed his hands together, savoring the next leg of the journey. Once more he felt invigorated. His body burned to feel the rhythmic power of paddling as his mind raced with the visions of Great River. Far away, he could imagine the beginnings of a colony and marveled at the arc across the continent New France might cover, the strength it would give her, the control. The route to the Orient no longer seemed important as La Salle envisioned his conquest of the American interior.

Nika responded to La Salle's growing excitement with a relieved smile.

"We must return to New France," La Salle explained as he crouched next to a crackling campfire that evening. "We'll need more men and boats. It's pure folly to think you and I alone can contend with whatever may lie ahead.

"I'm certain I can convince the governor, or at least Intendant Talon, of the importance of a series of strongholds down the length of Great River," La Salle went on, "but it'll mean building ships big enough to carry the necessary cannon and men, and fast enough to make the journey in one warm season."

Nika had stopped listening to his companion. He had lost track of the words—governor, strongholds, they did not mean anything to him. But as he watched La Salle detail his plans, he again saw that flame of intensity consume him. It would be an arduous journey heading back north, but Nika felt certain it would not be a wasted one.

CHAPTER EIGHT

THE CHIEF ELDERS SAUNTERED ACROSS the clearing to the low stools semicircled before a tall-backed gilt chair. As they settled in, their wives and selected tribe members moved to sit on the mats and carpets covering the ground behind them. Each tribe, in their distinguished costumes, delineated one of the Iroquois nations, and the chiefs were the most splendidly arrayed among them. In heavy face paint with their striking headdresses and robes, they appeared savage and regal.

La Salle thought the Frenchmen, even with the Sun King inspiring their fashions, could never match such ostentation. Carefully, he adjusted his broad-brimmed hat with its plume and straightened the thick, gold-trimmed cuffs of his prized crimson greatcoat.

He looked over at Nika, who over the past year had developed a unique mix of Shawnee and French dress. He remembered back to when the only thing differentiating Nika from the buckskin-clad woods runners had been the way his hair was fashioned in a roach. Even that had changed. Years of plucking had left him almost bald except for his roach. When they finally had made it to Montreal, after that frighteningly frozen journey over new, uncharted northern routes, Nika had taken to wrapping his chilled skull in a loose turban of striped Lyonnaise broadcloth. It was a unique fashion he had retained throughout the seasons.

The small troop of drummers hired in Quebec, and transported by longboat to this eastern edge of the Iroquois Lake where the first major French stronghold would be erected this afternoon, struck up a rhythmic beat that culminated in a sustained drum roll. La Salle looked around to see if he could spot from where the governor would emerge. Yesterday, as the final preparations had been underway, La Salle had received a letter warning him that his collaborator on this event, and in the venture of establishing a fort, would make a dazzling entrance.

La Salle remembered how Louis de Baude, Comte de Frontenac, recently replacing Courcelle as governor of New France, had turned up his nose at La Salle during their first meeting. He had even gone so far as to sniff his highly perfumed handkerchief all during the interview.

It was amazing, La Salle thought, that such a frivolous-looking personage as Frontenac had turned out to be such an astute businessman. Within a few weeks of his return to New France, La Salle and Frontenac had launched into elaborate plans for constructing a series of strongholds to control trade on the great lakes: at Niagara; guarding the straits of Detroit and Michilimackinac; at the Chicago portage, the shorter route from Great River to the lakes La Salle and Nika had learned of during their arduous return; along the Illinois; and then down the length of the yet uncharted Meche Sebe itself. It had been fast and furious on paper but the actual development of the initial stronghold at Fort Frontenac, as it would of course be called, had taken much too long. La Salle was worried that building the first few forts alone would take his lifetime.

The drum roll grew. At the shore a longboat landed. From beneath the shimmering silver fringe of an unusually large canopy, quite awkward on that rough colonial craft, a specter of pale yellow and gold emerged. Every eye turned to watch Governor Frontenac gingerly place upon the rocky ground a thick-heeled shoe topped with a wide, stiff golden bow. With a large knobbed walking stick he ambled to the gilt chair facing the seated Iroquois council. The dense layers of lace at his neck, cuffs, and knees danced. His gloved hand, glittering with a fat ring, brushed the dark curls of his long wig from a shoulder. As though he were the Sun King himself, Frontenac commanded everyone's attention. Standing now before the Iroquois, a clerk hastily unfurled a proclamation for the governor to read. La Salle moved to the governor's side.

"Kneel, you fool," Frontenac hissed at the clerk. The older man looked confused. "Kneel! You're blocking their view of me!"

Quickly the man went down on one knee, holding the paper above his head. With the slyest of glances, Frontenac almost winked at La Salle, whose large plumed hat seemed suddenly a careful miniature of the governor's.

"Everything ready, monsieur?"

La Salle nodded. With a flick of his hand, Frontenac silenced the drummers.

"My children," he proclaimed, "we the powers of New France bestow upon you the strength of our protection." He paused while La Salle repeated his words in precise Iroquois dialect. "Our father, the Sun King, welcomes you in peace for fruitful trade and to live long in harmony. You will do well to respect his wishes, for his strength in peace is equalled only by his strength in war."

Frontenac continued on, embellishing the agreement that all trade would pass through the fort and all surrounding nations would thrive through such an alliance. Finally he pointed over the chiefs' heads. When they turned to look, La Salle gave the prearranged signal.

Behind the Iroquois, the four walls of the fort, painstakingly prefabricated and laid out, were pulled up by an enormous contingent of waiting men. To the great surprise and admiration of the natives, Fort Frontenac, thanks to the meticulous engineering of La Salle, sprang up as if by magic. Awed by the entire event, the Iroquois embraced the calumet ceremony and exchange of gifts.

As he and Frontenac strolled through the celebrating groups to a roughhewn log and stone cottage outside the walls of the fort, La Salle briefly caught sight of Nika assisting woods runners and Indians in bracing the newly raised stockade. Nika nodded in La Salle's direction. They had stayed up late last night planning how to approach Frontenac, but the governor's directness made La Salle uncertain how to proceed.

"What's on your mind, dear son?" Frontenac inquired as he smoothed his finery into a small, stiff chair.

"The fort will be finished in a week's time, your honor. Commerce for New France will soon reflect the advantages to such an outpost. . . ."

"Get to the point, René," interrupted Frontenac.

"I must go to France to garner support to continue down Great River." Frontenac raised his eyebrows in surprise, as La Salle continued, "To begin immediately building the chain of forts we have planned, and establish allies among tribes we haven't even heard of."

"But with you managing Fort Frontenac," the governor frowned, "and the money we'll both be taking in, you'll be able to follow through with our original plans in a few years. . . ."

"I know there's more than a fortune to be made here, but the Jesuits and Joliet have already claimed the discovery of Great River."

"River St. Louis?"

"As they call it. But why not River Frontenac? If we don't move now the trade along the greatest river in the continent will fall into other hands, Spanish or English or . . ."

"I've no doubt many non-Jesuit parties would jump at the opportunity to send such a representative as yourself into the heart of the continent. The costs, however . . . After all, Louis is building his new palace at Versailles."

"But with letters of support from you and your allies I could convince the king to give me the royal patent for trade down the river in return for my charting it, claiming it for France, for him. With that patent—"

"Monopoly?" Frontenac suggested.

La Salle disliked the word but that was what he wanted. If word got out of his possibly obtaining a royal patent on southern trade before he had solid supporters, the political scheming among government factions as well as religious ones could very well undermine all his plans for Great River.

"Very well, with a monopoly," he said in a low voice, "I can raise enough credit to outfit an expedition and hire skilled artisans to build ships, and establish forts."

Frontenac held up his hand to quiet La Salle. "And your response to the fact that such trade could very well ruin Montreal and Quebec?"

"I'll relinquish any right to trade in furs north of the great lakes for the right to the trade of the south."

Frontenac was astounded. If such a stalwart businessman as La Salle would voluntarily relinquish trade from the known northern region . . .

"Your Great River is so rich?"

La Salle could not reply. He knew Frontenac was close to saying yes; he could not jeopardize it now by painting a picture of the prosperous empire he could see, but which others were hard pressed to envision. As he searched for a response an image came to mind of himself greeting a council of Indians far to the south. He would be dressed in French finery like Frontenac.

"Very well, René. But why you crave such an impossibly harsh life is well beyond me. This fort is certainly far rugged enough for my palate." He let out a sly chuckle. "Did you see the Seneca chief's reaction to my calling him 'my children'? I thought his buffalo headdress would gallop away."

La Salle smiled absently at Frontenac's self-delight as his mind filled with the imperative victory of his next voyage.

Nika finished helping with the western face of the fort and lingered behind the other Indians and Frenchmen as they went to share the copious spread of food with their newly established Iroquois allies. He was ravenously hungry but more anxious to learn the outcome of La Salle and Frontenac's meeting, a meeting he knew could change everything.

If they voyaged into the lands of Meche Sebe, Nika would be indisputably the most successful Shawnee trader ever known, even greater than his uncle who had perished at the hands of the Seneca. He thought back to the events leading to the day they were captured as he wandered toward the cabin La Salle and Frontenac had entered.

He and his uncle had traveled very far, trading salt for Osage bows and flint knives. They had been returning with their profitable exchange when captured by the Seneca raid. Then La Salle had intervened and now Nika was part of something else. The Europeans had weapons and items most Indians did not possess. Nika had heard the legends about strange bearded men dressed in silver with exploding sticks. With their viciousness they had ravaged many tribes. But that was long ago.

La Salle was not interested in wiping out tribes, Nika reflected. He wants trade. Things the Indians had in abundance were worth things they had not at all. The old ways were changing. Utensils and tools meant an easier life. Nika was eager to figure out how they fit into his world.

"Nika," La Salle hailed, stepping from the cabin. Nika knew from La Salle's demeanor their journey would begin again.

"We'll need to build canoes?"

"Not canoes, Nika. Ships. But first, we go to France."

Nika adjusted his beaver hat until the image in the shop window reflected its straightness, then he focused on the merchandise displayed within. Cascades of dark curls sat atop wicker heads. Plumed hats of fine fur adorned the shelves against the wall, furs that might have been trapped by the Illinois, then traded to the Shawnee, then stolen by the Iroquois, then bought by the French, then . . .

La Salle guided Nika away from the window. He'd had to backtrack a half-block when he'd realized his companion was no longer following.

When they had first arrived in Paris, La Salle had enjoyed Nika's fascination with all that was so new to him (and much that was new to La Salle, for this was an age of great discovery and progress) but today La Salle was annoyed by the Shawnee's curiosity.

As they continued through the maze of Parisian streets, Nika thought, not for the first time, what a shame it was that such a huge, grand city should smell so bad.

"This Seignelay we're going to see is a very important man," La Salle admonished for the fortieth time. "His father is Colbert, who has the ear of the king. We must do nothing to offend him. If we win him to our side, his father will give us an audience. If we can sway his father . . ."

After they had reached Paris, La Salle had found out his rival Joliet had been refused permission to build a fort on Great River. That had been good news, yet La Salle could not help but worry if the refusal was because of Joliet's Jesuit ties, and the Jesuits were currently held in less favor amidst the intricate religious politics of court, or if the sentiments of the anti-expansionists had gained the upper hand in the equally intricate commercial politics engaged in for diversion and profit by anyone who could claim an intimacy with an intimate of an intimate of the king. La Salle sighed. To think it was said Indians were hard to fathom.

Seignelay kept them waiting a very long time. When he did appear, he brushed aside La Salle's carefully prepared explanations. Barely did he glance at La Salle's precisely drawn charts, shaking his head in noncomprehension, dusting them with a fine coating of snuff that he had sloppily sniffed and that La Salle inconspicuously tried to brush away. With a final disinterested gesture Seignelay flung aside La Salle's arguments, then led him and Nika through the huge double-pane doors into an inner courtyard where a handful of guests milled.

La Salle sighed, straightened his coat, and in frustration whispered to Nika.

"Once again we're the afternoon's spectacle."

Nika didn't mind. He'd already grown used to the stir his presence caused and had worked at improving his French in order to embellish the repeated stories of his and other tribes in the New World.

Getting down to what was for him the business at hand, Seignelay waved forward a large, brawny man as the trio stepped from the last stone step into the manicured garden. Though outfitted like a thousand other courtiers, something in the man's demeanor set him apart. It wasn't just that his silks were more gaudy and his mustache the most finely trimmed. If the arrogance of the world-weary fop, Seignelay, came from family connections, this man seemed confident because he could probably back up any boast with real action.

"Monsieur La Salle," Seignelay introduced, "and Chief Nika," he added at La Salle's sidelong glance to his native companion. "I would like you to meet Monsieur Henri de Tonti, late of the king's army."

La Salle noticed the hilt of the man's sword. It was worn almost smooth. For comparison he looked at Seignelay's sword hilt, pristine as if the only hand that ever touched it had been a servant applying polish. La Salle looked back at Tonti and raised his eyebrows at the stiff metal hand where Tonti's natural appendage would have been. Nika, too, showed surprise as they watched Tonti sweep into a graceful bow. Seignelay had mentioned something about finding La Salle a lieutenant with an iron hand, but La Salle had presumed he was speaking figuratively.

Seignelay followed La Salle's gaze. He laughed lightly as he touched La Salle's shoulder. "Don't worry. He's quite capable."

La Salle's taut jaw showed his displeasure. His eyes glimmered as he looked Tonti up and down. Wasn't it enough that he himself had offered to undertake the entire expense of the voyage down Great River in the name of King Louis? Was he now expected to relieve the court of a no longer useful follower? La Salle spurned the peacock silks of the big man.

"I am very capable, monsieur," Tonti said loudly to everyone within earshot. Seignelay dropped his hand from La Salle's shoulder and cleared his throat.

"Monsieur Tonti's hand was blown apart in some Sicilian backwater. He cut it off cleanly," Seignelay paused for emphasis, "with his own sword. Then led the charge that won the day. Braver, Monsieur La Salle, you will not find."

"Three hundred leagues through Iroquois country?" challenged La Salle. "Another two hundred down Great River past unknown natives? Even with the ships we'll build, there will be much paddling."

"I'm stronger than any two men," Tonti countered. "I'll hold the paddle's end with my good hand, and pull it back with my bad. That's the stronger arm anyway. I've practiced in a rowboat on the Seine."

"A rowboat on the Seine? We'll be traveling the greatest river of the New World through lands never seen by any Frenchman, through seas the Spaniards patrol with ships of war."

"I'm a soldier by profession, monsieur. I do not disappoint."

"We have arranged a demonstration. If you'd like, Monsieur La Salle?" offered Seignelay, pulling La Salle away.

A swordsman came forward. He and Tonti stepped clear of the small crowd of hangers-on. Bowing to each other, the two men drew their swords. Immediately the crowd formed a circle at a respectful distance.

Steel clinked against steel. The men thrust and parried, displaying footwork and style. Tonti was indeed adept, La Salle admitted to himself, but he was still not prepared to have his expedition saddled with a cripple. He saw Seignelay beaming at him.

"In an arranged demonstration, yes, but against a less predictable opponent?" queried La Salle.

Before Seignelay could respond, La Salle tapped the swordsman on the shoulder and took his weapon. A murmur went through the crowd.

La Salle plunged in, trying to remember techniques from his brief training as a youth. But he could not recall a single one of the moves or steps that had seemed so important to him as a boy. They aren't necessary, he consoled himself as he rolled his shoulders to loosen his lean, strong muscles. I won't fight like a dandified French swordsman but then neither will any enemies we encounter.

Amused by La Salle's daring, Tonti casually countered his blows. I'll let this little rooster strut just enough to break a sweat, decided the soldier.

Angry at having each of his thrusts parried so easily, and at having become a sideshow, exactly what Seignelay had hoped for, La Salle let out a roar and lunged. Immediately the soldier's dander was up. He began fighting almost in earnest as La Salle became more aggressive. Seignelay held back anxious intermediaries who feared the growing seriousness between the two men.

"Tonti knows what he does," Seignelay said to comfort himself as well as the others.

"Watch that you don't kill him, Monsieur Tonti," shouted one of the entourage, "else how will the savage get home?"

The surrounding crowd tittered at the witticism but La Salle could not respond. All his efforts were in parrying Tonti's calculated advances. The crowd gasped as the two came face to face, swords locked high above their heads. Tonti bumped La Salle with his formidable chest and sent him stumbling back.

Nika moved to Seignelay's side. "Stop them."

Seignelay shook his head calmly at the worried Indian and waved his hand to lower the frightened cries of the crowd.

Nika wondered what he should do. La Salle had entered this fight willingly, yet there was clearly a danger that he might be wounded. Nika grasped Seignelay's arm, a firm warning.

Seignelay did not like being touched, especially now when he'd somehow managed such an entertainment as this one-sided sword fight. He tried to pull free but the savage tightened his grip. He looked into Nika's eyes. In that look came rushing back the nightmares of childhood, when the raconteurs at court delighted and terrorized him with tales of New World savage bogeymen.

"Monsieur La Salle," Seignelay cried out, "enough!" Nika released Seignelay. The courtier sighed relief.

Cautiously Tonti and La Salle stopped. Sweat trickled down La Salle's forehead. As Tonti turned toward Seignelay, La Salle tried a surprise blow to knock the sword from his hand. The crowd gasped and shielded its eyes but Tonti did not even flinch. Instead he raised his eyebrows as if to ask why the hush had fallen over everyone.

La Salle was impressed. He bowed in acknowledgment. The big man smiled confidently, showing no signs of fatigue. La Salle returned the smile before giving Seignelay his attention.

Seignelay moved Nika, La Salle, and Tonti apart from his excited guests.

"You are a most curious man, Monsieur La Salle," observed Seignelay. "I must speak to my father about you."

CHAPTER NINE

LA SALLE AND HIS SISTER, Catherine, strolled the treelined path. Well in front of them, Nika gestured broadly in explanation to Maurice, Catherine's husband, and Colin, her son. La Salle watched his friend's gesticulations.

"Monsieur Nika appears quite at ease amidst what must be a very different world for him." She brushed a sandy curl back up under her large brimmed bonnet. "You most likely feel the same when in his land."

"It can be harrowing. But, yes, I feel more comfortable there than I do in France or even Montreal."

"Poor Jean," Catherine sighed, glancing sideways to affirm her brother's surprised reaction. "His jealousy of you must reach hysteria over there. I feel terribly sorry for him."

"How can you say that, Cathy? He's one of the highest ranking priests at St. Sulpice."

"Oh, René, you take off into the wilderness and make a fortune while he's bound to the seminary. You're free and he's not!"

"Free? The demands of traveling into who knows what, directing others, negotiating with Indians, all require a very resolute . . ."

"But they're your own demands. Demands you place on yourself."

"You make it sound as though I pack my bags and head off for adventure. There are governmental policies to contend with, quarreling factions . . ."

"But you're changing them all. Our grandparents could never have dreamed France would have an entire other world connected to her. It's men like you who sculpt the future. Your name might one day be spoken alongside Cartier's and Champlain's."

La Salle could not respond for fear of sounding as vain and ambitious as their brother Jean had always accused him of being.

They walked on in silence. Catherine studied the changes in her brother since she had seen him last. Surely his body was different, with broad shoulders and thick forearms and a face beginning to turn to leather. But his spirit had changed too. He was no less intense; no less demanding of himself and of others; he still burned with the zealot's fire that had propelled him into the seminary, and later off to the New World. But tempering the fire now was a certain confidence, not just the arrogance he had always possessed in full measure, but simple confidence. It was as if he had absorbed the odd combination of exotic wildness and inner peace that she had decided made the savage, Nika, so interesting.

"René, Monsieur Nika says something about boats on Great River," Maurice said when his wife and brother-in-law had caught up with them.

La Salle smiled, happy to be on the subject that consumed him. "Not boats. Ships. I've shipwrights ready to voyage back as soon as King Louis gives his permission. To begin a fleet for the great lakes, another fleet for Great River."

"Is it really that big, Uncle?" Colin asked.

La Salle delighted in the boy's bright-eyed eagerness. If it carried forward to his father, La Salle would be sure of his brother-in-law's investment. "Much wider than the Seine. Wide enough that frigates will transport us much more effectively."

"And frigates will be much more defensible if there are others on the river, like English or Spanish, I imagine," Maurice concluded.

"There is that possibility," La Salle admitted. Catherine winced at the idea of her brother in such danger.

"But the main reason for large ships are the huge numbers of furs and hides we'll transport out the mouth of Great River back to France. Gold and silver perhaps." La Salle watched for Maurice's reaction.

"But no one has yet found any gold in New France."

"The regions I'll explore will be beyond New France as we know it. A vast territory. I'll name it Louisiane for King Louis, but perhaps I'll name a river Catherine, and a mountain range after Colin. And perhaps, Lake Maurice."

"Only if I invest, of course," Maurice chuckled.

The small group meandered towards the stone steps of the house.

"I haven't decided, René, if such a scheme is a wise investment or not. Quite frankly, I'm beginning to think that you're more a madman than a genius."

"Maurice! How dare you say such a thing about my brother?"

La Salle smiled. "You wouldn't be alone to say such things about me. Others have argued that point, as they counted the money my expeditions made them."

The morning had dawned gloomy and cold but from the tall arched window where La Salle stood a bright streak of blue appeared behind the gray. He smoothed his crimson coat and readjusted his cuffs. Once again, he partially unrolled the stiff parchment map to study the Spanish bay into which Great River flowed, to retrace the river's line up to where Joliet and Marquette had ended their journey. Not even halfway the length of Meche Sebe, he estimated. Nervously he rerolled the map and glanced to where Nika sat on a damask-covered bench.

Several weeks had passed in anticipation of this moment, an audience with Colbert, chief advisor to the Sun King.

Letters of introduction and support from Governor Frontenac and especially his ally the Prince de Conti had eased the way but it was agreeing to hire the one-handed soldier, Tonti, which had somehow settled some debt for Seignelay, Colbert's son, that finally won him the audience.

A small price, La Salle thought, and besides, the more time he spent with Tonti, the more impressed he became. Beneath his overly bright silks, the man was a professional. La Salle remembered the night he, Nika, and Tonti had spent discussing the proposed expedition down Great River. In an unexpected moment of camaraderie Tonti had removed the metal hand fashioned like a normal one to reveal an iron hook beneath. At that moment La Salle had understood the seemingly contradictory appearance of Tonti the fop and Tonti the soldier. Even Nika, with a silent glance to La Salle, had conveyed his approval of the man. La Salle felt certain that in the New World Tonti would command awe and respect instead of the stares of French courtiers.

The New World, La Salle thought. Over there, his plan to request permission to explore Great River, establish forts, and trade in the name of France had seemed so obvious and simple. Here in the Old World the political and religious factions had confused his entire mission. It can only be advantageous to the crown, La Salle reminded himself to chase away his anxiety. Strategically it is time to reinvest in New France, he would insist to Colbert. Silently he rehearsed his arguments again.

From around a corner at the end of the corridor, two men appeared. Nika quickly moved next to La Salle, ready to bow in greeting as he had been shown. The approaching men were bedecked in the excessive refinement dictated by King Louis XIV's court. Their square-heeled shoes sported ribbons of the same color as their sleeves and knee-length breeches. Bright contrasting stockings covered their legs and their short coats were looped with fanciful braiding. Both wore thick wigs of dark curls that hung down their shoulders.

La Salle bowed gracefully as the two men neared. Nika did the same, almost losing his headdress of a preserved eagle with beady eyes and cawing beak. Amused, the courtiers strolled past at the odd sight of the simply clad man and his Indian companion. Nika shrugged and moved back to the damask bench, adjusting the cougar skin wrapped around his shoulders. The string of deer toes clasped from one edge of the skin cape to the other clattered as he moved.

La Salle could not suppress a smile as Nika picked up the elaborate six-feathered calumet from which dangled wings of woven hair and small fetishes of carved bone. He could not remember the last time he had seen Nika in native array. It had to have been around the time the men had deserted at the Oyo. No, before that. As it had grown colder Nika had accepted the men's woolen clothes. Since then Nika had dressed more like a woods runner than an Indian, except for the loose turban he had adopted in New France but which he'd replaced with a large beaver hat for the streets of Paris. La Salle doubted Nika had ever worn such an amalgamation of Indian finery as he was outfitted in today.

Colbert's secretary appeared in the corridor with a young porter who gathered the heavy box of New World offerings La Salle and Nika had prepared. Checking to see that everything was in place, they were shepherded into Colbert's audience room.

"Of New France. René-Robert Cavelier La Salle and a noble Indian chieftain."

Colbert nodded tiredly, not even looking as the pair before him caused a titter among his court. He had been briefed about La Salle and his desires. His cause was strongly supported by some, and his son Seignelay had wholeheartedly approved of La Salle's use of his own funds to support the venture in return for a trade monopoly in the unexplored region. Others objected that the venture was too dangerous for France should it not be successful. Wearily Colbert sighed and looked up to address this next tedious task.

As La Salle bowed deeply, the huge feather of his hat swished through the air. He glanced over to make sure Nika had bowed too, but saw that his companion stood staring at the huge tapestries behind the minister, which depicted a

particularly violent and colorful boar hunt. Nervously, La
Salle whispered, trying to catch Nika's eye to signal him down
but instead saw him break into smile as if he were returning
the gaze of someone who smiled also. Quickly La Salle
glanced up.

Colbert, with one foot still delicately perched on a foot-
stool, gripped the chair's armrests to pull himself forward.
His mouth was pursed in a bemused smile as he studied Nika's pagan finery.

We have made an impression at least, La Salle thought. He
opened his mouth to address the minister but was silenced by
Colbert's motion to the porter, who placed the pile of New
World bounty before La Salle and swiftly stepped away.

"A warm water route for trade. Not subject to attack by
northern tribes increasingly wary of our expansion," La Salle
again emphasized. Wearily, he shifted his weight from one
leg to the other, and glanced over at Nika, who had stood almost without moving for the hour or so they had been with
Colbert.

"Minor tribes, long ago pacified," countered Colbert.

"Hardly pacified! Monsieur le Ministre," La Salle interjected, "I offer a new empire. With more furs than Quebec.
More fishes than Cape Breton. With more farmland than
Acadie. The possibility of an entire new colony that will lead
us into the forefront . . ."

"Or lead us into war with Spain," warned Colbert with a
wave to silence La Salle. He paused, letting the explorer
squirm. "France can ill afford the soldiers to hold the forts
you propose building."

"You won't need them," La Salle countered. "I'll post my
own men at each. The surrounding nations of Indians wait to
embrace King Louis as their father, France as their ally. With
their allegiances to support each fort . . ."

"And you would finance the entire venture in return for
the monopoly on trade in that region?"

"Yes," La Salle agreed emphatically.

As La Salle assailed the minister with another argument, Nika watched. For the last half of the audience he had no longer made the attempt to sort out the familiar words from the new ones exchanged between La Salle and the minister. Instead he had begun to wonder why Colbert continued to raise argument after argument, when it seemed to Nika he had made his decision shortly after La Salle had begun his explanations. Had they been in a Shawnee or a Miami council, Nika might have been able to decipher the head elder's intent, but here he could not even guess.

Colbert raised a hand to silence La Salle's impassioned speech. Everyone awaited his answer.

"Your zeal is impressive. I will present your request to His Highness." He stood, satisfied he had pressed La Salle hard and long enough to extract from him his final terms. He paused to look more closely at Nika, who had finally bowed awkwardly along with the others.

Colbert wondered if La Salle could succeed in his plan to bring hundreds of thousands of savages under the scepter of King Louis. It was a risk, but if France did not act now to claim this Great River and ally the tribes along it, the English or the Spanish would soon do so. In that, at least, La Salle was surely correct.

Poor La Salle, the minister thought as he walked past his footmen out of the room. He has no idea of the real reason King Louis may let him embark upon this venture.

"And how long does he ask to accomplish such a feat?" King Louis XIV inquired as he surveyed the odd assemblage of New World goods strewn before him. He plucked a belt of delicate beaded wampum from the chest that had been conveyed to his chambers.

Colbert directed several aides to hand the sovereign a large buffalo skin with its huge, wooly head attached. King Louis's eyes lit up with delight as he took the heavy beast's head.

"Ten years, Your Majesty."

"But my dear Colbert, that will never do," the king retorted, angrily thrusting the buffalo robe away from him.

With an impatient gesture he drew his advisor toward a small antechamber. When the door was shut the king swung on Colbert.

"You had estimated it would take no doing to convince him of three years' time," King Louis accused.

"Indeed, Your Highness, I believe . . ."

"We will not be in position to counter Spain if it takes ten years to dally down some waterway. What does this La Salle intend to do that would take so long?"

"Build forts, establish native allies, all things Your Sovereign needs to support an attack on Spanish lands," Colbert explained. "Mexico is rich with gold and silver. The Spaniards will not surrender it easily."

"But ten years!" the king huffed.

Colbert continued hurriedly at the flare of irritation in the king's eyes. "Yet I'm sure Monsieur La Salle could accomplish all this in five years' time, given Your Majesty's concerns."

"He must not know of Our concerns. If word spread that We were positioning Ourselves for an attack on Spanish Mexico . . ."

"There is no reason for him to know, Your Majesty," Colbert risked interrupting the king. "And, Monsieur La Salle is so anxious to have your full endorsement, not just the royal seal, that you are free to place upon him any restrictions you desire."

"So you did not tell him his venture had even intrigued me," King Louis clucked as he divined Colbert's scheme.

"I thought it best to let him plead for his plans. The more he doubted your approval the more willing he was to agree to anything." The minister paused to accept the king's smile of approval. "And I told him nothing of our plans to use his venture to confront Spain lest he realize the danger and insist on more soldiers and arms."

"Well done, Colbert," Louis muttered as he paused before a mirror to check his attire. "Draw up the agreement of Monsieur La Salle's plans with the stipulation that he complete them in five years, not ten." Louis fingered the trim of his robe.

"Excellent, Your Majesty."

"Colbert," Louis proclaimed loudly as the two men stepped from the antechamber into the midst of the sovereign's entourage. "Convey upon Monsieur La Salle the title 'Sieur de La Salle' in appreciation for all he has done for Our kingdom." Then he added in a quiet aside, "Such glories make men like La Salle strive past the difficult and beyond the impossible."

"It is done, Your Majesty," Colbert agreed, lowering his head in acquiescence of the royal order as he helped the king onto his throne. As King Louis smoothed the golden cloth of his breeches he shared with Colbert a conspiratorial smile.

CHAPTER TEN

W AR CLUBS SWIRLED ANGRILY above the painted faces of screeching Iroquois warriors. Muskets and bows jabbed the calm sky. Tonti sank back down to cover. The plain at the bottom of the low bluff was covered with warriors hungry for battle. Among them were groups of Miami and Anadonga allies, even more bloodthirsty than the Iroquois, to whom these temporary partners hoped to prove their mettle.

Tonti rested against the rough bark of the stout palisades surrounding the Illinois village. Nika, Father Zenoble, and, behind them, Illinois men stood facing him, waiting for an answer to the peril before them.

Yesterday, when news had come of the advancing war party, the Illinois had gathered all women and children in canoes and sent them south away from harm. Last night rumors had flown through the village that the women had all been captured, but by morning, when the breeze blowing from the Iroquois encampment carried no scent of burning flesh, the men knew their wives, mothers, and children were safe, at least for today.

Now the same Illinois men stood painted, dressed in war finery and, in appearance, ready for battle. But in their faces Tonti saw the look he had seen in men only once before, years ago, on the same day he had lost his hand. It was the look of men facing an enemy vastly superior in numbers and arms, an enemy who they knew would give them no quarter. It was the look of men preparing to die, too scared to hope and too proud to be anything but brave.

"Bloody Iroquois," Tonti sighed as Father Zenoble and Nika crouched beside him.

"Monsieur La Salle will have a time returning through those villages siding with the Iroquois," Zenoble worried.

"That's probably best. Not much to return to, is there?" Tonti reminded them.

The three shared a miserable expression. Both Fort Crève-coeur, their forward base for launching the Great River expedition, and the ship so painstakingly built there had been burned to the ground by their own men.

Tonti blamed himself. The three had been gone but a few days, hunting to replenish the larder, when the carpenters and woods runners remaining at Fort Crève-coeur had convinced themselves of La Salle's abandonment in spite of Nika's and Tonti's ardent persuasions that their leader would never do such a thing.

I should never have taken Nika and the friar with me, Tonti reproached himself, but by that point it had turned into such an us-against-them atmosphere with the overworked and seldom paid shipwrights that Tonti feared for the priest's and Shawnee's safety if he was not there to shield them from the disgruntled men.

When the trio had returned, woodsmoke still lay thick enough in the air to make the one-handed soldier's eyes burn. The dozen carpenters and woodsmen were gone. Of the ship, nothing remained but charred ruins. On a burnt board protruding from the skeleton of the half-built hull the fleeing men had scrawled, "We are all savages," as if to explain their desperation.

We are all savages, Tonti thought. Indeed.

Tonti, Nika, and Father Zenoble had been forced to seek refuge in the nearby Illinois village. That had been tense enough, for the Illinois were also beginning to believe La

Salle would not return. Was not the burning of the fort and of the strange structure the Frenchmen called a "ship" proof that La Salle had abandoned the enterprise? Without the French leader to protect them against ever bolder raiding parties of Iroquois, the Illinois feared being wiped out.

Now the very situation that Tonti's, Nika's, and Zenoble's Indian hosts had so feared faced them. Among the 700 Illinois warriors there were perhaps ten guns, two of which belonged to Tonti and Nika, and very little ammunition. Across from them a huge army of Iroquois danced about, shrieking their war cries and brandishing their weapons, almost every other brave with a musket. Even at this distance Tonti could smell the acrid smoke of burning matchlock cords.

Squeezed by the flood of French and English penetrating the interior to build fortress trading posts, the Iroquois had reacted by expanding southward and westward. These new European colonists were as ready for trade as their predecessors had been, but Iroquois lands had been exhausted of beaver. Likewise the lands of the nearby tribes, whose trade the Iroquois had long controlled, were fast becoming depleted of furs. At the same time, bold Europeans were proving ever more eager to bypass the Iroquois middlemen and trade directly with the distant tribes. For generations the Iroquois had fought to stop the westward growth of the European colonies. They had adeptly played Dutch against English, English against French. They had won many battles, inflicted much hardship, but still the relentless white men arrived in ever greater numbers, settling on tribal lands, poaching on Iroquois hunting grounds, arming Iroquois enemies. After long deliberations, a consensus had emerged among the Iroquois elders. Containment of the Europeans had failed. For the Iroquois to survive, they must do just like the encroaching Europeans and expand westward.

The Iroquois had annexed nation after nation of surrounding tribes—wiping them out, making them slaves, or occasionally converting them into allies. They now fixed their sights on the Illinois, the large nation whose lands were the strategic key to the upper Meche Sebe, Great River. If the

Iroquois controlled Great River, they once more had a chance of stopping the white man.

Looking through the gap between two posts of the palisade, Nika studied the field. The Anadonga and Miami would be temporary allies for the Iroquois, he knew. As soon as the strength of their added numbers gave the Iroquois victory, they too would be done away with. If La Salle were here, Nika knew he would bargain with them. He would remind the Iroquois that they dare not harm Frenchmen, and if they hurt the Frenchmen's Illinois allies, they would suffer. And all the time he spoke, the spirits that followed him would fill the air, whispering their own warnings that no one must harm this odd Frenchman who had become a legend among them.

Nika tried estimating the number of Iroquois facing them. A thousand? Two thousand? Certainly enough to extinguish all trace of La Salle's allies in this region.

"We must greet them," Nika said, "with the calumet in the name of La Salle."

The three men glanced at one another. In the past three years, since securing his charter from King Louis, La Salle had built forts next to or across from the major tribes of each region he traversed in his reach toward Great River. He had brought trade and firearms to help strengthen each nation against marauders. Almost alone among the Europeans who had wandered in and out of Indian lands, he had learned their ways. Within his network of forts he had remained among them. They had grown to respect and rely on him. Like a great chief of their own kind, one remembered for bravery and vision, he was revered by the Indians.

"Nika's right," Tonti consented. "If they know La Salle is coming back and has established allies among the Illinois they might not be so ready to wipe them out. I'll go."

Tonti thrust his musket into an Illinois's hands and returned to his hut to prepare.

"We must pray," Zenoble announced. Walking to the spot where he'd convinced the suspicious Illinois to erect a cross, he knelt. One by one, many Illinois joined him. The Iroquois threat wins the Lord more converts than my teachings ever did, Zenoble reflected.

After a quick search for a calumet and pouch of tobacco, Tonti grabbed a long strand of fat white trade beads and began wrapping it around his metal hand.

"I'll accompany you," Zenoble said, rising from his prayers as Tonti walked to the gate.

Nika nodded, "Me too."

Tonti frowned. He didn't like the idea of endangering them any further, but seeing a priest and a Shawnee might make the Iroquois hesitate.

"All right, then. Pick a few Illinois, Nika. We'll make a peace party to meet those damn savages."

Nika smiled, remembering how at first Tonti had given much offense by using that term as indiscriminately as most Frenchmen did, but the soldier had soon learned to do as La Salle and Nika, and apply the term "savage" only to one's enemies.

The handful of Indians and Frenchmen moved cautiously down the bluff. A wave of angry warriors broke apart from the rest and rolled to the center of the plain. Tonti raised the dangling trade beads in his metal hand and the shiny red stone calumet in the other. With coaching from Nika he shouted that the Iroquois must not harm the friends of La Salle.

The Iroquois moved uneasily at the mention of the Frenchman's name, screaming furiously at one another. Tonti advanced upon them with his signs of peace, quickly outpacing his small contingent. This was a dangerous mission, he knew. The Iroquois could not be counted on to respect an offer of peace. And even if their leaders would speak with him, would the wild, young warriors allow him to pass?

He was in among them now, pushing through as they crowded around him. Many stared in wonder at his metal hand. Tonti tried hard to hold an expression of strength, enough strength, he hoped, for these Indians to fear and respect him.

Behind him Tonti heard Nika's shout just as an enemy brave jumped forward with a glinting blade. Tonti dodged, but a second blow found its mark, piercing deep within his breast. The calumet flew as Tonti dropped to his knees. An Iroquois snatched the strand of beads from his still-raised iron hand.

Tonti looked down at his wound, deep and ragged. It didn't hurt. He wished it would hurt, for the pain might mean he wasn't dying, but he didn't feel a thing. Tonti pressed his good hand against the red flow gurgling from his chest, staring in disbelief at the frantic savages dancing around him.

"To shore," La Salle shouted wearily. His two companions, the Mohegan Saget and a humorless woods runner, directed the canoe toward the edge of Cayuga Creek. After weeks paddling the great lakes, entering the Niagara River that afternoon had seemed confining. This creek was narrower still, but now La Salle felt the elation of having reached his destination.

They paddled past the shipyard he had built to house the *Griffon,* and with discomfort, noticed no sign of the ship. Below Fort Conti, the blockhouse that guarded the passage between Lakes Erie and Ontario, they beached. The wooden structures he had erected here should have long since been replaced with stone, as had been done with Fort Frontenac, to establish more firmly the French hold on this edge of the frontier. Rebuilding in stone the string of forts he had established along the great lakes and those he intended to establish along the Meche Sebe would require the strength of hundreds, even thousands, of men, and would cost a fortune.

Lord, he prayed with a subtle caress of the rosary around his neck as the light craft beached, permit me to finish the ship on Great River in time to meet the king's deadline. I have come so far to be stopped now.

Almost three years had passed since he and Nika had stepped off the sailing vessel from France along with Tonti and several craftsmen, ready to launch the arduous adventure of opening up the continent. Those days when they had sat around tavern tables finalizing plans; hiring Saget, the Mohegan scout; making the last negotiations with those of his investors who lived in New France; those days were a faded memory.

Back then La Salle had warned such a great expedition could not begin in haste. It meant building two ships. One, to be constructed at Fort Conti, near the shores of Lake Erie, would traverse the great lakes to ferry home the furs and riches they would send north from Great River. The other, on the Illinois River, would speed them down Meche Sebe as they built fortified trade posts, allied tribes, and staked the French cross and the king's plaques. If his information was not wrong, the Spanish had yet to erect strongholds on Great River, or even reassert their claim on the territory supposedly established by Hernando de Soto more than a century earlier. But no one was certain. Barring disaster and the Spanish, or as yet undiscovered cataracts that might block the lower river, they would sail directly back to France after claiming the Meche Sebe valley for King Louis XIV at the river's mouth.

He had figured building the two ships would necessitate a year to a year and a half. His backers had protested but agreed. The craftsmen from France had been the hardest to convince. Most had desired to be done with their commission and return home or settle down in the cities of New France to open their own shops.

The eighteen months La Salle had anticipated to complete his mission had stretched to three years of isolation between Fort Frontenac and the Illinois River. After building the first ship on Lake Erie many of the craftsmen had deserted, unwilling to endure the rigors of wilderness life. Long winters had been spent on scarce rations in Indian villages as La Salle and his men went begging tribes to shelter them.

Tonti and Nika had understood, but the long delays and innumerable preparations had worn on them too. Most of all, even as he preached patience, La Salle was more impatient than anyone else.

Yet fortified posts throughout the lakes and northern rivers had gradually been constructed: Fort Conti at Niagara, Fort Miami on the southern edge of Lake Michigan, Fort St. Louis below the Chicago portage, and finally Fort Crèvecoeur, where he had left Tonti, Nika, Zenoble, and the others. And to La Salle each had been a personal accomplishment, as though he himself had hewn every timber, for each fort marked a visible reminder to all the Indians a hundred leagues around of the power of New France, extended into the heart of the vast continent by his work.

With a hand trembling in fatigue, La Salle pushed back the hair at his temples. Let me be done with this delay soon, he prayed as they climbed the path. The bundles of buffalo hides I have here are a worthy sampling of what trade will be. I know I can persuade the investors not to call in their loans but to refinance. My projects have been delayed, not aborted.

A huge, red moon rose above the trees as a chill wind swept the three men. La Salle sighed. He was not looking forward to more financial negotiations, nor to the questioning of the forced postponement of his claims on Great River. Time was running out. King Louis had given him five years, instead of the requested ten, to complete the mission. Over half his allotted time was gone.

"René-Robert Cavelier, Sieur de La Salle," he responded to the sentries' shouted inquiry as his group approached the fort gates. "Returned from the Illinois post at Fort Crèvecoeur with two men and bundles of pelts."

A sharp cry rose as the gates swung open.

"M'sieur La Salle?" the oldest sentry squeaked in surprise.

La Salle remembered the man from the first days of Fort Frontenac when he and the governor had convened the council of the five Iroquois nations. The man's experience and loyalty is well put to use at this more distant outpost, La Salle thought.

"You've no fire against this chill night?" La Salle asked as he ushered in the rest of his group. Another sentry stared with mouth wide open, backing away, then finally flew toward a cabin glowing with warmth. The old man pulled La Salle aside.

"They said you was dead," he whispered.

"Well, you see," La Salle responded lightly, "I am not."

The old man's face twitched. He nodded towards the cabin. "Careful, m'sieur. They've taken over."

"Who?" La Salle demanded, then saw the lean outline at the cabin's door.

"René," came Jean's familiar voice. "We feared you were lost."

If there was real concern in that voice, any joy in finding a missing brother alive, La Salle chose not to hear it as he strode to the cabin, directing Saget and his other man to take shelter in the nearby bunkhouse. La Salle pulled the old sentry along, propelling him into the warm cabin where a man he recognized as Monsieur Plet, one of his investors, stared in surprise.

"Take these," La Salle ordered as he tonged glowing embers from the hearth into a small metal bucket, "and build a fire at the sentries' post. Gather more fuel from the woodpile as you see fit."

Afraid to glance at Jean and Monsieur Plet the old sentry eyed the floor, nodding at La Salle's commands, whimpering his thanks as he let himself be led back outside.

The despair La Salle had yielded to when approaching the fort was gone. His brother and at least one of his creditors had well taken advantage of his absence. Without confirmation, they had declared him dead and taken over his estate to benefit their own pockets. What La Salle saw here was only a fragment of what he would find in Montreal and Quebec. He steeled himself to regain what had obviously been taken.

La Salle ignored Plet's stammering to address Jean directly. "So you had me declared dead in order to pillage my estate?"

"I despaired when I heard the rumors of your death," Jean pled in angry defense. "I left my duties in Montreal and came all this distance in search of you. It is a relief to have you back."

La Salle was unmoved. After all, if Jean's often repeated predictions of his death and failure had actually come to pass, would he have sincerely been disappointed?

As Jean watched his brother's eyes glaze to hardness, he wondered at his ever having grieved for him. René was as conniving, arrogant, and coldhearted as ever. He would never appreciate the predicament Jean had been put in when the creditors had decided to declare his brother lost to the wilderness, tired of waiting for hides to cover the money he owed.

"You speak of your estate as if it were something of great value. In truth, your finances are in terrible shape," Jean began.

La Salle held back his temptation to throttle Jean and addressed the creditor. "You two are in this together?"

"What the Abbé means, Monsieur La Salle, is that we've managed to cover a few of your more outstanding debts but most of your estate remains . . ." The merchant fell silent under La Salle's glare.

It had taken a few seconds to register the word "Abbé." La Salle turned to his brother in disbelief. With the huge amounts his estate would have brought in over and above his debts, Jean would have undoubtedly become one of the wealthier colonists of New France. No one could deny a wealthy Abbé of St. Sulpice was stronger than a poor one. How long, he wondered, could Jean have planned this scheme?

"Congratulations on your promotion, Abbé," La Salle snickered before flinging himself into a chair and grabbing a mug of wine. "I'm sure your influence will drive many into the arms of the Lord. Faith will be all that's left them, if you pick their purse as clean as you've tried to empty mine."

"You're being very unfair." La Salle's investor finally recovered the courage to speak. "Both to the Abbé and to me. We've been doing the best we could devise under very trying circumstances. Very trying indeed."

La Salle laughed aloud, remembering all the nights he had spent hungry and shivering in some miserable hut or overturned canoe, sometimes under no more shelter than a blanket.

"Laugh if you will," the man went on, "but your brother and I are clearly not the businessman you are. We've not your gift of persuading creditors to wait indefinitely. Leaving aside the money you owe to me personally."

"The hides I sent back to you on the *Griffon* should have covered most payments," La Salle spat. "Where is the *Griffon* anyway? I expected its cargo months ago. My second ship is almost ready for rigging."

The *Griffon*, La Salle's first ship built for traversing the great lakes, had been loaded with hides going to Fort Conti for transhipment to those in charge of La Salle's trade at Montreal. It was due to return, long overdue, with the sails and cordage to complete the second ship at Fort Crève-coeur. La Salle had just paddled hundreds of miles in an attempt to decipher its delay.

La Salle's heart sank at the look of surprise in the faces of the two before him. The merchant confirmed his fears.

"But the *Griffon* left here months ago. With all the supplies you'd ordered. The dozen additional carpenters from France you'd requested arrived not long after its departure. We held them as long as we could, but when the *Griffon* never came back to pick them up, well, we had to assume you and party had perished. The Iroquois have been restive."

"Perhaps the Iroquois captured the *Griffon,* and burned it after looting its cargo," Jean suggested. "Or perhaps the crew deserted . . . disappeared into the woods to live with natives."

As the magnitude of the loss sank in, La Salle felt the blood pound through his temples. The *Griffon* represented months of effort and thousands of louis borrowed at 38 percent interest. If it had sailed when they said, only a catastrophe could have prevented it from reaching its destination by now. Over the huge expanse of barely chartered land and water La Salle knew there was no place to begin looking. But he also knew that on this unforgiving frontier there was no time to stop and mourn.

"I imagine now you will have to abandon your expedition," Jean stated, too stubborn to indulge his little brother in a display of the sympathy he actually felt.

"To the contrary, my expedition has just begun, Monsieur l'Abbé. Tonti, Nika, and Father Zenoble . . . , you remember Zenoble? A Recollet priest. Very reliable fellows, the Recollets. They are at this moment leading the crew in building the ship to carry us down Great River. I'll simply have to buy new sails and cordage."

"Financed with what?"

"I don't presume you've managed to wrest away my patent from Louis XIV investing me alone with the right to trade along Great River."

"Monsieur La Salle," Plet asked indignantly, "do you accuse us of such a thing?"

"Have you?"

"No, René," Jean replied, irritated that his brother automatically expected the worst. "It could hardly be considered unless your . . . permanent absence had been affirmed."

La Salle nodded. So Jean had probably tried, but Governor Frontenac and his expansionist allies had prevented it. La Salle rubbed his forehead. His temples still pounded, but already the pain was diminishing.

Tomorrow morning he would leave for Montreal. It would take some doing, or undoing, to get his estate back in order. He would have to go to Quebec to reaffirm his alliance with Frontenac and straighten things out; face the creditors who had supported his venture and ask them to replace the equipment; then hire more boats and boatmen, perhaps a few Indians. . . . But there was time enough to compose a list on the journey.

The inevitable haggling was not a prospect La Salle was savoring, but a quick calculation told him that the time it would take to go to Quebec, reassure investors and pry a few more louis from them, then buy new supplies, and return to Fort Crève-coeur was about the same amount of time Nika and Tonti needed to finish the ship that would sail them down Meche Sebe.

Within months, if they didn't butt up against the Spanish, La Salle told himself, they would plant the cross where Meche Sebe spilled into the Gulf of Mexico. In the same ship they would cross the Atlantic back to France. Then they could return with the proper artisans and colonists to build a settlement on Great River. As the southern capital of New France laid down its streets, the forts along the river up through the lakes could begin being rebuilt into stone strongholds like Fort Frontenac. It was not a vision easily conveyed, but La Salle suddenly felt up to the challenge of convincing everyone of its necessity.

CHAPTER ELEVEN

"Over here," Nika whispered.

He steadied the canoe as Zenoble pushed Tonti's bulk into it, then clambered aboard. The two men glanced about worriedly as Tonti cried out some unintelligible oath. Darkness had finally come, giving them cover to make their escape. It was doubtful the Iroquois would post sentries after so total a conquest, but one could never be sure. As the canoe drew away from the bank, Nika strengthened his strokes. Unless Tonti began to cry out too loudly, the victory songs of the Iroquois and the death chants of the captives would cover any noise they made.

As the Shawnee shoved the paddle into the water, Tonti let out another agonized groan. "Keep him quiet," Nika warned.

"Dear Mother of God," the priest mumbled as he tried to lift Tonti's head. In their haste to get away, they'd shipped a lot of water, putting the semiconscious soldier in some danger of drowning where he lay in the canoe's bottom. Nika looked at the muttering priest and saw Zenoble's hands and robe were stained red with the soldier's blood, and doubtless that of many others killed that day.

It was La Salle who had saved them, Nika decided.

It wasn't until after Tonti had been stabbed, when calmer

heads among the Iroquois had paused at the thought of killing a Frenchman, that the wild braves had been deterred
from finishing him off. Barely able to stand, with blood flowing freely from his chest, Tonti had nevertheless been
dragged to meet the Iroquois chiefs, as Zenoble, Nika, and
Illinois had been shoved back to the Illinois village.

Hours later, Tonti had returned, pale from loss of blood.
Before he had collapsed and lost consciousness, he had re-
counted how he'd lied to the Iroquois chiefs, warning them
of the many Frenchmen and guns in the Illinois village, but
he hadn't been sure they'd believed him. They hadn't, and
when they finally attacked, the carnage was terrible.

In the hut they had shared since arriving among the Illinois, Nika and Zenoble had spent the battle trying to keep
Tonti alive. Whether they were overlooked because the hut
the unhappy Illinois had relegated them to was so miserable,
or saved by the Christian God as Father Zenoble had assured
them, Nika knew there was some purpose to their survival.
Nature was not random; there was order to the universe, and
if the Iroquois had bypassed them when so many had fallen
at their hands, it had to be because they had some mission yet
to fulfill.

And whatever that is, Nika thought, it has to do with La
Salle. For hadn't he brought Tonti, Nika, and Zenoble together into this country?

Tonti seemed to rest more comfortably, and Father Zenoble had begun to pray. Nika wished his uncle were still alive,
the wise uncle killed and eaten by the Seneca the night Nika
had first met La Salle. Nika needed someone to talk to, but
Frenchmen seemed so ignorant of spiritual matters.

Four canoes moved around a bend, creasing the glassy water of early morning. La Salle sat up high and renewed his
paddle strokes. Soon the log palisade walls of Fort Crève-
coeur would be in sight. His excitement grew.

Though La Salle hadn't been able to secure any shipwrights, such craftsmen being in great demand in the colony, he had found, upon returning first to Montreal then to

Quebec, that his resurrection from the dead had increased his reputation. Financial problems aside, he'd been able to pick and choose the men he needed. Among them was a Monsieur le Barbier, a man of surgical skills who would make an admirable ship's doctor. Perhaps most useful of all, however, was Prudhomme, the armorer. The wilderness was hard on firearms and if any southern tribes proved as fierce as the Iroquois, or if the lower reaches of Great River were already guarded by the Spanish as many feared, the expedition would need every musket in proper working order.

True, La Salle had brought a good solid troop with him, but he had to confess he was eager for the company of those he'd left to run Fort Crève-coeur.

Burly Tonti saw the exploration of New France as a new chance to put all his talents to the test and rid himself of the awkwardness his battlefield deformity had inflicted on him. Old World armies had no use for one-handed soldiers, but the New World was hungry for daring men of any shape. La Salle tried to remember the last time he had seen Tonti slide the normal-shaped, metal hand over his hook, then recalled it had been just before a calumet ceremony during which he had slowly, tantalizingly revealed the vicious hook attached to his forearm. The hesitant Fox leader had then agreed to let the contingent winter with them, and had even suggested they share his private reserves of food. From that moment on Tonti had been called Ironhand. Tonti has taken full advantage of the New World, La Salle thought.

And Nika. La Salle acknowledged that his own renown as an Indian diplomat was in large part thanks to Nika's increasing adeptness at translation. My negotiations, La Salle reflected, are effective only when completely understood. Nika had always been able to take La Salle's words and relay them imbued with Indian nuance and significance.

And Father Zenoble would be there, too. La Salle remembered how he had fretted that governmental policies would inflict on him another Sulpician like Father Casson or worse, a Jesuit spy in the guise of a priest. But to avoid religious and political infighting, the court had appointed a Recollet.

Zenoble had quickly discerned the success of incorporating native thought into his sermons. After all, was the Indian belief of a great spirit, a manitou, so different from European Christianity?

"Crève-coeur!" Saget shouted. The call was echoed.

Then they turned the bend and La Salle saw the remains of the ship a few hundred feet away. "Forward!" he commanded.

As they neared, every member of the expedition realized what La Salle had first discerned. The fort had been attacked. The ship's blackened keel looked like the decaying skeleton of a roasted whale.

Silently, canoes bumped the bank. La Salle stumbled to the scattered pile of sharpened logs that had been the fort's palisade. Nothing but charred wood. He nudged a pile of ash. Cinders blew into a miniature black cloud that wisped into nothingness on the breeze.

The vessel had been near completion when it burned. From the keel charred ribs extended above La Salle's head. He touched a bit of planking. The fire-eaten board crumbled in his hand. La Salle sank to his knees. His fortune was gone; his friends were gone; his dreams were gone, too.

"No bodies," reported Saget.

"Let's hope they took refuge with the Illinois," La Salle answered, wavering to his feet. "We must go there immediately."

The drained men piled back into the canoes. As they approached the bluff where the Illinois village had stood, they began to gag at the smothering stench.

Bodies covered the plain, bodies that had been dead and rotting for two, maybe three weeks. La Salle directed the devastated group to check the corpses for any sign of those he had left behind. The job took half a horrible day. Flocks of buzzards, grown bold by their long-running feast, squawked at the interlopers. The searchers found nothing of the missing men, only decaying Illinois, Iroquois, Miami, and Anadonga.

The men numbly launched the canoes once more to set up camp away from the nightmare battleground. Unable to concentrate on anything other than his loss, La Salle allowed Saget to choose a site.

Late that night, as the sentry threw more wood onto the campfire, La Salle pushed his quill across the parchment spread before him. Desperate as things seemed, he was determined to send word back to Frontenac of the present status of the expedition. They had encountered the Iroquois's reach into the Illinois valley; these Indians were flanking the French in an attempt to bottle La Salle into the great lakes.

Listing his estimates of the numbers annihilated—so many Illinois, so many Iroquois, so many Miami, and on and on—La Salle grimaced at the resemblance to the accounts he'd kept, the books full of columns of numbers he'd scribbled over the years to calculate his sales, costs, and profits.

The field of dead Illinois allies, was that to be counted among the costs? Indians had massacred Indians for millennia he knew, but had the weapons he'd handed out, the alliances he'd made, the furs he'd requested and the appetites for European goods he had so carefully sponsored, hadn't all those things worsened the carnage? Would the ghosts of dead Illinois haunt him? The soldier, Tonti, may have been destined to die on a battlefield, but what of the gentle priest Zenoble? What of Nika?

To clear his head, La Salle turned back to strategy. He would have to head north to Fort Miami on Lake Michigan to take stock of and reassure allies there. If Tonti, Nika, and Zenoble had survived he could only hope they had returned to safe territory. From there he would summarize the situation, and begin again. He dipped his plume into the inkwell to inscribe his plans to Frontenac.

La Salle paused as Saget and a few of the men approached. He recognized the stout figure of Prudhomme, and the bald head and red beard of Barbier. The back of his throat seized as he recalled Normandin and the others who had deserted at the Oyo. It's happening again, he realized, just as we near Great River.

Quickly he moved to stand before his accusers, but even as he did Saget sat and motioned the others to do the same. Warily, La Salle eased himself back down, choosing a spot that would put him in shadow, but would let him study their faces in the orange glow.

The men waited as La Salle covered his inkwell and re- placed his quill in its wooden case. He used the moment to speculate on how to counter this newest obstacle, but no ob- vious tactic came to mind. He looked up to face them.

"We have decided," the Mohegan began in his French-In- dian jargon, motioning to include the men behind him, "that if you want to journey down Meche Sebe from here . . ."

La Salle tensed. He had pushed them too hard. He knew that. Just a few more days and they would be back in friendly territory. They could rest and eat well. He would allow a tem- porary retreat. He would not force them to go on, not after seeing the fate of the others at the hands of the Iroquois. His thoughts jumbled inside him, colliding so he could not sort them out to say anything.

Saget saw his leader's trouble and motioned firmly to keep him silent. "If you want to go down Meche Sebe now, in ca- noes," he said pointedly, "we are not afraid to go with you."

Saget glanced at the men behind him. Each affirmed the offer with a weary nod.

La Salle placed his hand across his eyes. The fear of deser- tion was replaced by an overwhelming gratitude. When he dropped his hand, his eyes gleamed with appreciation. He nodded his thanks.

"If you want, we are ready," Saget reiterated.

"We must go back north," La Salle explained. "We will need more supplies and men to rebuild our ship."

The men seemed relieved he had not accepted their offer as they moved to stretch out alongside the fire. Saget was the last to move away, with a final nod.

Saget is so different from Nika, La Salle thought, in more ways than just the difference between Mohegan and Shaw- nee. While Nika dressed in French trousers and had made a turban of Lyonnaise broadcloth his trademark, Saget still looked unmistakably Mohegan. While Nika embraced some of the French ways and beliefs, even as he argued obstinately how ridiculous some of them were, Saget held to what he'd been taught as a child. His tribe had been all but annihilated, and now he worked diligently and loyally for the French. He'd let himself be baptized but it'd left no mark upon him. He was a pure Indian, La Salle decided, and Nika was something else—no longer Indian but not a Frenchman.

An arm crooked across his eyes, La Salle offered prayers of thanks for the courage and loyalty of Saget and the others, then added an ardent hope that Tonti, Nika, and Father Zenoble had somehow survived.

The men's proposal was naïve, of course. Going downriver in canoes would mean having to return upriver. One could not cross the ocean in canoes. And even a whole flotilla of them couldn't hope to carry enough supplies, much less cannon, to establish the forts along the river that the king's charter required; nor could they return with enough hides to make the expedition turn a profit.

The thought of profits reminded La Salle of his investors. Those he had spoken to on his return to Quebec and Montreal had been outraged by the loss of the *Griffon*, but La Salle had nevertheless pried open enough purses to resupply. Now with the second ship gone too, how would they react? How would they take the news of the men he had lost and the hundreds of Illinois allies dead?

Looking over to the rounded shapes around the fire, La Salle thought of the offer the men had made, to follow him downriver, and to do it in canoes. An idea sprang to mind, making him sit upright.

Would the expedition seem a failure if he could travel down Great River without a ship? He could still put up a fortified trading post or two along the way to seal the king's claim on the valley. Of course, they'd be meager structures, and he would not have the personnel to leave them properly manned, definitely no cannon, but they'd stand proud on the map he'd carry back to Paris. If his New France investors were losing patience, then those in the mother country must be seduced to lend a little more money, enough to buy a ship, if not build one.

La Salle suddenly realized the strategy he'd carefully followed for the last three years had been wrong. It was foolish to build ships in the middle of the wilderness when fine vessels could be had at half the cost in La Rochelle or Le Havre or St. Malo. Once he had found the river's mouth by canoe, and made friends with the natives living there, he could return to that spot by ship directly from France to found the trading colony that would become the capital of his empire—the colony that would complete the arc he envisioned from the St. Lawrence to the Spanish Gulf, bringing France a stronghold on the trade of the New World through control of its main waterway.

La Salle laughed aloud. A few men, still awake, glanced curiously over. They think I'm crazed after all we saw today, he thought. Well, people have been thinking that for quite some time.

Again La Salle pondered the men's offer. They are loyal, he thought gratefully, and I must be loyal to them. He remembered when he had heard the news of the loss of the *Griffon*, and how quickly he had dismissed the idea of searching for its crew. Now he had lost other men, good men: Nika, Tonti, and Zenoble. Yes, La Salle would lead the canoes downriver, but first he must find out what had become of his friends.

Weeks later, after following rumors that had led nowhere, La Salle came upon his three colleagues in a village near the shores of Green Bay, not far from Lake Michigan. He nearly wept when he first saw Nika and Zenoble, both thinner and looking haggard, but La Salle held back his emotions for fear the men would be embarrassed.

Silently he followed them into a rounded wigwam, ducking the stray leaves of thatch interspersed among dangling conical baskets and pots, to the bulky form of Tonti on a low wooden cot. Nika motioned the other men following into the hut to be quiet as Zenoble gently raised Tonti's head and put a steaming cup of liquid to his lips.

"Damn it, Zenoble," Tonti muttered, coming fully awake, "you better not be giving me last rites again."

"I suspect you'd prefer a ration of brandy," La Salle said.

"Ah, Monsieur La Salle!" With a huge grin Tonti grasped La Salle's hand. "I feared you were dead."

"And I feared the same for you."

Tonti nodded at the priest. "Thought I might as well take advantage of having a manservant while waiting to hook up with you again. This won me much sympathy, but it's really no more than a scratch." He pushed aside his covers and lifted the flat plaster across his chest.

A pungent aroma of herbs penetrated La Salle's nostrils as he bent to inspect the red scar glistening with salve. La Salle observed that the wound had been much worse than Tonti implied, but the Indian medicines had worked well. Tonti would soon be ready for travel, if not paddling.

"You saw Crève-coeur and the ship then?" Tonti asked. "The crew abandoned us after burning the whole thing while we were out."

La Salle glanced at the men. Suddenly his grand plan to continue the expedition down Great River by canoe seemed a pipe dream. What could I have been thinking? he asked himself.

"Got our work cut out for us, La Salle," Tonti said. The rest of the men voiced agreement. Tonti flung off the furs and with a suppressed groan righted himself on the cot. With a swift, if painful, move he swung his legs onto the ground.

"I'm ready to travel as soon as you are. As I said, I just didn't want these nursemaids to be idle," he said with a chuckle at Nika's and Zenoble's reaction to his newfound strength. Then Tonti grew serious and leaned toward La Salle.

"I was the captain you left in charge at Crève-coeur, so if you haul me back to Quebec in chains I won't blame you."

Tonti looked at the others. He wished they weren't here, listening, and listening they were, he realized, their ears pricked all attentive. To hell with them, Tonti thought, and continued.

"But I'm asking you for a second chance, monsieur."

La Salle moved to stop the soldier's embarrassed confession, but Tonti stayed him.

"Now that I'm healed let me go down the river in your name. All I ask is a canoe and a bit of corn. I'll pass the spot the Jesuits got to and report back. If I find any gold I'll bring it back for you, and if I run across Spaniards I'll bring back their heads."

"You'd never survive such a journey," Zenoble objected.

"If I died, Monsieur La Salle'd have no worse troubles than he's got now."

Each man there had invested in this voyage, financially and personally, La Salle saw. Whether Frenchman or Indian they had decided their future lay on Great River. No matter how they traveled—by ship, by barge, on foot—he knew they would go. A flotilla of canoes did not seem silly now.

"Yes, you will go down Great River by canoe."

When he heard La Salle accept Tonti's offer, Father Zenoble gasped. How could a God-fearing Frenchman consider sending a sick man into Indian wilderness alone? Only Nika saw that La Salle had a different vision, one that included them all.

By late winter the Illinois River leading to Great River itself was free enough from ice floes to begin the journey. One by one the loaded canoes were launched.

Of the almost two dozen Frenchmen, half wore European dress, others the buckskin of Canadian woods runners, and Father Zenoble his brown Recollet robes. Some wore large brimmed felt or leather hats, others decorated woolen caps. At the front of their canoes were pennants or symbols painted in the fashion of the gay emblems decorating their buckskin leggings.

Near as many, the natives too were full of contrast. The recently hired Abnaki wore tailored buckskins. Others wore loincloths and thigh-high leggings under cloaks of fur or

European blankets clasped at the shoulder. Saget wore a skirt and cape. Each Indian had feathers in his hair, either tied to the top standing up like ears, or hanging from scalp locks or ponytails. About ten Abnaki women, a few pregnant, and a couple of children accompanied the party.

La Salle had donned his crimson greatcoat and plumed hat to initiate the launch, although later he intended to fold his coat into the chest behind him. It would be his ceremonial robe, he had decided.

Nika wore a French shirt and vest with buckskin pants and leggings decorated in gaudy Shawnee fashion. His turbaned head was unique among his fellow natives. Tonti sported a hat similar to La Salle's but replaced the feather with a racoon's tail that dangled off the back. As if his iron hand were not ominous enough he had attached a stout cutlass and a pair of pistols around his waist.

The first few days of travel passed. La Salle relaxed as natives and woods runners, equally adept, measured their paddle strokes for maximum efficiency. Some sat on the canoe's crossboards to paddle; others knelt on its floor. Between the men were packs of merchandise for trade: beads and knives, axes, pots, awls, cloth, and tobacco, although the latter was as much a bonus for the men and the Indians.

The burning of the ship had rendered useless the sails and cordage that had cost La Salle so much time, effort, and money. He traded them for provisions, and had given pieces to thank the natives who had succored Tonti, Nika, and Zenoble. The locals had been delighted by the heavy canvas, less colorful but infinitely more durable than the cheap broadcloth usually traded.

La Salle watched the shoreline. With a finger, he traced a bend on the map in his lap. A ragged line marked the flow of the tributary they traveled into Great River. The flotilla caught a swift current around a bend. Paddles bit the water to avoid the whirlpools and eddies, guiding the fleet of bark boats across a plume of brown water.

"Great River!" La Salle shouted with a wave to the men. "This river! Meche Sebe!"

A hooray swelled up. La Salle had calculated a week to reach it but they had done so in only five days. The milestone renewed the men's energy. Paddle blades sliced the water in exaltation.

Although some called it the St. Louis, others the Colbert, and the Indians referred to it each in their own dialects— Meche Sebe, Mesa Saypi, Mesha Sepe, Missi Sipi—La Salle still referred to the Father of the Waters that split the continent as Great River. That is the French translation of the Indian, he told himself, and that is what it is: the great river that will lead to the prominence of New France, and to a new colony for King Louis.

CHAPTER TWELVE

THROUGH MUCH OF THE TERRITORY they had navigated the past days, the banks had been lined with abandoned cornfields, their native farmers dead or moved on, but here woods reached the shore.

Tonti instructed the men to position the canoes in a circle horizontally against trunks to provide a semblance of protection. The soldier was being overzealous, but the good humor born of being underway kept anyone from minding his attentive command.

La Salle stood on the bank, water lapping near his feet. He studied the shoreline, contentedly making note of its differences, how the water changed color as Great River grew wider. Behind him, around the blazing campfire, men ate, sang, or bedded down. Nika walked over to hand La Salle a bowl of sagamité, the corn mush the Indians had taught them to sustain themselves with. La Salle took it but didn't eat.

"This river shall cover us with glory, Nika."

"I thought you told your king it would cover you with hides," Nika chided.

"Is it wrong to hope for glory?"

Nika considered his friend's question. He imagined a time

of his children's children. Would they tell stories around the fire about Nika and his deeds? He would try to make certain his memory would be a glorious one for his people, and he was certain La Salle would strive for the same. But did those two paths lead in the same direction?

"Glory is a cruel master," Nika decided.

For days they traveled under high bluffs, past the Oyo through wooded lands. No Indian villages greeted them. No change in the shoreline broke the monotony of paddling until a tributary spilled from a large plain where buffalo grazed near water's edge. On La Salle's signal, canoes fanned out to flank the beasts.

"More than we've seen thus far," La Salle exclaimed.

The group moved on shore, but the wind was wrong for so direct an attack. The beasts smelled the hunters and moved on, gathering speed until finally the whole herd broke as one into a thundering gallop.

The men and women of the expedition watched in awe as a dust trail rose from the disappearing herd. All had seen buffalo before, though the hide trade was already making them rare around the Illinois plains, but no one had ever seen the creatures congregated in such numbers.

La Salle was elated at this proof that the richness of the interior would dwarf the wealth of the seaboard and St. Lawrence valley. That night as they fed on cornmeal and jerky, Saget and Tonti discussed the techniques of a buffalo hunt. If the animals they had seen had not moved too far away, they would eat fresh meat tomorrow.

La Salle made an entry in his log, then put away the journal to watch the group before him. They were excited about the full bellies and thick hides the buffalo hunt would bring, but the opportunity meant much more to La Salle. By estimating the hides in that one herd he could guess what the rest of the territory would bring. If it was as much as he hoped the voyage down Great River would be just the beginning. With financial success ensured he could actually begin planning the next leg, the founding of a colony.

Then La Salle frowned. We haven't yet made it to where Joliet and Marquette stopped, he chastised himself, and already I'm daydreaming like a young seminarian.

The next day, after the dew burned off, the party went in search of the herd. The tracks of so many hooves were easy to follow, but the trail seemed endless across the prairie. It was late morning when La Salle, after conferring with Tonti, Nika, and Saget, ordered the men to turn back. The hunters were disappointed to return to their boats empty-handed, for tough, chewy jerky could never compare with fresh meat, but La Salle knew that it was a waste of time to give more than a day to hunting when their provisions were still ample. If they had been in a ship, he thought wistfully, a ship with stowage belowdecks for all the skins they could gather, then the hunt would have continued with his blessing, for the hides from even one such herd would have nearly paid for a ship.

The next day was uneventful, except for a near miss with a drifting log, until late in the day when another, much smaller herd of buffalo was sighted, this time on the east bank. At the approach of the canoes, the creatures retreated into the woods, but Saget guessed that in the thick forest they would not travel far. La Salle agreed to attempt another hunt the next morning.

"If you'll permit, Monsieur La Salle," Zenoble interrupted the leader's supper, "I'd like to offer prayers for tomorrow's hunt."

At La Salle's look of surprise, Zenoble continued, "The men express such excitement at having fresh meat, I thought they might appreciate any extra help after the other day's disappointment." He didn't add that a couple of the Abnaki had asked if his God could help their hunting spirits bring a good feast, and Zenoble had seen it as an opportunity to lead them in Christian prayer.

"Of course, Father," La Salle hastened to reply. "I'm delighted to give my approval." He watched Father Zenoble, so pleased with himself, walk back to the campsite.

The next day Saget tracked the buffalo to a small meadow. He indicated that half the men should go downwind to form a musket and arrow line past which the others would direct the herd. They should shoot at will as the galloping beasts approached while the other group would try to isolate a few; thus they'd be doubly assured of game. When the line of musketeers had assembled they signaled the others to begin their approach.

The group, led by Tonti, moved slowly toward the small herd. The buffalo looked up. At the prearranged signal the men rushed forward. The small herd bolted in confusion, galloping toward the ambush.

Saget aimed. His gun belched noise and smoke. A young buffalo took the hit on a jowl. Hollering its rage, it charged straight for Prudhomme, who flung himself out of its way. For a moment it looked as though the animal would escape, but an Abnaki and a woods runner came running to send it back into Saget's line of fire. Another shot was fired.

The buffalo wavered in the center of the clearing, snorting, blood staining its wool. The wind played with its heavy mane. It stumbled. Tonti raised his cutlass. A third shot toppled it. The hunting party fell upon the prey.

The party noisily tramped into camp, flaunting their prize at those who'd been directed to stay behind to build frames for drying meat and hides. The good spirits were contagious.

"The bounty of our new land," Zenoble proclaimed.

Spits soon held roasting meat. Abnaki women scraped the skins. Tonti was the first to notice something amiss.

"Where's Prudhomme?" he asked.

Accusing eyes searched apprehensive faces after a quick scan revealed that Prudhomme, the armorer, was indeed not among them.

"Who saw him last?" La Salle inquired.

"He was with us when we brought down the beast," Nika said. They all recalled him dodging out of the way when the buffalo had charged, but no one could remember seeing him afterwards.

Dread swallowed the group. Prudhomme was their armorer, in charge of all firing weapons. If something had befallen him, the repercussions for the expedition would be enormous.

Tonti paused to watch the felling of trees. A team of two worked at each, alternating ax blows until "all clear" sounded, and the tree crashed down. Others cleared it of branches, then hauled it back to camp where it was sized and sharpened at each end, one pointed to drive into the ground, the other to provide firing slits and impede attackers from clambering over the top.

"Time we get to Mexico, we'll be doing this in our sleep, no?" Tonti called out brightly to the sweating men.

He closed his eyes, feigning sleep, while at the same time pretending to chop. He faked a snore, then swung his imaginary ax and uttered a loud "chop." Snore, chop, snore, chop. The men chortled as they paused to mop their brows before returning to their tasks.

It's working at least, Tonti thought.

He knew hard physical labor would be better for morale than sitting around wondering what had befallen Prudhomme. Most assumed he'd been kidnapped or killed by hostile natives, though no one had seen any, only a few footprints. Tonti knew the men worried that what had happened to Prudhomme might happen to any of them. He didn't mind them thinking that; a little threat of danger did wonders for discipline. But he guessed the greater peril was what could happen without an armorer to keep up the weapons. He himself was a decent hand with firearms, but no replacement for a proper craftsman. Tonti had seen matchlocks backfire in men's faces from lack of proper upkeep.

Tonti headed to where La Salle sat bent over maps, calculating distances traveled and, unable to curb his impatience, speculating on the distances to come. The expedition leader set aside his documents and rested his head against a tree trunk as Tonti squatted beside him.

La Salle pressed his eyes closed with ink-stained fingers, then opened them on a watchful Tonti. A report sent back from Nika's and Saget's search party stated they'd found no sign of Prudhomme, but had seen markings that Indians had recently been near. Tonti knew the expedition would be pressed to continue on soon, with or without Prudhomme, and had regretted placing the difficult decision before his leader.

"It's possible Prudhomme was injured and the Indians have carried him off to heal him. . . ." La Salle's explanation died as Tonti shook his head.

"Saget would have noticed such trackings—a difference in weight, something being pulled." Tonti fingered his thin mustache. "Two more days, at the most, and the fort will be finished."

"In all those wars that were your livelihood, Tonti, in your advances and retreats, were you forced to leave men behind?"

"Sometimes. But that was different," Tonti said quickly. "That was war. Had an enemy on our heels, and always had more than one armorer. Traveling on water, half our arms'll jam in a fortnight. Without Prudhomme to repair them . . ."

"Can't someone else keep up the weapons?"

"I can appoint someone. Prudhomme's tools are still here. But if we do come upon Spaniards, we'll be in a bad corner without a real armorer to replace parts and do more than just keep them functioning." Tonti poked the ground with his hook. "And if we leave with no sign of Prudhomme, every man will worry you'll do the same to him farther downriver."

That truth affected La Salle deeply. He had known all along, since the night Prudhomme was missed, the dilemma would focus on what Tonti had just said.

"Don't rush construction, Tonti. And let's take time to hunt, dry more meat. Perhaps we should venture after the Indians whose tracks Saget spotted. . . ." La Salle's voice trailed off.

Tonti nodded in sympathy and headed back to the construction site. La Salle reached for the comfort of his silver crucifix.

Nika didn't like taking orders from Saget, but realized the Mohegan was the best tracker of them all.

I just wish he wasn't so proud of it, Nika thought.

Saget raised a hand to bid the others to stop, and bent to inspect tracks. Nika pushed past the two woods runners and three Abnaki who had come along. He squatted beside Saget, who carefully studied the faint impression on the ground, so faint Nika could not discern it.

"Someone has passed this way," Saget announced, "but not the Frenchman."

Surprised, Nika studied the spot more closely but still did not see anything. He stood and hurried after the party already following Saget through the woods. When the Mohegan next spotted tracks Nika once more elbowed his way to study them. This time even he could make them out, clear impressions in the soft ground. When Nika looked around, he could make out several. Whoever had been here had passed more than once to leave so many footprints. He must have been wandering in circles.

"These prints are more recent but they are not the Frenchman's," Saget intoned.

"Whose?" a woods runners asked.

Nika spotted a mark on a tree just beyond the tracks. It was typical of the indication an Indian party would make to show they had crossed this way, that this land was theirs. He was surprised Saget had not seen it. Proudly, Nika pointed it out.

"Hunting party? Scouts? They aren't far," Saget declared as the men nervously checked their weapons.

A shout sent men scurrying for arms. Tonti saw Father Zenoble rush toward the wood's edge as Nika came out at the head of the returning search party.

Tonti shouted for the men to return to their work as he caught up with Zenoble. "Did you find him?"

Nika shook his head. "Only those two." A young brave and an old man were carefully guarded by Saget and the others.

"There were five of them," Saget interjected. "We could have caught all five."

"It was all we could do to run down these two," Nika

declared. "They shot arrows at us to try and get away. I preferred not to cause a skirmish."

Tonti hoped the Indians who had escaped had not sounded an alarm to bring more warriors.

"No sign at all of Prudhomme?" Zenoble asked.

"Neither seen nor heard of such a man," Nika added.

"Of what nation are they?" inquired La Salle, who had appeared shortly after the sentry's shout. He studied the first Indians to be encountered on Great River. They wore skin tunics and large medallions of bone strung with deer toes and feathers.

"They speak Chickasaw, the trade language of the southern nations, and call it the tongue of their tribe," Nika informed La Salle.

"Release them! Give them food," La Salle commanded. As quickly as he could he moved to his wooden chest. Carefully folded inside lay his crimson greatcoat, calumet, and pouch of tobacco.

The old Chickasaw quit gnawing a buffalo rib to look up in wonder as La Salle sat before him.

"I bring greetings from the Sun King," Nika translated.

When the old Chickasaw saw the calumet he excitedly turned to the young brave at his side. "We will smoke with this wealthy tribe."

Days earlier the old Chickasaw had been sent away from his village with his youngest grandson and three others. He had grown past the useful age of any warrior and it was time to invite the spirits to take him. The small group had followed as he awaited the signs to have them build his final resting place. Then they had seen the strange assortment of men in the woods. The others had fired arrows, fleeing in fright. It was an omen, the old Chickasaw had believed, not that he was supposed to journey to the other world but that he would finally find glory in old age.

"Nika, tell them we invite the young tribesman to travel with us to be a guide and learn our language."

When the old Chickasaw heard La Salle's intentions and understood he was to be left behind, he began rattling off such a stream of supplications Nika could not keep up. All the while the grandson became more frightened, and tried to draw his grandfather away from the strangers.

"Have the old man take these to his people," La Salle said as a woods runner opened a trade pack at the explorer's signal. "Tell him they come from La Salle, the French trader, and the Frenchman's fort at the river's edge. We will trade tools for hides and food."

"You go back to the village with these things," the old Chickasaw told his grandson. "And tell them your grandfather has been taken by the great spirit in the form of a white man with much power."

The young Chickasaw was terrified. He had heard stories of what happened when one's spirit was whisked away but never anything like this. The old Chickasaw smiled. He may have become useless with his tribe but they would never forget him after his grandson reported what had happened.

When La Salle realized the switch between the two, he insisted Nika straighten things out. The young brave would be useful, if he desired to come, and fresh enough to learn the French-Indian trade language and European ways, but the old man would be a burden.

The expedition pushed onto the expanse of Great River. La Salle looked back at the fort, scrawny but with tenable log palisades. Just as important, it was easily visible, perched on the bluff for all to see. La Salle caught Tonti's eye and nodded approval. They had decided to call it Fort Prudhomme.

To the great relief of everyone, especially the armorer himself, Prudhomme had finally reappeared. He had floated down the river, clinging to a log and so gravely ill from exposure that Barbier the surgeon had marveled at how he had even managed to hang on.

To continue on with so sick a man would be impossible. Thus leaving behind their only armorer was the only, albeit unpleasant, solution. La Salle put him in charge of the rest of

the men selected to stay behind to garrison the first fort on
Meche Sebe. A small group would strike out for the Chickasaw village as soon as possible to establish an alliance and
trade. To care for Prudhomme, the Abnaki were persuaded
to leave behind the pregnant women and children.

The reduced expedition, lighter still since pelts and hides
had been left for transport north, traveled quickly. In the bow
of Nika's canoe the old Chickasaw idly enjoyed the scenery.
The Shawnee had failed to convince the frightened young
brave to come along. As for the old man, he had been told he
would receive no more presents, but before any of the expedition had even finished packing their belongings, Nika had
found the old Chickasaw seated in one of the beached canoes.

In short time the men were loosening their shirts and shed-
ding their headgear. Sweat glistened as strong shoulders
slung back and forth to dig paddles into water. A song broke
out amongst the men, faded off, and was picked up again.

The first glimmer of spring had not yet reached the forest
but La Salle could tell that by March, no later than April, the
rolling woods would be a lush green.

"It's a blessed, bountiful land, monsieur," Father Zenoble
remarked as his canoe pulled alongside. "Can't you see the
even fields neatly lined with stone walls?"

For a moment La Salle envisioned a countryside of wheat
fields and woodlots, here and there a stone farmhouse with
smoke rising from the chimney.

"Yes, Father, I can."

"And where are the Chickasaw in that picture?" Nika interjected.

"Oh, I see them," Zenoble continued, "in that church down
by the spring."

He and La Salle shared a smile, but Nika did not join in.

The first two days of travel from Fort Prudhomme were
uneventful, but late on the third an alarm cry broke the
steady rhythm.

"Guard to the right!" Tonti yelled. Half the men looked in
that direction while the quicker half sped to the left as the soldier had instructed. "Watch your weapons. Keep them dry!"

Arrows arched from the right bank and fell short of the nearest canoe. As the others shouted to hurry, La Salle craned toward the source, then reached toward his wooden chest in the waist of the canoe.

"Turn back! We must greet them," La Salle ordered as he tugged on the crimson coat. His paddlers glanced fearfully at Tonti, who signaled the rest of the men to cease paddling as La Salle's determination became clear.

"La Salle, to the other bank," Tonti implored. "Let them come to us!"

The old Chickasaw began ranting. Beside him, Nika shouted, "La Salle, stop! He says they are the Arkansas, enemies of the Chickasaw." Nika paused as the Chickasaw burst out with another tirade. "He says they will eat us!"

La Salle ignored the warning, notwithstanding his paddlers' reluctance as they moved toward the right bank. Straightening the collar of his coat, La Salle unwrapped his calumet of peace. Tonti frantically motioned the others to gain their leader.

As La Salle stepped to the bank, Tonti and several woods runners lurched from their barely landed canoes to form a tight group around him. Their guns were lowered but ready. The rest of the canoes hugged the shoreline.

"I bring greetings from the Sun King," La Salle boomed in the Chickasaw words Nika had taught him that morning, as he raised the calumet. From the brush a few feet within the line of trees came rustling.

"Caution," Tonti warned. "They may yet attack."

"We didn't return their fire. They know we are men of peace," La Salle insisted. The feathers hanging from the calumet quivered. La Salle told himself it was just the breeze.

Tonti scanned the trees. It was a great effort to stay erect for he longed to drop to a defensive position flattened against the reddish sand. Several Indians appeared. Arrows were stretched tautly across long bows pointed directly at the Frenchmen. La Salle commanded the men to keep their guns lowered.

CHAPTER THIRTEEN

THE WOODS RUNNERS FINISHED HACKING notches in the logs and moved to fasten them into a huge wooden cross. Tonti watched a couple of young Arkansas braves jump up to help the Frenchmen with the heavy task. He smiled at how well things had gone. When first he'd looked into the arrows of the Arkansas warriors on the riverbank he had anticipated a skirmish. But they were only being cautious.

Just as I was, Tonti remembered.

La Salle, too, was pleased by how well the visit was proceeding. After the Arkansas's initial agitation over the presence of an enemy Chickasaw had been set aside, the two groups were getting on well. La Salle had realized he was fortunate to have ended up with the old man, who seemed to pose so little threat, instead of the young Chickasaw brave he had originally wanted. Once again, fate had intervened to help him out as it had long ago when he had met Nika.

They quickly learned that although the old Chickasaw called this tribe the Arkansas, they called themselves the Quapaw, and were the tribe that marked the southernmost extent of Marquette's and Joliet's voyage a few years before.

La Salle watched the woods runners and Indians lash the two logs together to form a cross, as Tonti helped prepare the spot to erect the symbol that France reclaimed this land. No sign remained of where Joliet and Marquette might have placed their own marker. Perhaps the Arkansas had dismantled it as soon as the Jesuits had gone back upstream. La Salle frowned when he realized the same fate probably awaited his own monument.

"Raise the cross," Tonti shouted at La Salle's signal.

Closing his Bible, Zenoble returned chalice and chasuble to their wooden chest, lingering over his movements with all the formality of a High Mass for the benefit of the Arkansas who watched curiously. When Monsieur La Salle had informed him this was one of the tribes visited by Father Marquette, he had feared he would have extra work to overcome any Jesuit influence, but in reality he had been able to discern not a trace of Christian ritual since arriving here, let alone Jesuit.

The rough wooden cross slid into the prepared hole. Baskets spilled loads of dirt, which bare feet quickly tamped down around the base. The symbolic claim on the land where Joliet and Marquette had brought their explorations of Great River had been renewed. La Salle smiled. He had nearly equaled the accomplishments of the Jesuits and his competitors. Soon he would surpass them.

"Best not to bury the plaque," Tonti said as he stepped to La Salle's side.

"The king's arms belong with the cross."

"Last night," Tonti related under his breath, "one of the men saw a piece of the plaque Joliet buried here decorating an Arkansas woman's ear,"

"No doubt he was mistaken," La Salle suggested with eyebrows raised.

Tonti shook his head. "He could read the lettering."

"What was he doing that close to her ear?" Father Zenoble interrupted, having overheard the exchange.

"Monsieur La Salle," Zenoble continued after an awkward silence, "you must lecture the men on fornication."

"It seems they understand that subject quite well already, Father. Will you lead us in another Te Deum?" La Salle requested, clearing his throat. "Men, we shall sing. For the glory of the Lord and the salvation of your souls."

The Arkansas shared puzzled looks at the discordant chant.

By the next afternoon, most woods runners had become even more friendly with their Indian hosts, while their leaders, La Salle, Tonti, and Nika, had become certain there was trouble brewing, trouble that began with the presence of the old Chickasaw.

Once the old man had assured himself the rules of hospitality prevented the Arkansas from bashing in his head, he had grown bold, even obnoxious. Never out of sight of La Salle, and thus certain of his own safety, the old Chickasaw had become insolent enough to eat from the Arkansas's stewpot uninvited and to chastise a troublemaking young boy as he might in his own village. When he went so far as to offer a gift to one of the Arkansas maidens, the chief berated him in front of everyone.

The old Chickasaw had taken the refusal of his gift as a grave insult, and had insisted that the expedition's leadership follow him to a spot near the water's edge, just outside the village.

At a shallow pit of freshly dug earth, the old Chickasaw scooped three fingers into the wet ocher and held up the daub for the others to see. He looked at La Salle, who asked for an explanation. By way of answer, the Chickasaw smeared three parallel lines across his cheek. La Salle looked from Tonti to Nika, not wanting to accept what the demonstration of war paint meant.

"They need a military demonstration," Tonti suggested. "They'll not attack us once they see what our muskets can do."

"It is not us they want to attack," La Salle thought aloud. "He's asking for protection. But for himself, or for his people? Ask him, Nika."

Nika interrogated the old Chickasaw, who claimed to have no fear on his own account, but to be worried only for the sake of his tribesmen. The Chickasaw and Arkansas had been at war since before he was born, but in the last several years there had been much sickness among the Chickasaw. They were no longer as numerous, no longer as strong. The Arkansas must not be allowed to destroy them.

"Maybe we'd best steer clear of it," recommended Tonti.

"Peace among the tribes is necessary to support Great River trade," La Salle retorted. "We can't let our alliances fall to petty disputes."

"Their disputes are not petty. The weapons they'll soon be trading for will see to that," countered Nika.

"If they fight, then sooner or later we'll be drawn in. One tribe or the other will call us their enemy," La Salle objected.

"Yes," Tonti admitted. "Once it starts it'll be hard to keep out of. And it's not much of a garrison we left back at Fort Prudhomme."

"If we don't stop it here, now, then eventually the English or the Spaniards will arrive, and take the other side, and we'll be left with the same bleeding wound that has held back the growth of New France," La Salle forewarned.

"The two tribes have been at war since before this old man was born," Nika reminded. "You are strong, La Salle. You are helped by powerful spirits. But you cannot stop a war."

"Maybe I can. Maybe if I . . ."

"Were you strong enough to stop the Iroquois warring on the Illinois?"

The question silenced La Salle. Tonti held his breath. And as Nika walked away, even the old Chickasaw realized a wedge had been driven between the two friends.

Firelight slid through the open walls of the dance house to ebb at the edge of the gathering. Lines of Arkansas men and separate lines of women moved to rhythms thundering from hide-covered hollow log drums. Dried gourds filled with pebbles rattled in accompaniment. Creels of corn, dried fruits and meats, pottery, and basketry hung from the posts supporting the flat thatched roof. Central in the dance house stood a sinuously carved pole strung with finer baskets woven in intricate designs of red and black, round loaves of coarse corn bread, pottery painted with details of hunting rituals, and calumets, each distinct with stone bowls and shafts laced with bright feathers, woven hair, and beads.

Amidst the tribal elders, from a large reed mat where young braves sat ready to do his bidding, the Arkansas chief rose. The elders fell silent beside him. The chief walked to the central pole, slapped it, then began to sing.

Across from him La Salle and his group watched. Tonti, next to La Salle, wiped his mouth on his sleeve before passing a platter of food on to Father Zenoble, next in line, who dug in hungrily. Nika leaned back from questioning an Arkansas about the song.

"The chief once fought a great bear, bigger than a buffalo, hand to hand, and killed it," he narrated as the elderly chief illustrated his proud song with elaborate movements of the hunt.

Next to Nika the Arkansas who had explained scooted closer, smug at his role as translator to the strange group that had built the mysterious totem at the edge of the village today. Though it was the mother tongue of their sworn enemies, like most tribes in the region the Arkansas used Chickasaw as their trade jargon.

As La Salle watched the chief's performance, he recalled his friend, Bertaud, who told a similar tale of killing a huge bear. If that Montreal innkeeper and this Indian chieftain were ever to meet, La Salle wondered if they would realize the bond that made them not so different as they might at first seem.

The chief ended his song and unhooked a calumet and disk of bread from the post. Lowering them from high above his head, he presented the gifts to La Salle. The Arkansas announced their approval by patting their flattened palms quickly back and forth on their rounded mouths, emitting a "hoo-hoo-hoo" of applause. La Salle's expedition, Frenchman, woods runner, and Indian, exchanged looks of astonishment at the strange sound. With the quickest glance, eyebrows raised, La Salle silenced their possible breach of etiquette as he stood to bow acceptance of the chief's largess.

As he reached into the bundle of gifts he had carefully placed beside him earlier, La Salle was stayed by the old Chickasaw. Nika brushed the old Indian's hand away even as he listened to his words.

"Old Chickasaw says you must recount your own brave deed before you make your gift," Nika translated. "The Arkansas chief honored us with his story. You must do the same."

La Salle looked around at his men as they teased and cajoled him to participate. Finally, he consented. Walking to the post he slapped it as the chief had done. Whisking around, he moved his arms out wide in front of him to address the chief and his entourage, making certain his crimson coat billowed grandly.

"I traveled the ocean, the big water, from halfway across this world," he paused to let Nika translate.

Instead Nika heckled, "Joliet visited this village, too."

La Salle continued his movements, ignoring Nika's comment. "Joliet got no further," he said emphatically, throwing his hands up high in the air. "Just translate, Nika," La Salle added with a stomp of his foot as if his exchange with the Shawnee were part of his story. Nika grinned and the other men laughed as La Salle spun around once more.

"I follow Meche Sebe, Father of the Waters, to the sea, creating an empire to rival the Spaniards' or the Turks'. Or the great and ancient Mound Builders of these lands," La Salle added, remembering the remains of that Indian civilization he and Nika had come across. He grabbed the edge of his coat to make it flare out wider.

"The Arkansas are part of this mighty alliance." He spread out his arms then gathered them in, enveloping the Arkansas nation under his protection, as he finished his performance.

There was polite hoo-hoo-hooing from the Arkansas. Several of the woods runners countered the Indians' lackluster applause with their own clapping and shouts of "bravo." La Salle presented the chief with a pair of small hatchets, bending to show how finely the tools would replace the stone ones he had noticed men in the village using. Those behind the chief approved the gifts with oh's and ah's. The chief passed the tools to the inquiring elders at his elbow.

When La Salle had taken his seat the chief filled a calumet with tobacco. At a terse command, a young warrior leapt to fetch an ember from the fire. The chief nodded the pipe in the four directions then up high, and low to the ground. Silence fell as he puffed, then indicated for the pipe to be carried across to La Salle, who graciously accepted the calumet, puffed, and nodded his satisfaction. La Salle passed it to the old Chickasaw.

A rumble of consternation roiled up from the Arkansas. Warriors jumped to their feet, gesturing angrily. A bark from the chief sent a warrior to pull the calumet from the Chickasaw before he could touch it to his lips. Tonti's hand automatically checked the cutlass in his belt.

"He says," Nika began in translation of the chief's barrage, "that with our guns and his warriors we could wipe out the Chickasaw."

"Tell him we are allies to all nations along Meche Sebe. The Chickasaw are our friends, and that if he . . ."

The chief interrupted with a retort that angered the old Chickasaw. La Salle raised his hand to prevent the old Indian at his side from replying.

"You need not be so cautious," Nika continued his translation. "Chickasaw are bad allies. They fight like women."

The chief directed for the calumet to be offered to Tonti, who anxiously looked to La Salle for guidance.

"Don't insult them further," Nika counseled. "The Chickasaw are not in favor. You should not let the old man smoke."

With a nod from La Salle, Tonti took the pipe and inhaled deeply, too deeply, and coughed out a lung full of smoke. The Arkansas elders nodded approvingly.

"I believe," Tonti suggested as he smiled at the Arkansas, "that I should spin a tale."

Tonti made great show of bounding up to slap the post.

"Tell them how you got your hook," Zenoble urged, his eyes wide with delight at the thought.

La Salle looked back in surprise at the priest. If it had been his brother, Casson, or innumerable other clergymen, they would have chastised the men for participating in pagan rituals.

Nika moved from his cross-legged position to a kneeling one, the better to translate as Tonti dramatized.

"I was on the isle of Sicily serving the great and glorious king of France. Surrounded, we were." The soldier strode over to one side and grimaced. "We were dead men and we knew it, but we were going to make it cost them." He marched around the edge of the circle scanning the perimeter darkness, looking for his Sicilian enemies. He growled like an angry, caged animal. Many Arkansas searched the darkness too.

"But this Sicilian general was a sly one. Wanted to save his men. So he tried doing us in by lobbing grenades amongst us. You know what grenades are, don't you? Boom!"

He made the noise and gestured with his arms, but the Arkansas merely watched, not the reaction Tonti desired. He pulled a log from the edge of the fire and threw it hard into the center of the flames. "Boom!" he yelled as it hit and showered sparks into the night. The Arkansas jumped. The drummers, who had remained silent after their chief's tale, began punctuating Tonti's speech with rhythms.

"That's a grenade. And they were flying in all around us. . . . Boom! Boom! Boom! Tearing my men apart."

The drummers accented Tonti's noise with thunderous beats. The Arkansas jumped with each imagined explosion.

"Boom!" Tonti clutched his chest. "Boom!" He pretended to strangle. The Arkansas were spellbound.

Suddenly Tonti stopped. He looked around at his imaginary fallen comrades and his eyes filled with tears. Hoarsely, he continued. "Then one grenade fell right beside me." Tonti watched it land at his feet. "I knew I was crossing the final river that time. Then something told me different. Like a voice it was, that said, 'Hurry, you fool. Save yourself!' I'll not die if I be quick, I thought!" Tonti reached down and grabbed the grenade.

"I picked it up to lob it back! To plant it like a hat on that Sicilian general's head." He pointed to the general, who stood outside the circle. Everyone, Frenchman and Indian, followed his aim.

He drew back his arm and readied himself to throw, when: "Boom!" Everyone jumped, even the expedition members who had heard it all several times before. Tonti clutched the wrist above his iron hand. In his mind's eye it was still a mangled pulp of flesh.

"Was my good hand they took. The one that held the sword. That lifted the glass. That touched the women tender. For that, they would pay."

He pulled his cutlass from its sheath at his waist and swung it to cut clean the bloody stump hanging from his wrist. He shrieked as he grabbed his wrist and fell to his knees. Panting, he stuck the blade into the ground and pantomimed tearing off his shirt to wrap it tightly around the wound. Then he took up his cutlass and jumped to his feet. Bravely, he waved the cutlass over his head, as if it were his thick-blade battle saber. He signaled the charge.

"Follow me, men! We'll not die here like rats!" Tonti loped around the post, looking back to encourage his men. "Like the Bible's heroes, they followed. Even the wounded, all but the dead, rose up and followed."

Tonti danced around the circle, thrusting, parrying, slicing, drunk with the adrenaline of battle. When he ran the last imaginary enemy through, he calmed, sheathed his cutlass, and addressed the Arkansas chief.

"I lost my hand but that Sicilian general lost his head. I slew eighty-seven enemy on that field. And with my men behind me, we carried the day."

In a grand final gesture he detached the iron hand that fit over his gleaming metal hook and held both out for all the Arkansas to see. Their mouths dropped open. The low roll of their voices burst suddenly loud, with excited hoo-hoo-hoo's, their equivalent of a standing ovation. Tonti picked up a knife from the trade packet and placed it as his gift before the chief, then returned, bowing, to his seat. The Europeans clapped and whistled their approval, slapping their captain on the back as he repositioned himself among them.

"When you told it before, it was only fifty-seven you had killed," Zenoble chastised Tonti.

"Got a bigger audience tonight," Tonti winked at the men.

The chief, hearing this last comment, asked about it. With a smile Nika translated. When the chief heard the response his pleased look at Tonti's performance disappeared. The drummers stopped their pounding and an eerie silence descended. The chief walked to the story post and rubbed it with a buffalo robe, reciting a mournful incantation as he did. The members of the expedition exchanged nervous looks, knowing something was amiss. La Salle directed Nika to ask.

"He is cleaning the lie off the post, and apologizing to it for the insult."

The chief tossed the knife he had received from Tonti into the fire and walked away angrily, indicating that the ceremony had ended.

The next morning, the Frenchmen found their Arkansas hosts still hospitable, but noticeably less friendly. Yet it was another incident, perhaps trivial, that worried La Salle more.

Tonti had been making his way to the river to check on the canoes when two Arkansas men, each carrying a few switch cane, had appeared on the path. Arguing over who would tote the shiny new hatchet, one of the pair that La Salle had given to the chief the night before, they hadn't seen Tonti until they were upon him. Startled, they'd hustled around the foreigner.

After they had disappeared down the trail, Tonti had picked up a cane reed they had dropped. Surprised how stiff it was, he had sighted along it and found it straight and true, perfect for an arrow shaft.

Toying with the cane, Tonti had checked the canoes and walked a little farther upstream. An extensive patch of cane, much more than what the men had been carrying, had been harvested. Soaking his moccasins in the soft mud, Tonti had affirmed what he had suspected. The cuts had been fresh. He had smoothed his thin mustache and grumbled. Making full use of their new tools, the Arkansas were preparing for battle.

La Salle had not reacted well to the news. His sour mood grew worse at Tonti's suggestion that they remain neutral, allow the war to proceed, and make alliance with the winner on their return upriver. Even Nika seemed to agree with the soldier.

"Who are you to decide the Chickasaw are undeserving of attack?" the Shawnee demanded.

"I am their governor. They are my children. My children will not fight one another," La Salle exclaimed in exasperation.

"You did not father them. They were here long before you. What power do you have over them? If they chose not to trade you corn you couldn't even continue on your journey."

"I shall be their father. I have the power. I will prove it."

"We must be careful, Monsieur La Salle," Tonti interjected. "As we saw last night, it's easy to be misunderstood."

"I will prove I have the power," La Salle reiterated. Why was Nika, so helpful on all their journeys, suddenly such a thorn? He acted more and more like La Salle's brother, questioning the wisdom of every move and the motive behind it. Didn't Nika believe La Salle knew the best methods to make this journey a success?

Nika ignored Tonti's reproaches as La Salle stormed off. Nika regretted angering and hurting his friend, but at the same time he could not deny a certain exhilaration.

Arms loaded with trade gifts, La Salle strode to the dance house. Close behind him, the old Chickasaw nervously watched the Arkansas crowd following them. La Salle arrayed his goods and sat, stealing the small crowd watching Father Zenoble pantomime the mysteries of the saints.

Hoping the priest would not fault him for interrupting, La Salle began the calumet ceremony. La Salle drew on the pipe, eyeing the Arkansas warriors who were inquisitive enough to sit. After a few puffs he passed it, with a short string of bells, to the Chickasaw fidgeting at his side.

The old Chickasaw momentarily forgot his enemies seated across from him as he lifted the bells. With wide eyes he shook them and crooked a smile at their musical jingle.

"Smoke," La Salle whispered.

The old Chickasaw somberly returned to the task of drawing in the tobacco. The calumet returned, La Salle inhaled again, then extended it toward the Arkansas. In his other hand he lifted a longer string of bells. The Arkansas pointed and talked among themselves, but no one reached forward. Ignoring their refusal, La Salle handed the Chickasaw an awl and passed him the pipe. La Salle retrieved the pipe and offered it to the Arkansas along with another awl. Once again he had no takers, but the circle of warriors grew closer.

Rumbling rose among them as La Salle handed the old Chickasaw a pair of scissors. He toyed with them as he puffed the pipe, snipping a lock of his long gray hair. La Salle next offered a hatchet. This time an Arkansas warrior, defying his friends' objections, sat before La Salle and reached for the hatchet. La Salle extended the calumet instead. With reluctance, even distaste, the Arkansas took the pipe and puffed on it. La Salle gave him the hatchet. The Arkansas walked off to show the treasure to his friends.

After another puff for the Chickasaw, La Salle offered a mirror, holding it toward the Arkansas, who craned to see themselves in it. A young warrior, more gaudily arrayed than most, sat to smoke for the looking glass.

"If this buys peace, it'll be cheaply purchased," Tonti mumbled from where he and Nika watched.

The Arkansas warriors had started to queue for their turn to smoke with the Chickasaw when they parted amid sheepish whispering. A row of tribal elders, and then the chief himself, his face a thundercloud, marched forward to confront La Salle.

CHAPTER FOURTEEN

THE TWO LEADERS STARED at each other. La Salle gave the Chickasaw the pipe to puff, then offered it to the Arkansas chief, holding up a fine ax as a gift. The chief remained impassive. La Salle added a small copper kettle to the offering. Still no reaction. La Salle added a long string of glass beads, looping them into the kettle. Not enough. He began to wonder if his plan might have backfired, if the chief was so angry that La Salle might be answered with the blow of a war club. The Arkansas were certainly numerous enough to slay all the Frenchmen and keep the trade goods La Salle was bargaining off.

La Salle added several knives to the pile before him. Then, with quiet dignity, the chief sat.

La Salle offered the calumet, still holding out the trove of gifts, but the chief ignored both. He reached out to stroke La Salle's coat, feeling the fine crimson cloth between his fingers. The chief pointed to the coat, then to the calumet. The chief would smoke the pipe of peace with the Chickasaw, but he would name his own price.

And a high price it is, La Salle thought. Not only was the coat worth several times more than the whole pile of trinkets between them, but it also had great personal value. La Salle had carefully chosen it to make an impression on the nations he visited. Too much of an impression here, La Salle thought ruefully. Its deep crimson, the color of blood, represented power to most tribes. Its weave was richer and its brocade more ornate than anything even the native-born Frenchmen traveling with La Salle had ever seen. Nothing anyone in the expedition possessed would serve half so well as his coat for conducting the diplomacy necessary to complete the voyage.

La Salle emptied the rest of the bundle of trade goods in front of the chief—three dozen items, any one of which would make its owner a rich man in the eyes of his fellow Arkansas—but the chief pointed to La Salle's coat.

La Salle grimaced. What price for European trappings if they stop a feud between two nations? he consoled himself. Still he felt a physical pang of remorse as he reached to un-button the coat. It was as though he gave away a piece of him-self, a piece of what he represented, of New France and French power. La Salle shook off the notion as he pulled off the coat.

At the back of the crowd, Nika smiled.

Arkansas escorted the expedition to their canoes. The chief strutted along in his crimson greatcoat. Its fine cloth and vivid color would make him a legend in villages through-out the region, which would make up for some of the glory lost since agreeing to peace with the Chickasaw.

Several Arkansas men stepped forward. They reached out to pass their hands over the bodies of their departing guests. It was a gesture unfamiliar to the Frenchmen and to the In-dians of the northeastern tribes.

"They do that to give us courage," Nika explained.

Tonti enjoyed it. He puffed out his chest and raised his arms. The woods runners laughed. Arkansas joined in.

La Salle's group boarded the canoes. Several Arkansas launched pirogues to see them off. Paddles began their rhythmic dance through the water as those remaining on shore mimicked the white strangers' odd custom of waving good-bye.

Rain fell hard and cold. For three days it flooded the canoes, adding the tiresome chore of bailing to paddling. It filled hat brims and brought on aching chills. It transformed the men's cupped palms of parched cornmeal into thin porridge. It washed away the memory of comfort and warm meals among the Arkansas.

La Salle concentrated on driving his paddle through the plane of rain-pitted water. A couple of woods runners watched him for the signal to send them ashore before nightfall.

It's better to press on through this miserable weather, La Salle repeated to himself, ignoring their looks. The solace of taking refuge would only weaken their performance the next day. They would be sluggish in anticipation of being released early again from their duties. And that would postpone reaching the mouth of Great River.

Too many delays had already piled up against La Salle, as huge a pile as the buffalo hides he should be acquiring. But all would be rectified when word spread they had voyaged the length of the river, and fulfilled the king's commission. Then he would focus on restrengthening the fortified trading posts, renewing alliances, and, someday, populating a new colony at the river's mouth.

They would paddle in shifts, La Salle decided, and sleep in their moving canoes. It was too dangerous to camp anyway, he convinced himself. Rain would mask the sound of any attackers. Rain would blur a sentry's vision, and make him inattentive. La Salle pulled his paddle up, eyes ahead. The woods runners surrendered their hopeful watch.

Days later the rain finally drizzled to a mist. Tonti suggested that the company stop at the island just coming into view, as it would provide a safe campsite and its sand would drain faster than the muddy banks. La Salle finally relented.

When the last man abandoned his attempt to light a fire from the waterlogged wood with a gripe of "I wish I'd never come," Tonti ceased giving directions and studied the faces of the others. Many agreed with that sentiment, he saw.

In his years as a soldier he had heard much complaining, and knew enough not to put too much stock in it. Nevertheless, he fervently hoped the weather had changed for good. With the condition of the arms and the lack of time to care for them properly in this land verging on enemy territory, he would be only too happy to make it down to the mouth of the river, lay claim, then speed back to surer lands.

With a shudder he considered that La Salle might want to explore the coast when finally they reached the sea. His leader had never outlined the plans for that leg of the journey. He never did offer up what he had in mind, Tonti grumbled to himself.

The soldier liked being second in command of what could be a history-making and lucrative voyage. He appreciated that La Salle had signed him on back in France when no one else wanted him, and even more La Salle had kept him on after the Fort Crève-coeur disaster. Many another general would have sent Tonti back in chains, only too happy to have a convenient scapegoat to blame for failure. Yet La Salle had not done so. And what about Tonti's gaffe at the Arkansas story post? La Salle had not mentioned it, had not even hinted at reprimand.

Loyalty came easily to Tonti, and such a leader as La Salle was worthy of loyalty. If La Salle pushed the men too hard, didn't he push himself harder? If La Salle quickly dismissed his own failings, wasn't his memory just as short for the failings of those who served him? Even after all that had happened, he still had faith in Tonti, and Tonti was determined to be the perfect captain, worthy of that faith. Still he couldn't help but wish La Salle would be more forthcoming with his plans. The trick La Salle had pulled to keep the Arkansas from warring on the Chickasaw had worked, but it had been risky.

It would have been a safer bet had he told me what he had been planning, Tonti thought, so I could have at least had our muskets ready lest the whole thing go awry.

And now they were entering the lands once traversed by Spain. Even a small, ill-disciplined Spanish garrison would be more than a match for his own unsoldierly crew. Hopefully he would find time to drill them in a few basic battlefield techniques. But now the weary lot was being pushed to its limit. As much as Tonti disliked the thought, and the odds of its acceptance, he would have to approach La Salle again about easing up on the men.

Silence burdened the sandy campsite. La Salle passed Nika a bowl of cornmeal mush, barely warmed by the wavering fire the men had eventually wrangled. Nika accepted it, glad for even a small change in the monotonous diet demanded of careful rations.

The division between the two had deepened during the morose silence of exhausting travel. La Salle longed for the honest, although wry, Nika of the past. But lately he'd gotten little response to his questions.

"Will the Shawnee consider this voyage a success?" La Salle attempted.

"It has begun well. We have not been killed," Nika stated warily. "And the Frenchman?"

"This is a voyage of exploration to establish legal claim," La Salle began, trying to gauge Nika's reaction to each word. "I built Fort Prudhomme. I've made allies of the Chickasaw and the Arkansas. And each day we travel I bring new lands into the kingdom of France. So far a success, yes."

"You hardly met the Chickasaw, and you bought the friendship of the Arkansas."

"You don't understand diplomacy," retorted La Salle, staring hard at his friend.

It could have been Jean, Jesuit detractors, or any number of other enemies making such a comment, but it was Nika, the man with whom he had shared the last several years of travails, his trusted liaison to the thousands of natives whose land he traveled.

If Nika doesn't understand the importance of what I do, La Salle wondered, why should I bother explaining to anyone? Disappointment filled each step as La Salle crossed the campsite.

"Monsieur La Salle," Tonti intercepted, "we should take a day or two to hunt."

The persistent rain had managed to enter their supposedly watertight provisions. Much of the food had spoiled, but even so La Salle was reluctant.

"We've discussed this before, Tonti. The lands along Great River have been robbed of easy prey by the locals."

"But we've seen no sign of Indians for days."

"Are your eyes good enough to spot their cook fires in the driving rain?"

"The men can't keep up paddling at this pace. Their bodies need diversion, and sustenance."

"We will continue on to the next tribe closest to river's edge. We can trade for food and establish a post at the same time."

"Let's hope the next Indian village is near," Tonti warned, lowering his voice before turning away. "And can be as easily won over as the last. We're in no condition to fight."

La Salle watched Tonti's broad shoulders retreat to where Nika observed from the campsite. He rubbed his forehead to erase the accusations of his cohorts. Distress propelled him onward to where Father Zenoble studied his catechism at the end of the treeless island.

The priest's eyes fluttered open at La Salle's approach. He righted the prayer book tilted on his knees.

"I've awakened you," La Salle apologized.

"No, not at all, monsieur. I was only resting my eyes," Zenoble stammered as the expedition leader came into focus. He pushed himself up onto the driftwood log against which he had been leaning, and followed La Salle's gaze to the men easing into camp.

"Will you confess me, Father?"

Blinking himself fully awake in surprise, Zenoble motioned for La Salle to kneel. La Salle dropped to the sandy ground. By rote he recited the introductory ritual, wondering how long it had been since last he uttered those words. Moments of awkward silence passed with only a shared sigh.

"What is it, my son?"

"I'm not certain."

"Yet something troubles you."

"The men suffer," admitted La Salle. "Their discomfort, even your own . . ."

"You cannot blame yourself," Zenoble offered. "The men signed on knowing it would be a hard experience, as did I."

"It's not that I blame myself. I believe the obstacles the Lord throws up before us are meant to test us."

"Yes, yes. We must take strength in that. What we are sent to endure should fortify our resolve in our mission."

How often the priest had tried to remind himself of that when discovering a new way to incorporate Christian dogma into the natives' spiritual understanding. His few, small successes had made him want to crow with pleasure at his own cleverness, a sin of pride he knew, but when successes were so few was pride so sinful if it nurtured the spirit? When La Salle once again spoke, the priest reprimanded himself for letting his thoughts wander from the matter at hand.

"I fear, Father," La Salle paused, "I push the men too hard."

Zenoble could not respond. He feared the same, and knew Tonti would agree that La Salle demanded too much from them all. Yet it was never more than La Salle himself was willing to endure. They all knew there were time constraints on the mission, that precious years had been lost and no one could be certain how long it would take to get downriver without ships to carry them, and how long to paddle back. The man kneeling before him risked losing everything if the voyage were not completed in time.

La Salle's burdens are much more than anyone can imagine, Zenoble knew, for to someone who had invested the span of his manhood in this quest it would be as huge a spiritual and emotional loss as a financial one.

"Sometimes I hear the voice of my brother, and the Jesuit fathers, condemning me. I fear," he stumbled on, "each lap I gain is in spite of them.

"My goal seemed so clear. To ally the Indian nations, establish trading posts among them, bring them Christianity, all for France." La Salle paused, knowing that sounded hypocritical. After all, if he accomplished such a feat he would be a very rich man. "I know I've much to gain from this voyage, yet I can no longer sort out . . ."

Such anguish prompted Zenoble to place a comforting hand on La Salle's shoulder. The usually stoic leader slumped forward, his folded hands against his forehead, to rest his elbows on the log where Zenoble sat.

La Salle couldn't believe he was being so forthright with the Recollet priest. These were not sins as he usually construed them. He wasn't even sure they were failings per se. But they weighed heavy on his soul, heavier now that Nika, and to some extent Tonti, seemed to question, and yes sometimes undermine, his every action.

As the pause grew uncomfortable, Zenoble felt compelled to speak.

"It is a tremendous responsibility," Zenoble concluded, clearing his throat. "And should be a humbling one. You are absolved, my son," Zenoble rushed. "Say five Hail Mary's for the next fortnight."

La Salle allowed a day of hunting, but the results were meager. A woods runner shot a turkey, and Saget managed to snare a couple of rabbit.

The next morning, the bad weather abated and the brisk chill they had become accustomed to didn't survive past the early morning. The river changed. Its width grew to embrace treelined bluffs of red on the east bank opposite an indefinite encounter of river and forest on the west side of the river. La Salle's fingers moved to the expedition's location on his map: the spot past the Arkansas River where Great River ended and uncertain sketches began.

Tonti worried after a canoe became lost to sight along the low bank where it had gone to inspect the gray vegetation that veiled the trees. He sighed relief when he spotted it making its way back.

"We have now gone farther than Monsieur Joliet and Père Marquette," La Salle announced as he folded the map. "We enter lands never seen by any Frenchmen. We enter the un-known!"

La Salle had expected the men to cheer but they didn't. In-stead the vast reaches of the continent swallowed up his words as if he had never said them. He looked around at their tired and hungry faces. But how, he wondered, could those sensations be enough to quell the excitement of this moment?

Tonti watched La Salle survey the men. They are ciphers to him, Tonti thought. Tonti knew La Salle was a great man but that greatness sometimes put him on a level where he could not understand what drove normal beings. Tonti had served under many great men. Even the wisest generals always had blind spots. It was the captain's job to cover that flank. He must do something to lighten the mood for the many leagues to come.

The canoe paddled back from the bank, steadily fighting the eddies until it regained the expedition. Pulling beside Tonti, Barbier tossed him a length of the plant that hung from the trees. Tonti inspected the long, tangled strands.

"Have any of you seen this before?" he asked. They shook their heads; it was as unfamiliar to them as to him. He held it to his chin, bouncing his jaw and making it wave.

"Like a Spaniard's beard," he shouted over the hoots of laughter.

Being at the edge of the known world doesn't excite them, La Salle scoffed in silence, but this bit of horseplay does.

Then one by one their laughter died. Eyes moved above Tonti's false beard of gray moss. Mouths dropped open as fear crept into their faces. Tonti's eyes grew wide, and he spun around.

On the high, rock bluff above the river an enormous crea-ture was painted across the blonde stone. It was black, red, and green, some twenty feet high and thirty feet across.

"Dear Father, protect us," Zenoble mumbled as he clasped his cross to his chest. La Salle felt a chill go up his spine as he too reached to finger the rosary tucked inside his shirt.

The creature had the face of a bearded demon with a snarling mouth of grotesquely curved teeth. Its head sprouted sharp antlers and four huge talons extended from its scale-covered body. Wings sprouted from its back. A long, winding tail curved over its body and through its legs. From the end of its tail hung a fork like the devil's own.

The Frenchmen gaped. Saget and the Abnaki whispered uneasily, and threw handfuls of corn into the water to appease the creature.

"We enter the unknown," Nika echoed La Salle's claim as they drifted beneath the frightening gaze bearing down upon them.

CHAPTER FIFTEEN

On Great River's edge, under a freshly built thatch canopy, the Tensas king sat. Vivid feathers danced from the calumet he tapped idly against his thigh as he listened to his wives and children, who were reclining on grass mats near his feet. The sun had chased the cool morning mist, and now gnats stirred by the warmth swirled under the canopy. The king barked a command. On either side slaves widened the movement of their fans. The breeze stirred the delicate white clothes of the king and his retinue.

Tensas crowded the bank, talking in small groups. Now and then laughter rose above the general murmur. Unlike the king and his family the men wore short buckskin loincloths attached to thick, decorated belts. The women were dressed in loosely woven skirts of sun-bleached grass. A brave, farthest down the bank, suddenly stood up. Ignoring his brothers' inquiries he marched to the king, who stood to watch the river as a hush settled over his people.

For years he had anticipated this moment. He had heard of white visitors led by a black-robed shaman who had visited the Arkansas and left many gifts behind. Later when his own warriors had captured an Arkansas, a warrior of no special note, among his possessions was a steel ax. The Tensas king had of course seen such items before, and even owned a pair. But these were precious goods traded with tribes who had traded for them with other tribes who had traded for them with still other tribes. If an undistinguished Arkansas warrior could have such a tool then these white visitors must be the source.

The Tensas king was certain of two things. If his enemies the Arkansas had such weapons, then his own people must have them, too. And if he could convince these whites to trade with him but go no farther south, then he could exact whatever prices he wished from the tribes downriver. It would be an enviable position.

As the tail canoes of the expedition rounded the bend, the men took full stock of what awaited them.

"Sacred Mary," Barbier exclaimed as others echoed his sentiment. "Must be over a thousand of 'em."

La Salle raised his hand to silence the men and Tonti's inevitable orders to head toward the opposite bank.

"They've no arms," he called out.

"None that we see," Tonti cautioned as their canoes came alongside each other, gently bumping.

"We've been expected for some time," Nika added.

La Salle also noticed the family groups resting on mats to keep them off the damp bank, with baskets of food beside them. This was not a reception hastily arranged in answer to a sentry's cry. These natives had been waiting some time for the arrival of the Frenchmen. La Salle wondered at the network that had informed this tribe of their arrival

The Tensas stepped back just enough to allow the expedition to pull their crafts up the low bank. Tittering, they pointed at the strange Indians mingled in with the hairy pale men. They wondered at the long sticklike weapons some of the strangers held at their sides. A sharp shout quelled the buzz of their curiosity. Slowly, the Tensas parted to form an aisle to their king, seated beneath his canopy.

What a sight, La Salle thought as he scanned the men at his sides. Nika, dressed as part Frenchman, part feathered Indian, stood next to Tonti, enveloped in buckskin. His thick sword dangled from his side, pistols jutted from his waist, and his fierce, metal hook lay against his chest to give the Indians something to consider. Father Zenoble stepped up to join them. He had taken the liberty of putting on his brightly colored chasuble. La Salle looked at the other three and wished he still had his crimson greatcoat.

"Tonti, select a group to stay with the canoes."

The soldier smothered his objections at splitting the party as he instructed half the men and Indians to stay on the bank, the others to fall into line with arms and trade supplies. La Salle nodded at them to step up for the march to the thatched lean-to.

"I bring greetings from the Sun King," La Salle announced as he extended the calumet in a flamboyant bow.

The Tensas king's spies had been accurate. These foreigners' skin was of lighter color than his own people's, but what was most striking was their hair, with waves and, for some, tight curls. Several had hair brown in color or even yellow, and one red. And as the spies had foretold they let the hair grow around their face, making them look like bears. And they smelled. In truth they smelled worse than bears coming out of winter's hibernation.

Nika stepped to La Salle's side. Loudly and emphatically, he translated, "From the great, northern empire, we are children of the powerful king of the sun."

A nearly bald advisor stepped up to await the king's acknowledgment. If nothing else would have betrayed the importance of this event to the Tensas people, the fact that such a renowned warrior and widely traveled trader was acting as translator to the king, rather than the usual slaves, marked this as an extraordinary occasion. With a nod from the king, the advisor raised both hands and emitted an undulating howl in royal salutation before explaining in Tensas what had been said.

Children of the king of the sun, the Tensas king harrumphed to himself, ignoring the retainer's translation. He had heard and understood what the Indian had said in his mix of trade jargon and Chickasaw, but did not want the strangers to be aware of the extent of his knowledge. If they were truly children of the sun, wouldn't they decorate their bodies with pieces of it, to prove their pedigree so other men would worship them? These strangers were as boastful of their lineage as the Tensas's arrogant allies to the south, the Natchez.

With a frown the king studied the party, especially Nika, the old Chickasaw, and the other natives. The Arkansas prisoner who had told of the pale men had said nothing of many other tribes being with them. The king motioned his retainer over.

"Who are these others who look more like us?" he asked in quick Tensas.

Again the advisor raised his hands and howled before speaking. "I recognize Shawnee, a nation of wanderers from the northeast. The old one is Chickasaw, of course. The others I don't know."

"What are they saying?" La Salle whispered to Nika.

"I'm not sure. They're speaking in their own tongue. But it seems they're trying to decide what tribes we are."

He's never seen so many nations together, La Salle thought with a smile, and wonders what joins us. La Salle stepped abruptly forward. Mimicking the advisor, he let out a low howl and raised his hands.

"All children of the great northern king of the sun," he declared, stumbling over the jargon he had not mastered as well as Nika. He had barely pronounced the words when two burly guards stepped between their sovereign and the audacious foreigner.

The king leapt to his feet. He had not invited the man to address him, and was about to say so when he caught himself in mid-accusation. Instead, with an indifferent flick of his calumet as welcome, he walked away. Slaves rushed ahead to sweep the ground he would tread as his entourage hastened to follow. Tensas jostled to clear his path into the dense woods.

La Salle was momentarily chagrined that he had committed a breach of etiquette. But he also knew his group was too odd and these people were too curious for that to be the end of discussions. And sure enough, the advisor gestured for La Salle and company to follow the procession.

The path soon gave way to a mud and post wall behind which domed huts loomed. The Frenchmen filed past the skull-topped poles around the gates.

"We're at their mercy without more men for protection," Tonti warned.

"If they knew we were coming, they've doubtless heard as well of the power of our weapons."

"But we didn't unload a proper ration of powder and shot."

"We must be very near the ocean," La Salle changed the subject. "See the adornments in their ears, around their waists." Masses of shells and smooth conches decorated the Tensas's clothing. "We can't be far. We must find out tonight at the feast."

"If they give us a feast," Nika responded doubtfully.

"If they don't feast on us," Tonti muttered.

Inside the gates, a central plaza was dominated by a large building atop a mound three or four feet high. At first La Salle assumed it was the royal house, until the Tensas leader entered a small dwelling at its base instead. Several braves took a stance outside his door, challenging any approach. Evidently the visitors were on their own until summoned.

The structure on the mound was a temple. Through its entrance, guarded by a couple of old men, a fire blazed. Around the door were posts studded with skulls like those outside the village. In addition flat disks danced brightly on tethers.

"This is proof that we are nearing Spanish lands," La Salle indicated. "Temple mounds like those in New Spain."

A quiver of danger and fortune surged through all.

"By the saints, you're right," whispered Barbier, the barber and surgeon. "I had a customer once who knew all about New Spain. He visited its capital, the city of Mexico. Was just like this. Bigger I suppose, but it was after all a capital and the man was probably bragging. But just like this, with pagan pyramids and man-made hills, and all such treasure."

"Treasure?" Tonti asked. This rude village was barely grander than the Arkansas town they had seen a week before.

"Treasure. Imagine what's inside their pagan church, if they hang those big chunks of gold around the outside."

The men followed where he pointed. Tonti guffawed.

"I'm glad you're a barber and not a metalsmith. That's copper, not gold," roared Tonti, whose laughter was infectious as the nearsighted Barbier squinted toward the temple.

"Nor a jeweler either," chimed in La Salle, fingering the silver crucifix he always wore around his neck.

"And certainly not a paymaster, or we'd be seeing even less than we're making now," added Tonti, who roared again until he saw La Salle's face.

What with changes in plans and loss of the ships, no payments had been issued in quite some time. Many of the men had been promised fixed amounts, but by now all of them accepted that compensation depended on the success of the expedition, perhaps even the success of some future colony. Their fortunes rode with La Salle's.

La Salle dismissed being reminded of his financial obligations to the men. He knew they would be recompensed in good time depending on what they found along the river. *If any of us survive, of course,* La Salle thought.

Analyzing the Tensas temple, he remembered the abandoned mound he and Nika had stumbled upon along the Oyo. Were these descendants of those peoples? If this was a vestige of some greater civilization, it would explain the elaborate courtesies extended before addressing the chief.

The Tensas king reclined on a wicker throne just high enough to put him a head taller than anyone else seated. Gifts were presented; the calumet was passed; platters piled with food were handed around for each to eat his fill. Delectable fruit pulp shaped into men, deer, turtles, and fowl highlighted the meal for the men who'd been subsisting on cornmeal and jerked buffalo. Gratifying was their sweetness, especially to the Europeans who had come so far from the candy shops of France.

"Are others like us downriver?" La Salle asked. "Spaniards, English? Have they built forts?"

Nika translated. His Chickasaw was improving and he could even throw a few words of Arkansas, which the Tensas also understood, into his jargon. The king's advisor went through the perfunctory ritual, raising his arms into the air with a low howl.

"If there are more like you downstream," came the reply, "then you should not need to ask. If they are your friends."

"If they are the chief's friends, then he has no need for our trade goods," La Salle replied, gesturing to the pile of European tools beside the Tensas leader.

"King," Nika corrected before translating. "He is not a chief but a king."

"That's a pearl necklace she's wearing," Tonti whispered to La Salle while Nika translated.

La Salle hesitated. The gold disks that so excited Barbier had just been copper. The men, seeing no trove of furs accumulating to sell back in Montreal, were now desperate to find some other, easy fortune to claim. La Salle understood, but he hadn't expected Tonti to be caught up in treasure fever.

"Pearls," echoed the woods runners.

It did seem to be made of pearls, La Salle observed, but of what value he could not ascertain at this distance. The woman realized what the men were staring at. She clutched her necklace. The Tensas king noticed, too.

The king thought it very odd the strangers should take such interest in cheap river pearls when his other wives wore jewelry of seashells that had cost him quite dearly. But hadn't he resolved not to be astonished by anything these visitors said or did?

He had all but ignored them at the riverside. Once in his town, he had kept them waiting well past the fall of darkness and arrival of mosquitoes, without any offers of food or water. He had shown he did not fear them, or even consider them too important. Now he could afford to be generous. He had instructed his wives to show no excitement over tonight's feast, to pretend it was no more food than they enjoyed at every meal, but in truth he could not remember when he had counted so many overflowing platters brought into his hut. Not only had his hunters caught a large, though tough, buck, but he had instructed that four of the fattest dogs in the village be spiced and roasted.

Now the strangers' slaves or warriors (the king still hadn't figured out which) were still eating ravenously, while their leaders picked their teeth and looked around with greedy eyes. Perhaps these strangers would not be so hard to understand after all. His wives wore their finest jewelry, had even borrowed from their brothers or sisters if they owned finer still. Yet with so much on display the visitors took an interest in cheap river pearls. Were they playing a trick on him? The king decided not; his guests did not seem intelligent enough for such intrigue. If they wanted the pearls, then just as well.

The king snapped an order for the wife to give up her necklace. When her eyes flashed in response, he remembered what a temper this one had, so he quickly added he would replace it with something much finer. The young wife was mollified. Normally the king would not have bowed so easily to the girl's will, but it would not do to make a scene in front of the strangers.

The young woman removed her necklace and was prepared to offer it to La Salle, when the king issued another command. Instead of La Salle, who was clearly the leader, the woman gave her necklace to Tonti, which surprised both foreigners. The king was quite pleased. Perhaps these pale men would be inclined to bid one against the other. The groundwork had been laid. Now the king was ready to hear what they wanted.

Two hours passed. The discussions continued, and grew heated. The king had not liked La Salle's proposal that his people become part of an empire, but La Salle was insistent, and what exactly it meant appeared so open to interpretation that the king finally agreed. Now La Salle was bargaining for food. Food itself was all right with the king, but it was clear the food was needed so they could continue traveling south-ward. This the king would not abide.

He was determined to be the middleman between these men and the nations to the south. Already he was tallying the Natchez slaves and Koroa flints, Chitimacha baskets and At-takapas smoked fish he would get in exchange for the white men's tools. They must not be allowed to continue south. But of course, neither could he offend them so much they would refuse to trade with him.

When the king finally grew impatient with his own ruse, he interrupted his advisor, speaking directly to Nika in Chicka-saw.

"The king speaks Chickasaw," Nika stated in surprise, "bet-ter than I do."

Delighted, the old Chickasaw started to talk but was cut off by a speech aimed at La Salle.

"He says cannibals live downstream. We will be eaten."

"I'd like to ask him if they mount skulls on pikes like he does," Tonti grumbled.

The king began a steady harangue in Chickasaw. Nika tried to indicate that he should pause to facilitate the trans-lation into French, but the king was impatient. Nika launched into a running interpretation.

"He says the heat will melt the gum that seals our canoes. Leave your work downriver to him. His people have the dug-outs proper for the area. . . . He says we'll find no food down-stream. We will starve. That he cannot give us food because he has none to spare."

"No food to spare? What of this feast?"

Nika shrugged, and continued, "The Piasa, that thing painted on the cliff, is a living creature that hunts downriver. It plucks men from canoes, takes them to its nest, and eats them. Starting with their eyes."

The king glared, mustering all the menace of the Piasa bird itself. When it became clear La Salle was not to be so eas-ily cowed with supernatural threats, the king stood up and left. His retainers and wives hastened after him. Painted war-riors entered to usher the baffled Frenchmen to their hut.

Tensas voices gave counterpoint to night sounds. The deep croak of bullfrogs was so unlike their smaller northern cousin's that at first the Frenchmen had assumed they must belong to some other animal. By now their deep bass had become reassuring, because their silence was the first herald of danger's approach.

Outside the low door of a hut Tonti sat with musket resting between his legs, its muzzle in his hand. He scanned the village. Torches flickered down as the night wore on. A rustle made him right his weapon until he discerned that it came from inside. Zenoble stooped through the door.

"Expecting an attack?" the priest asked.

"A soldier lives as long as I by always thinking they'll attack."

As he eased himself down next to Tonti, Zenoble heard the laughter of a woods runner and a Tensas maiden. He blushed as Tonti acknowledged it.

"It seems some of the Tensas are friendlier than their king," the priest worried. Tonti roared with laughter, his mirth heightened by Zenoble's reddening face.

A heavy mist shrouded the barely risen sun. Tonti and Nika ambled to the shore where they had left the rest of the expedition and supplies.

"I don't like the looks of these people, Nika," Tonti divulged. "We should persuade La Salle to head on as soon as he reaches an accord with their chief . . . er, king."

"That may not be soon."

"Then let's get the rest of the men to the village where we can keep our weapons ready. At least I can drill the men; make certain the Tensas know our salt."

They reached the clearing of a fallow cornfield, a quarter-mile inland between the river and the village, where Saget had decided to make camp since the river's bank was so exposed to chill night air. Abnaki women were just preparing food. Men stretched, happy for a day that did not mean twelve hours of paddling. Tonti chastised Saget. The camp had not been made with an eye toward defense and, worse, the sentries had not been at their post with the canoes since sunrise.

The fog thickened as they neared the river. Stumbling, Tonti grabbed a stick, gave one end to Nika, and held onto the other so they would not lose each other. After shouting back and forth in growing frustration, they determined they'd indeed reached the place where the canoes had been propped up to drain the day before. But they were gone.

Tonti created havoc as he led into the Tensas town, in rough approximation of a military drill, the half of the expedition that had camped the night in the cornfield. Apprised of the missing canoes, La Salle immediately demanded to see the king but it was several hours before he considered the request.

Their canoes, the king explained, were cached in the temple. He'd had them carried there so they might be purified by the smoke of the sacred fire, a blessing to honor and protect his guests. No, of course they could not have them back just now, not until the ritual had run its cycle. How long would that be? Until the temple flame keepers declared the boats were thoroughly purified.

"How long will that be?" La Salle demanded again.

The Tensas king rose in silence. The audience was over.

Thus the expedition waited. Father Zenoble set about teaching Scripture. With mixed feelings he saw his catechism classes fill with Tensas. The priest guessed they attended not for his preaching nor from hunger for the word of the Lord, but because the king had ordered them to do so.

Nika used the time to perfect his Chickasaw, and to begin learning the Mobilian jargon, which a friendly Tensas had told him was the common trade language of the south. But the king must have heard of his efforts, because suddenly no Tensas was willing to converse with him in Mobilian.

"The king doesn't want you to go any further because he wants to control southern trade," Nika reiterated what La Salle understood too well. "Why is that wrong of him? Aren't you doing the same thing?"

"It's not the same thing," debated La Salle. "I deal in broad terms, offering peace and trade for the good of all. Indian nations see things so narrowly, thinking only of the benefits to their individual tribe."

"What about the Iroquois? Didn't they build a powerful confederacy? Don't they control a land as big as your mother France?"

"Don't talk to me about the Iroquois," La Salle spat. "You of all people should know. The Iroquois are savages."

It was a time of frustration for La Salle. Even at a distance he spied the canoes through the temple door, sacred smoke wafting around them. Once again he regretted the loss of his ship. Even the audacious Tensas could not have stolen that. He restrained himself from barging in. Such methods had worked before, but he sensed the need for more patient diplomacy here.

With tribes such as the Iroquois, where a council of elders argued major decisions, a bold stranger could rile one and pacify the other to manipulate decisions. Here the pagan king seemed his own sole council. La Salle worried that direct confrontation could be dangerous without equal rulers to intervene.

La Salle decided to outwait the king, and perhaps at the same time, outwit him. He instructed his men to begin a fort at the river's edge, but the day's work of sharpened logs was stolen as soon as the men went to supper. The green logs when finally lit made a grand, smoky bonfire around which the Tensas danced into the night. Some of the woods runners joined in.

The king beamed with such approval on the awkward footwork of the newcomers that La Salle did not stop them. Looking around, La Salle saw many woods runners pairing off with Tensas girls. Some wore bits of the Frenchmen's clothing, exchanged for what favors La Salle could well guess. If they stayed much longer, many of the men would not want to leave.

Since the beginning of the fur trade, woods runners had settled in with native tribes, to stay perhaps a year or two, perhaps forever. But on this expedition, La Salle could ill afford desertions. If more than a few men refused to depart, La Salle would be hard pressed to continue downriver.

And that was exactly what the king intended, La Salle realized when a quartet of adolescent girls sat beside him, Nika, Tonti, and, to his great embarrassment, Father Zenoble. Perhaps the king had sensed the priest's greater restraint, because the girl next to him was the boldest. His attempts to make her desist made the others, even La Salle, laugh.

La Salle studied the girl beside him. She seemed more demure than the others, more regal, perhaps. Could she be a daughter of the king? Her eyes certainly spoke of an intelligence equal to her monarch's.

La Salle grew wistful. Women had been such a small part of his life. While still young he had traded the self-denial of a young Jesuit seminarian for the single-mindedness of an ambitious trader. The average man leaves a dozen children behind, La Salle thought, and with luck three-quarters of them survive. He would leave an empire. Would it survive? Before he could think of taking a wife, he must see his greater dreams fulfilled.

La Salle turned to Tonti, to discuss ways of curbing the passions of the men, but Tonti and the young girl who'd been beside him had left.

At town's outer edge Tonti strode impatiently in front of the line of French and Abnaki. He stopped to check each man's musket. The steady scowl on his face and the terseness of his orders conveyed the importance of their preparations. Tonti sorely missed their armorer, Prudhomme. Even as he checked the weapons he guessed some would not fire. None, he hoped, would backfire. He had seen men killed that way.

La Salle paced, not at all sure a demonstration of military might would have the desired effect. Tonti had been anxious to drill the men, but Nika had pointed out that once the Tensas king saw the power of their guns, he would be that much more anxious to have them for himself, that much more determined not to let them trade beyond his kingdom.

There was a time, La Salle grumbled, when I would have announced my decision without taking the counsel of others. Witnessing the change in himself made him angrier. Everyone avoided his path, except Nika.

"What if he destroys them?"

"Then I will build new canoes! You taught me how."

Nika sprang up as the king arrived with a troop of warriors in full war paint. Slaves positioned the king's chair to block the path. The king eased himself down, eyes on La Salle.

"The time has come to be bold. Demand the return of my canoes," La Salle told Nika as they approached, but Nika couldn't finish translating before the king replied.

Nika turned to La Salle with the king's words. "As most powerful king, his duty is to save us from our . . . folly. He will return our canoes if you agree to return upriver. Our trade with the southern nations will pass through him."

"The folly is his," La Salle retorted. "Tonti! Fire when ready."

"Finally," Tonti grinned as he tugged his troop into the semblance of an orderly firing line. "Men, remember our drills. First group, advance!"

Tonti raised his cutlass as every third musketeer in the line of buckskinned Frenchmen and feathered Indians took a step forward. They raised their muskets to aim at a row of trees. The Tensas watched suspiciously.

"Fire!" Tonti shouted as he sliced his cutlass down.

The noise and smoke set off shrieks of pandemonium among the Tensas. Some bolted for the woods. Others fell to the ground. When the crash of severed branches and alarm of birds ceased only one Tensas remained unmoved: the king. He sat with no expression, watching the smoke clear, then called to his tribal members. Those flattened to the ground stood shakily; others crawled from their hiding places behind trees.

In a sudden rage, the king leapt up to gather his warriors. One still cowering on the ground he kicked with all his might. The brave yelped, stood, and joined the others. The king roared. The penitent group rushed to grab La Salle and Nika.

"Second group, prepare to fire! Choose your targets," yelled Tonti.

La Salle twisted in his captors' arms. "No, Tonti! Wait!"

The explorer wasn't sure even their superior weapons could defeat the Tensas's numbers. Even if he did win, they would make mortal enemies, and this stretch of river would never be safe.

The Tensas yanked La Salle and Nika toward the gates of town as double rows of warriors surrounded his men, arrows aimed at their hearts. La Salle glanced at Nika as the warriors pulled them on. The expression on Nika's face recalled the Seneca ceremony minutes before Nika's uncle, the Shawnee prisoner, was tortured. La Salle opened his mouth to reassure his friend but was shoved to where the king waited.

The king's face was ashen. He spit out words in Nika's direction.

"He . . . he admits your power is great," Nika stammered. "But his is greater. He will show you. Then you will bow down . . . down before him and do as he says."

The march continued in silence to the temple mound. The copper disks glinted in the sun.

"The Tensas killed the greatest warrior ever and ate his heart," Nika paraphrased in order to keep up with the king. "Years ago, generations ago. The warrior's ghost killed thousands and thousands, some entire nations like the . . . I don't know that name. Fevers and spells never seen before, but the Tensas ate his heart so they are strong. . . ."

"Tell him my father, the Sun King, is greater than any such warrior."

When Nika translated, the king waved the idea away and pointed to the copper disks Barbier had mistaken for gold on their arrival.

"He says the great warrior ate from plates made of pieces of the sun, as you see."

At the temple entrance, when the old men who tended the sacred fire protested the holy building's desecration by strangers, the king literally shoved their objections aside. Leaving his warriors behind, the king pushed Nika and La Salle inside.

A fire glimmered. An old man moved to stand between it and the strangers. Another fell to his knees, furiously brushing the hard-packed dirt, erasing La Salle's and Nika's every footprint.

The bulky shapes of the canoes gradually arose to dominate the smoky gloom. Piles of covered baskets lined the temple walls of brightly painted murals stained dark with soot. A huge effigy of an eagle hung from the ceiling, its wings outstretched as if soaring toward the far wall of the temple. The king marched to a large shiny object hanging there, and spoke emphatically.

"He says the great warrior wore robes made from pieces of the moon," Nika interpreted.

La Salle's eyes grew wide. He stepped toward the shiny object. A guardian moved to impede him but the king shouted him back.

"Nika," whispered La Salle, wanting to blurt it out, "this is Spanish armor."

"It is sacred," stated Nika.

"Ask him where he got it," La Salle insisted.

"He just told you."

"If it is as old as he says, it must be from the expedition of de Soto." La Salle's head whirled with the images of heavily armored Spaniards tramping through Tensas lands. They have been here, he thought, but generations ago.

He'd read of the expedition of the Spaniard, who had set out to survey Florida, and after many months had discovered a great river. He had died on the voyage, and his body weighted and sunk in that river to hide it from the Indians. De Soto had traveled with an army, yet had failed. La Salle had only a handful of men. How could he hope to succeed with all the disappointments endured thus far?

"Tell him his great warrior was just a man, like him or me, with no special powers. Tell him," La Salle repeated at Nika's hesitance.

The king grew furious at Nika's translation, and began a tirade.

"He says the king of the Tensas is not 'just a man.' If the great warrior had no special powers, why did so many die?"

"Spaniards carry the pox." Then La Salle added, as much to himself as to the king, "We French are different."

La Salle inspected the armor. At its collar, a fine silver chain hung. His curiosity aroused, La Salle pulled the chain from where it disappeared inside the armor. The king admonished La Salle.

"He warns you must not to desecrate it."

La Salle ignored the warning and the rising voices of the guardians as he continued to tug on the chain. On its end hung a silver crucifix. La Salle tried to lift the chain free but it held fast. He slid the silver cross to the end for the king to see, then dug inside his own shirt to the end of his rosary. He held his silver cross beside the other. Seeing that the two crosses were a near exact match, both the king and the guardians gasped.

"Tell him there is but one true God and that we all worship him." La Salle paused, not sure what to say. He wondered whether he should call for Father Zenoble, then decided he could handle this himself. "Tell him we will baptize him with the strength of this cross." La Salle shook his rosary at the king. "But that he must return our canoes."

The Tensas king held his breath. He had known from the beginning the visit was unprecedented, but this turn of events was completely unexpected. The strangers were different from any people he had ever met, but he had at least assumed they were human. Now he wasn't sure. This issue of trade suddenly seemed unimportant next to the more spiritual concerns at hand. Should he bow down before this creature? No, better to kill him and eat him, and thereby absorb whatever strange powers he possessed. The Tensas king was opening his mouth to call for his guards to bring him a war club when La Salle's approach stopped him.

"You have honored us," Nika translated as La Salle neared the king, "by blessing our canoes. Our shaman, Father

Zenoble, will bless your people in return. Baptize them, starting with you. But first you must return our canoes."

The monarch stepped back. He's afraid, La Salle saw, wondering how best to put the king's fear to use. La Salle looked
at the temple guardians, whose protestations had fallen
mute, their eyes fixed on his rosary. La Salle looked down at
the silver cross himself.

How many miles it has traveled, he thought, since the day it
was given as a gift from my family when I left to become a
Jesuit. That moment seemed lifetimes ago, and yet as clear as
yesterday. In the seminary, La Salle had considered the crucifix a symbol of his devotion. After he had left the Jesuits, it
had become a reminder that those avaricious black robes had
no monopoly on spreading the gospel. Lonely nights during
his years crisscrossing the vast pagan continent, the little silver cross had been his succor. Shivering in cold, endlessly
chewing a piece of his buckskin because there was no food, he
had cherished the rosary. It had been a constant promise that
God would not forget him on his missions.

But La Salle was not shivering now. It was hot and smoky in
the temple. To finish this mission, he needed to complete his
journey in the short time remaining that King Louis had allotted. To do so he needed his canoes. And to get the canoes
he must win over the Tensas king.

Slowly, La Salle lifted the rosary from around his neck, gesturing to the silver cross dangling from the Spanish armor.
He kissed the crucifix, then crossed himself with it in the
name of the Father, the Son, and the Holy Ghost before carefully draping it over the neck of the stunned king.

"Will he accept the true faith of these crosses, Nika?" The
king considered long and hard before answering.

"He accepts it, and accepts that you are a god."

"But I am not . . . ," La Salle replied, his forehead furrow-
ing.

"And now that you have accepted he is a god as well," Nika
conveyed, cocking his head, "he will return our canoes."

La Salle stared at the rosary around the king's neck.
Acutely he felt its absence around his own. He reached to rub

the back of his neck. Fine beads of cold perspiration formed on his brow. La Salle longed for the steadiness of Tonti's company and the consolation of Father Zenoble. The guardians' mouths moved but the sounds were slow and distorted. La Salle wondered why they swayed back and forth and how the murals had begun to throb.

Nika studied La Salle, remembering how often he had talked to his string of beads and silver cross. He knew his companion was feeling a pain he did not understand. That was all right, Nika decided. Pain would be balanced with joy, as was the order of things.

"La Salle," Nika called.

Nika's clear voice broke through the dull pounding in La Salle's head. The king came sharply into focus. He smiled as he moved his fingers up and down La Salle's rosary. Reluctantly, La Salle nodded his acceptance—acceptance that the Spanish armor was a god, the Tensas king was a god, and he was too. The king touched La Salle's chest where the rosary had hung, then his own. The guardians ushered them to the door of the temple. The king paused to allow Nika and La Salle to exit first.

The men emerged from the staleness. The sun dazzled off the bleached skulls, warning against desecration of the temple.

CHAPTER SIXTEEN

DARK CLOUDS BILLOWED as the afternoon grew warm. Silence was broken only by the splash of paddles and the cry of startled birds. Hushed conversations rose and died.

Tonti looked anxiously at La Salle, who forced himself to sit rigidly, each paddle stroke an effort. Since they had left the Tensas, the leader had grown sick, then sicker still. Tonti, even Nika and Zenoble, had tried to persuade La Salle to slow his pace, or at least let the others propel the canoe until he felt better, but La Salle refused.

"Monsieur Tonti! Look!" shouted Barbier.

Tonti's eyes followed outstretched arms to shore. An alligator twice the length of a man slid into the water. Only its nose, eyes, and the ridge of its back surfaced.

"What is it?" La Salle asked, roused by the men's voices. Tonti moved closer alongside La Salle's canoe. He inhaled sharply when he saw La Salle's red-rimmed eyes. The leader coughed, and clutched his chest. Tonti glanced at the other men in La Salle's canoe. Their faces showed concern but they focused on moving along Great River.

"The men have spotted some sort of crocodile. The Tensas eat them, and we are out of meat."

After returning their canoes, the Tensas king had had

second thoughts about letting them go. He hadn't stopped them, but had traded very little food in hopes they'd be forced to turn back. Tonti's threats had kept any woods runners from deserting, but a few Abnaki had stayed behind.

"Of course, captain. Shoot the crocodile for the men. Fire when ready."

"Monsieur La Salle says fire when ready!"

Several worked to light their matchcords, but Saget, with a newer flintlock musket, aimed and fired. The alligator, stunned but not hurt, sank beneath the water leaving the men to grumble.

Cautiously, Nika and Saget led the party to a group of huts they'd spotted atop a low bluff. Only black and crumbling sections of a few structures remained. The rest was charred rubble. Bodies picked clean by scavengers lay amongst the ruins.

"War party," Nika declared. Saget agreed.

Tonti signaled the men to relax their defensive formation. The only danger here was from ghosts.

La Salle staggered up the trail, and rested against a fire-scarred trunk. The others had pleaded with him not to come but he had felt the men's confidence in him weakening as he had succumbed to illness. Deciding it was important to demonstrate he was still able, he had made the climb. Perhaps they had been right. He was so weak and exhausted from the exertion that the opposite of his desired impression was achieved.

"Everyone dead," Tonti reported. "By their decorations, relations of the Tensas."

La Salle surveyed the huts through half-opened eyes. A coughing fit overtook him.

"No food stores we can find. Burned or taken," Nika concluded, joining them.

"Have Father Zenoble say a prayer. Then back to the boats," La Salle instructed.

Nika had taken advantage of the foray to send a couple of Abnaki in search of medicinal plants. Now he and Tonti moved off to speak with the Abnaki who had returned empty handed.

"We do not know plants here. They are strange," explained the older of the two.

"Everything is strange here," the younger Abnaki added, glancing around.

"We are far from their lands," Nika offered in excuse to Tonti after the Abnaki had started their descent to the shore.

"Not near as far as I am," barked Tonti.

"It's not their fault."

"I didn't mean that it was. It's just I was hoping they could help. I know Barbier's supposed to have that charge, but every time he bleeds La Salle, Monsieur looks weaker. He can say what he wants but if a man loses enough blood, no matter what ill humors it may contain, his life drains out with it. It's nearly happened to me a couple of times."

Nika remembered when Tonti had been first to fall at the Illinois massacre, and noticed the soldier unconsciously rubbing the stub of an arm above his hook. That must have been the other time, Nika thought. Tonti always told the story of losing his hand with such enthusiasm it was easy to forget such a wound could have killed him.

All of us are mortal, Nika mused. He glanced at La Salle, shivering under a buffalo robe on such a hot day, Zenoble by his side. Even La Salle was nothing but a man of flesh and blood, Nika knew, no matter what the Tensas king might have believed.

When Tonti saw where Nika looked, he worried. Perhaps there was no need to say it, but it was best to prepare.

"What do we do if . . ."

Nika flinched at the cold question. Could the spirits be deserting La Salle?

"Then you take command. As you have begun to do already."

"Only to lighten La Salle's load," Tonti quickly pointed out. He had known leadership would fall to him if La Salle died, but he was relieved to have Nika acknowledge it. It was not a question of ability—Nika was able—but of politics. Tonti saw the irony of the situation. Nika was a much better politician than he, but an Indian was not a suitable representative of France.

Tonti also knew that if La Salle died, the king's charter would be automatically revoked. Or at best, it would fall to La Salle's brother the Abbé, or to his creditors. Not to a soldier at arms like Tonti. Tonti didn't doubt he could get the party back to Quebec, but he wouldn't be able to pay them if he did. And finding the mouth of the river? What value in that if La Salle died? Knowing such a route might help Tonti find other employ, especially if he kept copies of the maps. But if the Jesuits had regained favor, they might have him locked up to keep his knowledge secret. It was all too baffling for one used to carrying out orders. La Salle must live, Tonti decided, for I'll be a shipwrecked sailor if he dies.

"Maybe he was bewitched," Tonti conjectured aloud, liking the idea more as he considered it. "As devious as the Tensas king was, it would not surprise me at all."

"We need a local shaman," Nika offered, not fully understanding what Tonti meant by "bewitched," but knowing a medicine man practiced in local herbs could ease La Salle's physical pain if not his spiritual one. Watching his friend, Nika regretted they had seemed at such odds of late. In spite of what he saw as La Salle's intrusion in the Indians' world, he still cared for the Frenchman.

Nika and Tonti looked at one another and for very different reasons came to the same conclusion.

"La Salle must finish the voyage," they agreed as they walked back to their leader, who was doubled over in Zenoble's lap.

The days grew warmer and the humid air caused everyone to fatigue quickly. Again the expedition was plagued by rain, sometimes squalling so powerfully that the canoes were forced to stop. Provisions had not improved. Except for a deer Saget had killed as the animal crossed the river, the Indians had been unsuccessful in hunting.

Early one day as the party rounded yet another bend in Great River's winding course, Saget spotted a small dugout carrying two people. A roar went up among the men as they waved and yelled to get the craft's attention.

"Catch them! They may have food," Tonti shouted. The starved paddlers increased their speed.

La Salle strained to sit tall in his canoe. Wobbling, he reached behind him for the calumet, his efforts frustrated by a coughing spell.

The alarmed locals paddled downstream rapidly, looking back at their pursuers. As the canoes of La Salle's crew closed the distance, the two natives could make out clothing different from any they had seen before. Was this a war party of some faraway tribe or were these malicious spirits of the river? If they are men, why would they be dressed so strangely? If they were friendly, why would they be yelling?

The natives wished to let these strangers come no closer, speeding as fast as they could to the safety of their landing.

Two canoes of strong paddlers and relatively light loads broke away from the rest of the expedition. The canoe carrying the locals moved out of sight. The party redoubled its efforts. One by one the expedition's canoes navigated around the bend. Paddles abruptly reversed to curtail the momentum they had built.

On the east bank at the foot of a towering bluff, poised with nets and arrows around a wicker fish weir, were nearly two hundred Natchez. Each of them wore white clothing like the Tensas king. Women set down baskets and rushed to the thin line of trees below the bluff. Men grabbed up their spears, war clubs, bows and arrows.

They're arming themselves, Tonti saw. Perhaps I should approach them with calumet raised high, as La Salle would likely do, he considered with a quick glance to the leader slumped forward in his canoe. Then Tonti recalled the day he had tried to do so with the Iroquois. His soldier's instinct took over.

"To the far bank! Build a fortification. Prepare all weapons. I'll cover Monsieur La Salle," he bellowed at his men.

Tonti shoved his pistols into his belt and strapped on his cutlass. La Salle's canoe pulled up. The explorer was confused by his men's swift retreat.

"We must greet them," La Salle babbled.

"Not on the river," Tonti replied as he directed the men. La Salle did not approve of Tonti's line of action but his paddlers did.

At the fish weir a Natchez warrior named Burning Serpent summoned his fellow tribesmen to repulse the intruders. Several countered that they should return to the village immediately and consult the War Chief. Others objected they had not prayed nor danced nor sang; they had not painted their bodies or made ready for battle. But Burning Serpent swayed enough warriors that all the men joined in for fear of appearing cowardly. They clambered into their dugouts, and set off in pursuit.

The expedition's canoes were dragged into a circle on the wide bank of sand. Weapons were checked. Steel axes slammed into brush to add cover. The last canoes, carrying La Salle, Tonti, and Nika, approached, but in the distance so did a hundred Natchez warriors. Tonti ran to supervise preparations for defense.

He regretted the men had not taken time to move beyond the tree line for greater cover. He glanced over his shoulder at the nearing Indians. They outnumbered his men three to one. Too late to move now, he cursed.

Zenoble and Nika grabbed the squawking La Salle and dragged him to the low fort of canoes and brush.

"My dignity before the natives, Nika," coughed La Salle, clutching his calumet.

The Shawnee and the priest managed to get their leader inside. Saget quickly helped clear a spot where La Salle might rest well protected from the fray. His coughing continued unabated as they lay him down. Nika and Saget exchanged a look, any rivalry forgotten now, pressed by the grave illness of their commander and the danger brought home by the distant cries of the Natchez, growing louder as their canoes sped across the water towards the expedition's haphazard stronghold. Saget picked up his flintlock and found a clear line of fire to where the Natchez canoes would soon beach.

Nika felt Father Zenoble's eyes on him.

"Someone should offer them the calumet. That's what La Salle would do," reminded the Father.

Nika glanced at Tonti, busy readying the men. With La Salle disabled, the soldier would be the natural one to lead, but Nika would not suggest it. He remembered too well what had happened at the Illinois village. He looked back at Zenoble and realized the priest was reliving the same events.

"Perhaps," Zenoble hesitated, "I should do it." Even as he heard his words, they sounded odd to him. He trusted his life to the Lord, but this sort of bravery was something else altogether. He tugged at the calumet in La Salle's hand. When La Salle, though near delirious, refused to give it up, Zenoble blushed, embarrassed by his own sense of relief.

The first of the Natchez' canoes touched shore. Warriors ran toward them and fanned out, circling with weapons ready. Burning Serpent waved his men into position.

Inside the flimsy bulwarks, muskets and pistols were ready too, but not sufficient to shoot all the Natchez.

"Choose your targets! Be ready to fire on my order!" cried Tonti.

Natchez bowmen drew back their strings, choosing targets themselves. Burning Serpent tried to discern what sort of weapons these strangers held. They were neither war clubs, nor bows, nor blowguns, nor even the atlatls, or spear-throwers, that some of the primitive tribes downriver still used. No matter, Burning Serpent thought, he had warriors sufficient to rout the group. And his victory song would be remembered all the more for their oddity. He looked right then left and saw that all his men were well placed for attack. He hesitated a moment more, savoring the glory this fight would win him.

On wobbly legs La Salle rose. He immediately became the target for several Natchez bowmen. But just as Burning Serpent gave the signal to attack, La Salle raised high his calumet. Both Frenchmen and Natchez wavered, unsure what to do next. A few Natchez lowered their war clubs, others unstrung their bows. Burning Serpent reprimanded them furiously.

From his spot behind an overturned canoe Tonti steadied the men. La Salle coughed again but kept the pipe high, turning to face Burning Serpent. It is clear this man is their leader, La Salle saw. He tried to push aside the fever that clouded his mind to study the native who eyed him with fierce disapproval.

Around Burning Serpent's waist was twisted beautiful white cloth, tightly woven from threads of mulberry bark. A flap fell in front and another behind. His short, black hair was cut in a thick fringe around the crown of his head, his body covered in blue-black tattoos of symmetrical designs and ferocious animals. An angry serpent coiled down his right arm.

The Indian stared back at La Salle, watching as the pale, feeble stranger muttered words in a language that Burning Serpent had never heard before. The stranger's arms trembled from the slight weight of the calumet. And Burning Serpent saw that still more of his tribesmen unstrung their bows and lowered their guards. If he pressed for battle now, would they follow him? He did not know. Better to wait for a more propitious time, he decided. But his anger at the sickly stranger who had robbed him of his chance at glory burned like bile in the back of his throat.

Burning Serpent cupped the fingers of his hands and gripped them in front of his chest. Nika recognized the gesture.

"It signals peace."

La Salle trembled a sigh of relief. "I bring greetings from the Sun King."

Nika shouted out his translation in Mobilian jargon. Burning Serpent replied in the same.

"He is Burning Serpent of the Natchez and he too gives you greetings," Nika faltered, "from his Sun King."

Girls and boys played on a wide grassy plaza. At opposite ends, serving as goal markers, earthen mounds ascended twelve to fifteen feet high. Large, thatched huts crowned them. Around the plaza, at ground level, smaller huts were arranged precisely. Women sitting in small groups chattered as they wove cane mats and watched with mild interest the game occupying their children.

One boy and girl on opposite teams were special rivals. A moss-stuffed, hide ball lay between them. Their eyes met. The girl moved her jaw up and down almost like chewing. It was a trick her half-sister had taught her. It made the designs tattooed on her chin dance. Sometimes it distracted the opposing player long enough . . .

But this boy and she had played together too often. He faked a dodge, kicking the ball with a knobby leg. His team shouted support. He dashed for the goal line and almost made it, but the girl knocked the ball away. Her team let out a whoop of victory. The ball flew across the plaza, through a group of women who ducked to avoid it. It bounced past their admonishments and into a hut. Instantly turning from opponents to allies the boy and girl shared a mischievous look.

They raced to the hut just as a woman came out robed in a magnificent cape of multicolored feathers. Brilliant hues of green, red, blue, and white brushed her thighs above the hem of the white sarong that circled her hips. The children knew that the intricate patterns of the cape were symbols of great power. The woman stretched out her arm, tattooed with beautiful forest flowers. In her extended hand she held their ball.

The two swallowed hard. Their downcast eyes timidly asked for the return of their ball. The woman, Tattooed Orchid, smiled and threw the stuffed deer hide back into the plaza. But as the boy and girl scooted back, their game was interrupted. Heralds ran into the plaza bearing long poles lined with feathers to mark their place in the excited crowd that quickly circled. Tattooed Orchid strolled over to hear the news.

The expedition crowded around their canoes on Great River's bank. Tonti had left express instructions that if the

sentries abandoned their boats here as they had done at the
Tensas landing, they need not worry about torture by the locals for he would happily take on the task himself. The men
watched the Natchez lead a few members of La Salle's party
up a narrow trail that climbed the sheer bluff bordering the
river.

Tonti looked down at the men, dragging up canoes and
preparing camp, then glanced up hoping to see some signs of
a village. He could only see the red, twisted path, dotted with
brush and knee-high grass. It was so constricted in places
ahead that the Natchez moved in single file.

Nika stayed close to La Salle. The explorer had marshalled
his strength to greet the attacking Natchez, but now sickness
overtook him. Agonizingly, he wavered up the bluff. Exposed
roots became handholds. Pretending to observe the vegetation, La Salle paused repeatedly. His body quaked with each
breath but he refused Nika's offer of support.

Finally, they reached a level area. Tonti moved toward La
Salle, waving Zenoble and Barbier over also. They would
walk together into the town that lay away from the bluff's
edge surrounded by thick mud and post walls blinding white
in the high sun. The party shuffled past the walls through
even rows of thatched buildings onto the grass plaza.

The children had stopped playing. The women had set
aside their tasks. Although prepared for the strange visitors
by the heralds, the curious Natchez could not help ogling.
Never before had they seen such colors and textures of cloth.
Barbier's red beard, grown long, so disgusted the Natchez
they were compelled to gawk. Children whimpered in fear.
The entire town, and even citizens of villages across the
nearby creek who had come running at the news, lined up
like a gauntlet, mesmerized by the bizarre parade.

Tattooed Orchid, as curious as the rest, studied the strangers. One in particular caught her attention. He walked un-
steadily between the one in the long brown robe and the one
with a shiny pointed hand. Then she felt a tug in her chest
that meant the War Chief, deathly ill and in her charge, was
again in pain. She heard, not with her ears but with her body,

a low moan inside his hut. The moaning grew stronger. Tattooed Orchid focused her mind on her duties and crossed the plaza to his hut.

"They must not see I am sick," La Salle panted, clutching Tonti's arm. The soldier nodded reassurance, even though La Salle's state was impossible to disguise.

Burning Serpent was irate that the warriors had not readily followed his lead to battle. He quickened his pace to move ahead and climb the Great Sun's mound. He reached the door of the large hut just as bearers arrived with the Great Sun's litter. Calling inside, he begged permission to enter. After a pause the Great Sun granted his request, annoyed at the interruption.

Flanked by aides, the Great Sun dressed. He pointed to his feathered cape. The glossy white feathers shone iridescent even in the half-light of the hut. Fingering the soft cape, the Great Sun remembered the heralds had said the visitors wore clothing of strange colors. It would be unacceptable to be outshone.

He rejected the feather cape and pointed to one of panther skin. With help, he put it on. The cat's snarling jaw and pearl-eyed head sat atop the Great Sun's like a crown. The tail dangled past his calves. The lining, painted in geometric red, yellow, and black, contrasted nicely with his white breechcloth. He faced his aide to facilitate the looping of pulls that tied one side of the skin to the other. The heavily decorated thongs fell to his wide, naked chest. The Great Sun turned to Burning Serpent, who had waited in agitation.

"They attacked two of our warriors on the river," Burning Serpent began. "I led a counterattack. . . ."

"I am sure you were brave," the Great Sun silenced him. He repositioned the blue feathers hanging from his short hair. "I heard the accounts of what happened. I will meet the strangers."

"But most high Great Sun, if we let them live . . ."

"You are so anxious to be War Chief that you would kill these strangers before we observe them," the Great Sun reprimanded. "Do you claim the honor of War Chief while the noble one that led this tribe to so many victories still lives?"

"Our honored War Chief is ill," Burning Serpent declared, "and these are dangerous times."

He was right, the Great Sun knew. For more than a generation the Natchez had seen items of trade unknown to the Suns of the past. Stories had come of bearded creatures with bodies of white copper and spears that shot fire. Thousands had been dying of strange maladies unmentioned in Natchez lore which frustrated shamans swore could only be attributed to some new and awful magic. Nearby tribes, weakened in number, had given up the old ways so that few besides the Natchez still built the tall mounds that reached their temples toward the sun.

Only last season Tunica traders had brought a creature much like a deer but larger and without antlers. They had called it a horse, and rode upon its back. In the direction of the setting sun, they had told, a great journey away but growing closer, white men had arrived causing great turmoil and upheaval wherever they trod. The Great Sun had long known that one day such trouble would appear at the foot of his mound.

He stepped around Burning Serpent and bent low to exit his hut. Gracefully he positioned himself onto the cushions of his litter beneath the cool shade of its tightly woven palmetto canopy. Grunting in unison eight slaves hoisted him up. In capes of brown turkey feathers the Great Sun's personal guard stepped alongside the litter bearers as they marched imperially down to the plaza.

The Great Sun of the Grand Village of the Natchez had power of life and death over each and every one of his bowing subjects. And over La Salle and his companions as well.

La Salle staggered forward with Nika moving beside to translate. The Sun's guards prevented any closer approach.

"I bring you greetings. . . ." A coughing fit prevented his continuing. Tonti and Zenoble moved to steady him.

"I bring you greetings. . . ." La Salle tried again but could not go on.

"This is the warrior you were going to prove your bravery against?" the Great Sun inquired of Burning Serpent. "He can hardly stand."

"Kill him," Burning Serpent advised. "Kill him now before he recovers. Then let me lead a party to the river and kill the rest of his people who wait there for his command to attack."

Nika listened carefully though he understood no Natchez. Through much practice he had become adept at reading the meanings of words he did not understand. It was clear Burning Serpent wanted harm done to them.

Nika addressed the Great Sun in Chickasaw. "Here is a great leader," he announced, "who has made a long and difficult voyage to bring presents to you, the great king. He fell ill but would not stop to rest and heal himself because he said he must pay homage to the greatest of kings. Now we beg your deepest wisdom and finest medicine to cure him so that he can properly bow to your glory."

The Great Sun understood. Nika sighed relief that at least the barrier of language had been surmounted. The Great Sun issued a command. A guard ran to the hut where Tattooed Orchid attended the War Chief.

"Their medicine man will treat La Salle," Nika explained.

"Monsieur Tonti," Barbier exclaimed, grabbing Tonti's arm, "you cannot put Monsieur La Salle into the hands of these tattooed barbarians. . . ."

As Barbier complained and Tonti reasoned with him, the Great Sun's guard led Tattooed Orchid toward them. Nika saw she was a powerful shaman, and told the others.

"She? A woman?" Tonti and Barbier curtailed their dispute to turn where Nika looked.

Natchez villagers stepped back to clear Tattooed Orchid's path. Warriors bowed their heads as she passed. She neared La Salle, glancing at the strange men around him. La Salle tried to bow to the royal lady but his head throbbed too much.

Tattooed Orchid pressed her fingers to the back of La Salle's hands, peering into his eyes and smelling his breath. Motioning for the men surrounding him to step away, she

placed her hands firmly on La Salle's chest, then shut her
eyes. For a brief moment, the Frenchman and the shaman
breathed as one. The calming effect made La Salle droop.
Nika quickly stepped up to brace his friend.

Barbier's mouth fell open. He started to inform Tonti that
this woman was certainly a witch when the Great Sun spoke.

"Her name is Tattooed Orchid," Nika translated. "She has
cured many sicker than our leader."

Tattooed Orchid commanded Natchez warriors to carry the
sick man to her hut. Tonti and the others hastened to follow
her the short distance, but they were pushed back roughly at
her door.

"Tell the panther king," Tonti demanded of Nika, "we insist on staying with Monsieur La Salle."

Nika indicated the Great Sun's entourage settling around
his now empty litter at the door of his hut. The Great Sun
had retired inside.

Much too ill to resist, La Salle was placed on a low cot built
into the wall. Tattooed Orchid examined his clothes as she
leaned to rub her hands along the sides of his thin face, re-
coiling at the stubble of whiskers.

The Indian shaman removed her feather cloak and put
several pottery cooking stones to heat in the glowing fire. She
poured water into a pot, then selected a small sack from
shelves holding many such skin bags along with bowls of
herbs and poultices. Withdrawing pieces of dogwood bark,
she crushed them into the pot of water. Even a cursory exam-
ination told her she must bring down his fever. Returning the
sack to the shelf she put aside a bit of magnolia, for he would
soon be having chills.

La Salle moaned as Tattooed Orchid removed his gar-
ments. She paused to rub a warm stone against his temples.
When he quieted she went back to removing his clothes. It
took her a moment to figure the strange fastenings, since she
had never seen buttons before. Finally she managed his shirt,
then drew off his pants, frowning at the sight of his hairiness.
His chest resembled the underbelly of a deer more than any
man she had ever known, either Sun, Noble, or Stinkard.

This should all be plucked, she thought. But first he must be made well.

When the cooking stones were hot, Tattooed Orchid tonged them into the water to steep the dogwood. She filled a drinking bowl with the brew, then soaked a cloth in the remaining mixture, as she pondered which sacred chant to sing. The corn chant was her favorite but seemed inappropriate for this strange patient. She decided on the song of the little forest people.

The little people were magical and clever, and cleverness would be necessary to heal such a creature. She closed her eyes and began. Slowly she moved the soaked cloth along her arms and neck, choosing the tattoos most likely to aid healing. The seeing eye, the cornflower, and the cross on her palm denoting the four directions soon glistened with the herbal bath. Finally, she circled the cloth once around her waist.

Again she dipped the cloth into the pot and moved to La Salle's side. Slowly, she cleansed him, all the while singing. La Salle's eyes flickered open. For a moment he imagined himself in a field of beautiful blue flowers as he looked into the blossoms tattooed across her chest and shoulders. Her song was hypnotic. He gave himself up to it.

Tattooed Orchid placed the cloth across the sick man's forehead and eyes, then carefully raised his head and angled the bowl to his lips. In a semiconscious reflex, La Salle swallowed small mouthfuls. When the bowl was empty, Tattooed Orchid reached once more to her herb shelf and drew down some fragrant pine. She knelt before the fire and dropped it into the low flames. Smoke and the aroma of fresh pine filled the hut. Tattooed Orchid leaned over the smoke and smoothed it over her body. Then with a flick of her hand she sent it spiraling toward the rising sun, the setting sun, north and south. Satisfied the initial cleansing ritual had been successful, she sat on a cane mat near the cot to wait for her patient's fever to break.

CHAPTER
SEVENTEEN

THE SUN HAD LONG SINCE SLIPPED behind the horizon. Outside Tattooed Orchid's hut, the men waited, anxious that they had heard no sound from within since a lilting song shortly after noon. The final glow of sunset faded and with it mosquitoes descended. Tonti lit a smoke fire as Nika handed around a pouch of bear grease. Hungry and apprehensive, the men slapped at the persistent insects.

Three Natchez boys appeared with food and drink. They set down the platters, then squatted to watch the men eat. Tonti brandished his hook for their amusement, stabbing bits of meat and licking the juice from the steel point. The boys lingered until a woman's shout spurred them home.

"Such round faces and wide noses these Indians have," Tonti remarked.

"Like Chinamen," Nika observed.

"You've seen Chinamen?" Barbier doubted.

"In books La Salle showed me." He remembered the days in New France, after the journey to the Oyo, when La Salle had shared his failed dreams of finding a route to China. It had been the first time Nika had seen such books. That Nika had been young and naïve, willing to follow La Salle. Today Nika felt ready to stand beside La Salle to ensure his people's place in the New World. In spite of their differences, Nika hoped La Salle would soon recover for he felt at a loss without the challenge of the Frenchman's company.

"If Monsieur La Salle is dying," Father Zenoble whispered, afraid to voice his worry, "he must receive absolution. That is our duty."

"He's not dying," objected Tonti with a scowl as he tossed pine needles onto the fire.

From his reclining position Barbier snorted, "But he may soon be with that woman tending him."

The anxiety provoked by Barbier's remark overwhelmed Zenoble. He grabbed his long wooden rosary from around his waist and kissed the wooden cross, praying for strength as he strode to the hut.

When La Salle's fever had lessened Tattooed Orchid had selected red, the color of power, to speed his cure and return his strength. From a tiny pot of pigment stirred with a willow switch, she daubed the color onto La Salle's face and torso. Rhythmically, she painted and chanted.

Zenoble entered the hut. On its earthen walls were signs and symbols the priest had never seen before but which he knew his superiors back in France would consider witchcraft. The acrid smoke and strong smells made him choke. Peering through the gloom, Zenoble was stupefied to see his leader lying disrobed and unconscious, being painted red by a half-naked woman.

Tattooed Orchid rose up to fuss at the stranger for bringing who knew what spirits into her hut. Zenoble apologized even as he tried to maneuver around the frightening woman to La Salle's side.

"I feel much better, Father."

Zenoble blinked in surprise. So did Tattooed Orchid, who had assumed the strength of the stranger's sickness would not be routed so quickly.

"I don't need last rites just yet," La Salle muttered, "but rest and quiet."

Relieved, Zenoble went out to share the news.

While La Salle's recovery consumed the next few days, his cohorts quickly integrated themselves into the pleasant patterns of Natchez life.

The old Chickasaw left the party at the river and found his way up the bluff to search for his benefactor. Allowed a peek inside Tattooed Orchid's hut he was much reassured to see the explorer painted red, and the hut smelling of herbs. The old Chickasaw soon latched on to Nika. The Shawnee had often spoken to him when interpreting for La Salle among the Arkansas, when the Chickasaw had been the center of controversy, but since then they had not dealt much with each other. Now as they conversed, Nika discovered he liked the old Indian. The Chickasaw possessed a wry sense of humor, a refreshing change from the ribald Tonti.

He also sparked in Nika an interest in trading. Explaining he wanted to return to his village with many possessions, he told Nika he had never been a great warrior and was seeking another route to comfort in old age. With La Salle's approval, Nika spooned into the expedition's cache of goods, and he and his wizened companion were soon partners in trade with the Natchez. Nika found the furs much inferior to those farther north but the buckskins were plentiful and cheap, confirming what La Salle had hoped.

The Great Sun's and Burning Serpent's knowledge of Chickasaw was the exception. The less educated spoke only Natchez, and most warriors the trade language of the region, the Mobilian jargon. Nika worked to master both tongues.

Twice daily Tonti climbed down to where the canoes, the supplies, and the rest of the men waited. On one trip Barbier accompanied him and did not return to the Natchez town. He said it was because he preferred the company of Frenchmen to Indians but Tonti believed it was so he could distance himself from the horrible fate the surgeon assumed would soon befall La Salle at the hands of the woman doctor.

Determined not to repeat their errors with the Tensas, Tonti kept the riverbank party together and instructed that the canoes be upended for use as temporary huts. They provided shade by day, shelter by night, and thus would never be out of sight of a credible guard.

The engineering behind the Natchez fishing weirs impressed Tonti greatly. The extensive network of wicker traps reaching out from the bank allowed fish to enter through a series of gates but confused the exit enough that the fish might be caught with bow or spear at leisure. The Abnaki joined the Natchez at their weirs and in taking short trips downstream and up to set trot lines.

Tonti was amazed by the order and civility of the Natchez. He began scouting a site for a fort and trading post to secure their future position with such worthwhile allies. He also spent time watching the ball games the villagers delighted in playing across the central plaza. It was not like the stickball he had seen upriver tribes enjoy. Here opposing teams kicked the ball toward goals at facing ends of the plaza. Primarily the game was meant as training for warriors who played hard and rough, but less serious matches were joined by children and old men. Sometimes a warrior or two took part in these milder games, careful to rein in his competitive spirit. Tonti had briefly joined in a match himself, after he realized there were no strict rules about how many players a team might field at any given moment.

The Great Sun was an avid fan of the sport. Off of his mound he never walked upon the ground, so he could hardly be expected to play. Often, however, he held court outdoors to watch the impromptu matches. At the same time he lent his wisdom, if not his full attention, to settling the disputes of his subjects who climbed his mound.

Father Zenoble took the delay to attempt conversion of the natives on a large scale. The other stops had been too restricted by time and tension to invest seriously in preaching. It was a formidable task since he was able to learn only the most rudimentary words to explain his beliefs, but the priest took great heart in the fact that the cross was an important symbol to them. It was painted on the stockade around their town. It was tattooed on their bodies. He had even seen it inside the medicine woman's hut. Any belief, Zenoble consoled himself, in the importance of the cross was surely a head start in teaching the Savior's torment and the Holy Trinity.

Judging by the crowd around the plaza, this ball game was a significant one. Only acknowledged warriors were allowed to play. One team had painted their bodies white to distinguish themselves from their opponents. The Great Sun, with his wives and children, watched from atop his mound with no pretense of carrying on the business of state during the game.

Nika, with Tonti beside him and others of the expedition who had been invited up to the village, sat among the Natchez on the slope of the Great Sun's mound. Father Zenoble tried to take advantage of the Natchez crowd to teach the Scriptures but he had to struggle greatly for even part of their attention.

Fervent side-betting went on. A point was scored and bets were paid off, with most of the winners Natchez. Some of the woods runners were becoming sore losers.

"Mind your manners or I'll put Father Zenoble after you," threatened Tonti with a grin.

Nika and the old Chickasaw, nearly alone among the foreigners, were winning, with a sizable pile of twigs, each representing a buckskin, in front of them.

Nika and several Natchez hollered encouragement to their respective teams. The game was fast, violent, and required brute physical strength as well as skill and speed. Burning Serpent, the star, thought nothing of flinging down an opponent.

Nika pointed out Tattooed Orchid's hut to Tonti. Braced against its outside wall, La Salle watched the game.

"I'd best go report."

"I'll cover your bet."

Embarrassed to be reminded of his gambling, Tonti walked over to La Salle. He wasn't sure how his leader would take to the men gaming with their Indian hosts.

"It is good to see you about, Monsieur La Salle."

"A very sporting people."

"I've allowed the men to wager," Tonti confessed, fingering his mustache, "as is their custom. That is," he corrected, "the Natchez' custom."

"Don't let the men win too often, Tonti," smiled La Salle.

Tonti let out a sigh of relief, but La Salle didn't notice.

On the playing field, with a swipe of his foot, Burning Serpent scored another goal as his vicious kick knocked a bit of Spanish moss stuffing from the ball. The crowd went wild. Injured players retired to the sidelines.

La Salle walked slowly with Tonti to the slope of the Great Sun's mound to sit with the others. The Great Sun sent slaves over with palmetto fronds to give La Salle shade and fan him. La Salle bowed his thanks.

"He is the Great Sun. The most powerful man in the Natchez kingdom," Nika explained as he crowded beneath La Salle's shade. He indicated other Natchez in the crowd, each distinguished by their dress. "Those are Suns as well. Those others, lesser Nobles. Most are merely commoners, called Stinkards."

"Much as in France, with nobility, a bourgeoisie, and the rabble."

"Civilized, aren't they?"

La Salle checked Nika for sarcasm. Tattooed Orchid came out of a hut and skirted the game as she walked toward them.

"Tattooed Orchid is also a Sun," said Nika.

"They will be good allies to the French."

The medicine woman took a place beside La Salle. The Great Sun dispatched a couple of slaves to shade her as well.

"Ask how she learned her craft. The history of her people."

"Not now. This game is a ceremony, a ritual. Would you ask questions like that during Mass?"

"But this is hardly Mass. They gamble over it. The game is chaotic."

Nika didn't answer, but instead pointed out Father Zenoble waving his cross and preaching the gospel to a group of confused Natchez. It was a strange dance which, out of earshot, had no apparent meaning. La Salle looked back at Nika, and chuckled. Nika also indulged a smile.

The ball players worked their way toward the Great Sun's mound. Taking a breather, Burning Serpent stared hard at the strangers.

"Is he the one who led the attack on the river?" La Salle asked.

"He tried to. You stared him down. Do you remember?"

"The fever was on me. But I think I remember."

"He is Burning Serpent, their fiercest warrior. He wants to be War Chief, and looks for a chance to lead the warriors into battle. The current War Chief is very sick."

The game resumed, and La Salle watched Burning Serpent drive the ball downfield. "But is that title not passed down like king to prince?"

"One must be a Sun to become War Chief but he must also earn the right. A Sun may not marry a Sun. Burning Serpent must marry a Stinkard. His children will be Stinkards. It is the Natchez' way."

"And Tattooed Orchid?"

"Tattooed Orchid must also marry a Stinkard, but since she is a woman, her children will be Suns. One of them could be the next Great Sun."

"She seems certainly worthy to be mother of a king."

"In the eyes of the Natchez, barbarians are Stinkards, too. You are an eligible Stinkard."

La Salle looked at Nika in surprise, then glanced over at Tattooed Orchid and blushed.

The Great Sun stepped into the cool dew of early morning darkness. He inhaled deeply air that had been scented by the new growth of spring, as he adjusted his white feather cloak and bent to lower his frame into the litter. Bearers hoisted him and began the march down the slope of his mound, across the length of the plaza, and onto the facing mound from which the temple rose toward the dark sky. Above the rhythmic breathing of his bearers, he could hear songbirds, an impatient cacophony calling him to duty. Humming, the Great Sun readied himself.

The bearers doubled their grips for the extra effort of climbing up the steep temple slope. Flame keepers exited to bow to the Great Sun, who acknowledged them with a nod. His litter lowered, the Great Sun stood and turned to survey his capital. Many subjects fringed the plaza, waiting to begin their day.

The time was near. The Great Sun cleared his mind, preparing for the rapture he would soon feel. The temple priests moved to his side. Facing east, the Great Sun extended his arms. Reaching deep into his chest he began a low song, and as he sang the sky grew lighter. The song grew in power until it reached a crescendo when the moment came. As the Great Sun's arms trembled with the strain, he slowly lifted the golden orb above the horizon. As morning rose from behind the hard line of earth and trees, the Great Sun's voice rose also in a melody undulating with solemn rejoicing.

The Natchez on the plaza below joined in. Once again, their great king had lifted his cousin, the sun, into the sky and blessed them with the gift of a new day.

La Salle and Nika enjoyed the warm rays as they casually inspected a typical Natchez field. Crops were mixed. Squash grew interspersed with potatoes between hills of melons. Bean vines climbed cornstalks to earn a share of sunlight. It was the edge of spring. Green sprouts rose through last year's brown husks. In the distance Natchez women poked the ground with sticks and dropped seeds into the holes, covering them over with an economical step of bare feet.

"The soil is rich," observed La Salle. "When we build a fort here, the Natchez will easily provision it. And many more besides, if we bring in French farmers to help the Natchez improve their methods."

"Do you know why there are no rows to keep their crops in order like a Frenchman's?" Nika asked La Salle.

La Salle sensed the kind of intellectual trap Nika had increasingly grown fond of during the voyage. He decided to ignore the query.

"What good are rows if you have no plow?" Nika answered his own question.

"We could trade them plows," La Salle suggested.

"What beast would pull those plows?" Nika tugged at a tall plant; its green leaves trailed through his hand. "A buffalo would not submit. Neither would a deer. A dog is too small."

Nika found a small tomato turning orange. He plucked it to give to La Salle but the explorer shook his head.

"Eat it."

"What is it?"

"Some Natchez fruit. Eat it."

"Perhaps it's poisonous."

"Do you think the Natchez grow poisonous fruits in their garden? Are even the Iroquois that devious? Are even the French?"

"If you're trying to make some point, say it directly."

But Nika said nothing. He'd been relieved, even happy, to see La Salle return from the brink of death, but in the midst of that joy he'd felt foreboding. This journey of La Salle's would change forever these people, the Natchez. Others too, to be sure, but somehow especially the Natchez.

He thought perhaps to link La Salle up with the medicine woman. Tying the two peoples together might avert catastrophe for both. But then again, no mortal could hope to confound the mischief of the spirits. With a pang Nika again felt that the spirits that guided La Salle would ultimately bring destruction to the Natchez. Just as they would bring death to Nika.

When he realized Nika was not going to answer, La Salle carefully picked his way between the haphazardly spaced plants. Nika hurried to follow.

"Are you afraid this is like the apple in the story that Zenoble tells? That if you eat the Natchez fruit you'll no longer be able to live in the Frenchman's paradise?"

"Who are you to mock me, Nika? When I first met you, you were as anxious as any maiden for ribbons and beads and printed cloth. You prized above all those cheap mirrors I had ordered by the gross from St. Malo."

"I have learned much since then."

But what has he learned? La Salle wondered. What have I taught him? Now Nika bargained for furs and buckskin as commercially as any Montreal trader. Even the proud Natchez, La Salle had witnessed, gave up their carefully tanned hides for the trinkets the expedition offered.

Soon their hunting parties would be going out to kill deer expressly for the trade: six bucks for a steel knife, eighteen for a copper cooking kettle. Bucks and does would grow fewer. Hunting parties would have to range farther, encroaching on the lands of other nations. The limited wars that were little more than raids to give young braves a chance to prove their manhood would turn into life and death struggles for mercantile supremacy. La Salle had seen such war in the beaver grounds farther north.

Again the Shawnee offered the tomato to the Frenchman, but La Salle strode away, careless now, treading on the plants in his path. Nika looked at the tomato and took a bite.

La Salle found Tattooed Orchid in the woods along the creek bottom. Wind rustling through the emerald canopy flickered shafts of sunlight to where she used a short stick to dig medicinal brown tubers from under thick, green moss. She brushed them off and tucked them into the buckskin sack slung below her breasts. Damp leaves and abandoned spider webs clung to her leggings. La Salle cleared his throat so as not to startle her, but she had long before sensed his presence.

At first she had ignored his arrival, intent on the ritual of harvesting her medicine. La Salle had watched her in silence and thought, not for the first time, that French physicians could learn much from the Natchez' knowledge. Perhaps that's what Nika was getting at, but Nika made it seem like a choice, French ways or Indian, and a choice that once made could not be revoked. La Salle wasn't ready to make such a choice. Once it might have been easy but now he doubted he'd ever be able to choose.

Finally Tattooed Orchid rested from her labor, sat back on her haunches, and looked up. He moved quickly to squat beside her, studying her as she brushed away a vine caught on the ties of her moccasin.

"Tattooed Orchid," he whispered.

She looked up, recognizing the sounds he used to call her. She scrutinized his features for any sign of what he was thinking, but these strange white men often defied her powers. Once again, she wondered at how he had responded so quickly to her cure, when even her own War Chief seemed to be dying in spite of her most careful magic. Without expression, she waited for him to continue.

La Salle sighed. He wished Nika were there to translate, but another part of him was glad Nika was not, as he relished being alone in these woods with this Natchez princess.

Why does he blush, Tattooed Orchid wondered. She touched his forehead, but felt no fever, and was surprised when he held her hand there. Perhaps he wants me as a woman, she realized. She had not considered such a notion before.

Like other Natchez women her age, Tattooed Orchid had already been with several men, each of her choosing, collecting from each items that would be her dowry when she eventually married. She had put off choosing a husband from among her lovers longer than most women did, as her sisters frequently chided. She knew they were right, for at her age she felt out of place participating in the sessions of girlish talk where unmarried women livened the monotony of grinding corn or weaving mulberry bark by trading notes on the skills of the young warriors who bid for their favors and by vaunting the gifts they added to their dowries.

Tattooed Orchid attributed her delay in marrying to the pressing importance of her duties as medicine woman, but in her heart she knew part of her reluctance was the idea of pairing for life with a Stinkard. Such a union was all that was allowed her under Natchez law. This she knew and accepted, but she didn't much like it.

But if Stinkards put her off, the idea of intimacy with this foreigner was hardly appealing either. The Natchez girls who'd coupled with them had reported most of them to be quite vigorous lovers, knowledgeable in new techniques but still willing to learn the Natchez ways. The tall one with the iron hand was a special favorite—good-humored, always hungry, and generous with gifts. Still, Tattooed Orchid thought, these foreign men were hairy and they smelled bad.

"We'll soon be departing," La Salle said as he tapped his chest and moved his hands to explain the meaning of his words. "I want to thank you." Then he repeated himself, this time using some of the Chickasaw he had learned. "I arrived here ill. Now I am strong. Thank you."

He examined her face, then continued even though he knew she could not comprehend.

"As a boy I wanted to be a missionary priest, conquering the New World and saving savage souls. But the natives on this Great River are not savage. Least of all the Natchez."

La Salle let out a small laugh. "You don't understand a word of this."

She continued to watch him, knowing that his words, no matter what meaning they carried, must be a step in his recovery of strength.

"There were nights, bundled under beaver pelts, when I was less afraid of frostbite than . . . than what? Debtor's prison? No, I could always talk my way past that. That the king might spurn my services? Why should he? I give him an empire at no cost to him. That I might die? Maybe that I'd die and all that I had done, all my years of struggle, would disappear in a season, like a cornfield left unplanted. What is it in the teas you give me to drink, or the markings you paint on my face, that eases those fears? For this moment, I feel more at peace than I have ever felt."

He looked at her impassive face, the tattooed flowers rising and falling with her gentle breathing. When he leaned on his knees towards her, she made no move away. As he touched his face against her cheek the bristles of his beard chafed her skin, but as they lay back on the grass, she accepted this as part of her healing of him. Then his urgent, awkward attentions overpowered her other thoughts.

CHAPTER EIGHTEEN

THE GREAT SUN GLANCED at La Salle and Nika, then indicated to his aide that they would be the next petitioners. As the pair climbed the mound to the throne, La Salle repositioned his dress sword and pulled at the stockings and breeches he had taken from his chest for the occasion.

The Great Sun stole a moment to watch the ball game on the plaza. This one was not a serious event—it involved mostly children and old men—but he was no less fascinated for the players' lack of skill.

Everyone took their place, waiting. With a final glance at the game, he wearily called for attendants to shield him from the sun's rising heat. Burning Serpent moved to the Great Sun's side, ready to counsel him.

"I bring you greetings from Louis of France, the Sun King."

Nika translated, speaking mostly Chickasaw but now and then showing off a phrase of his newly acquired Mobilian jargon. The Great Sun's reply was curt.

"He says he is the Sun King."

"And he is. Of this land and these people he sees before him. Yet my father, the Sun King, rules a land even more vast and wishes to extend his greetings to his brother, the Great Sun of the Natchez."

"Where are you from?" the Great Sun asked flatly.

In the translation Nika shortened La Salle's reply, omitting references to the Great Waters and sailing ships, distilling it down to a faraway land in the direction of the rising sun. The Great Sun was satisfied. His next question took La Salle by surprise.

"Do you ask to become subjects of the Natchez?"

"We ask to become allies of the great Natchez," La Salle explained as he unwrapped the ornate calumet he had kept for such an occasion. "We wish to embrace you in the protection of King Louis and to share with you the powerful blessings bestowed by our Savior, the Lord in Heaven."

Nika had translated the speech before among other tribes and was able to accomplish it quite literally. The Great Sun cut through the pretty words.

"You want the Natchez to become the subjects of your king?"

"Allies."

"It is not too late to kill them," Burning Serpent snarled in Natchez. Nika started to translate what he had understood of Burning Serpent's words but La Salle stayed him. He understood the import of the warrior's tone.

"How many warriors has your nation?" inquired the Great Sun.

When Nika translated countless tens of thousands, Burning Serpent laughed derisively. The Great Sun did not. It was not clear if he believed La Salle or not, for he maintained the opaque demeanor of a diplomat.

"And what would the Natchez gain by becoming allies of your faraway king?"

"Trade." La Salle extracted a small iron kettle, a steel knife, and a mirror from the bundle Nika had carried. The Great Sun examined the kettle.

"It is heavier than our pots," he said. "It would grow tiresome to carry. And our women would grow lazy if they did not make their own vessels." The Great Sun banged it on the ground at the foot of his throne. "It doesn't break," he said.

When Nika translated La Salle smiled. At least the Great Sun realizes the superior strength of a French-made kettle, he thought.

"This pot is useless to us. Each year at the New Corn ceremony we break all the pots in the village to start anew. What would we do with this?"

He placed the kettle on the ground and picked up the steel knife, testing its sharpness. Burning Serpent leaned in closer to have a look. The Great Sun withdrew his own knife from the belt at his waist. Formed from the jawbone of an alligator it shone white like ivory. Fanciful carvings decorated the handle. The Great Sun tested his blade and found it equally sharp.

"This comes from the powerful jaws of an alligator," the Great Sun explained, "and so keeps with it the strength of that animal. It lends that strength to the man who carries it."

Lifting the steel knife he continued, "From what great animal does this knife come?"

When La Salle could not answer, the Great Sun put down the knife and took up the mirror. He examined himself and obviously enjoyed seeing his image in the looking glass. Burning Serpent leaned over for a peek as well. The Great Sun beckoned a couple of his wives who lounged nearby and showed them the mirror. They gasped at how clearly their faces were reflected. Almost immediately an argument broke out to see who would get the gift. The Great Sun took the glass away and tossed it down.

"Such gifts would make us vain," he concluded. He leaned back in his throne. "Does your faraway king have anything to offer the great Natchez that we can use?"

It took La Salle a long moment to come up with an answer. "We will protect you."

Burning Serpent butted in. "The Natchez need no protection. It is you who need protection!"

"Natchez are the most powerful nation. Who will you protect us from?" the Great Sun demanded, ignoring Burning Serpent's outburst.

"There are many fierce nations who will come to prey upon the honorable Natchez. The Spanish to the west. The English to the east. They will come and try to enslave you."

"No one makes slaves of the Natchez," Burning Serpent frothed.

The Great Sun studied La Salle. The warning the stranger gave were things he had heard before, events he hoped he would not see in his lifetime that he had been warned of when he assumed the mantle of the Great Sun. Wouldn't we be equally enslaved by the tribe of this man as by the others called Spanish or English? he wondered.

La Salle took the pause to mean the Great Sun was considering the allegiance. He offered the elaborately decorated calumet. When the Great Sun took it La Salle's hopes rose but then the Natchez handed him the beautiful knife made from the alligator's jawbone. La Salle had intended ceremonial kinship by smoking the pipe, but the Great Sun chose to interpret it as a simple exchange of gifts.

"When a Natchez girl collects her dowry," the Great Sun stated, "she takes many men. When she finds one she likes above all others, they decide to wed. If her mother is wise she advises them to wait, for the ardor that cannot survive a time of courtship, nor withstand the attentions of other suitors, will never last a lifetime. As it is with lovers, so it is with nations. You are welcome to the hospitality of my capital. Join me tonight as we celebrate the planting of the corn." The Great Sun indicated they were dismissed. His aides began ushering in the next group of petitioners.

The Great Sun watched them go, then studied Burning Serpent. The troublemaker is troubled himself, he thought, by trying to deduce my intent. The Great Sun knew he had satisfied no one but at least he had bought some time.

Tonti joined La Salle and Nika as they gained the plaza.

"How did your audience go?" inquired the soldier.

"We made a good beginning," decided La Salle.

By the light of a roaring fire, concentric circles of Natchez danced on the plaza. Men formed a large outer ring, women a smaller inner one. To each the other ring became a swirl of excited faces as they danced round and round. Beyond the circles, shell shakers sang and shook gourds filled with rattling seeds or round tambourines fixed with clattering shells.

La Salle looked up from the dancers to study the Natchez seated on the slope. Suns, Nobles, and even Stinkards wore their finest attire. Tattooed Orchid, in her feathered cape, had chosen a seat far from him.

Had their meeting in the woods compromised her? he wondered. He wanted to give her some remembrance of his indebtedness to her, but he had been afraid such a gift might be misconstrued. Above all, he did not want to insult her with some token gift like what the woods runners freely gave in return for the women's favors. That afternoon La Salle had rummaged through the expedition's trade goods and had even gone through his personal stores but found nothing he felt was appropriate. It had been easier to find a gift he thought would impress the Great Sun, than to find something that even in some small measure expressed the gratitude he felt he owed this woman. She had restored his health, and somehow, though La Salle could not quite put his finger on it, she had awakened in him a deeper understanding of the peoples in this empire he had come to claim. He caught her eye briefly, but she immediately turned away.

She stole a glance at La Salle. The shadows of the dancers circling the fire played on his face, but even when in darkness there seemed a glow about him, an intensity that burned from within. I must not judge him as I would another man, she decided. He is different, not just different from the Natchez, but even among his own kind.

The dancing ended. A retainer returned from the temple at the far end of the plaza with a glowing ember. The Great Sun recited a speech as he lit a decorative calumet.

"He lights the calumet from the temple flame," Nika explained, "the same fire brought down from the sun by his ancestors many, many generations ago, tended through time by the flame keepers of the temple, under the direction of the Great Suns. Now the sacred flame will light the pipe we smoke to formalize the peace between the Great Sun of the Natchez and La Salle, chief of the French."

The Great Sun puffed several times then gave the calumet to the flame keeper, who carried it to La Salle. La Salle took the pipe, stood, and puffed ceremoniously.

"On behalf of Prince Louis, king of France and Navarre, Fourteenth of that name, I accept your allegiance and welcome you to the French Empire and the land I have named Louisiana." La Salle paused, allowing the translators to catch up. La Salle could see Burning Serpent mumble angrily. The Great Sun frowned as well when he understood La Salle's speech.

Their reactions were no more than La Salle had anticipated. After the Great Sun had so carefully belittled the gifts that afternoon, La Salle had given much thought to how he should proceed. From a pouch he took out a small tin box. To find a gift the king might not belittle, he had put aside the dwindling supply of trade goods and gone into the expedition's personal stores to find an item he hoped would make the right impression. With much ceremony, he gave it to the Great Sun.

The Great Sun inspected the box, pleased enough with the pretty object, but clearly did not understand its function. La Salle showed him how to open it, exposing the chip of flint mounted in the tiny mechanism, and the pan filled with fine tinder. The Great Sun admired this too but still didn't understand. When La Salle touched the button that released the spring, the flint hit metal and threw off a spark. The tinder flared, creating fire. The startled ruler jumped, then leaned in to see this magic at work. The Great Sun touched the flame and found it was actually fire, easily come by.

The Great Sun held the gift, his mind racing. If these men could create sacred fire instantaneously, what else could they do? They were potentially even more dangerous than he had thought. It was a worrisome situation, and now it grew worse, as a runner climbed the slope, begging to approach the Great Sun with portentous news.

La Salle studied those who clustered around the Great Sun to speak in hushed tones. Tattooed Orchid joined them, her face as stricken as the others. La Salle suddenly realized the dancers, singers, and shell shakers had stopped. Now the crackling of the bonfire was the loudest sound, until a sing-song keening grew among the Natchez.

The Great Sun heard out the runner, then listened to an impatient harangue from Burning Serpent, who kept pointing at La Salle. Tattooed Orchid spoke, and her words seemed to carry weight, but her somber expression frightened La Salle most of all. As the Great Sun pondered, other advisors lent their wisdom, but Burning Serpent repeatedly interrupted them and his ruler's reflection to make other points.

La Salle and his men knew something was wrong, something that could adversely affect them. Nika strained to hear, and tried hard to piece together what was going on from the little bit of Natchez he had learned. La Salle looked to Tattooed Orchid for an explanation but her eyes were on the conversation at the crest of the mound. Her expression showed deep concern.

Finally, the Great Sun rendered a decision that angered Burning Serpent. He addressed La Salle, in Chickasaw, but he spoke too quickly for La Salle's meager knowledge of that language. La Salle turned to Nika for a translation. Nika paused, his eyes on La Salle.

"Their War Chief died. It's unnatural for such a great and famous warrior to die in bed, so it must be the work of malicious spirits. In other words, you. Us."

Fear rose in the faces of La Salle's party as the men restated what Nika had translated and looked around at the angered Natchez. Burning Serpent addressed the Great Sun again, but now obviously played to his tribesmen as well. He gestured repeatedly at La Salle and his men. His message needed no translation.

"I fear the situation, Monsieur La Salle," Tonti exclaimed. "Let's return to our boats while we still can."

"I will not see everything lost over a misunderstanding. Nika, follow me."

La Salle approached the Great Sun, kneeling and bowing.

"I beg him to forgive me because he is great and wise and merciful. The French will make good allies for the Natchez."

La Salle had hardly finished before Burning Serpent renewed his harangue, fanning the anger of the crowd.

The Great Sun spoke, and Nika translated. "He suggests we leave immediately. The warriors loved their War Chief. He doesn't know how long he can hold them back."

"But the Great Sun is all powerful. Surely he can stop this uproar so we can speak calmly."

"Let's begin an orderly retreat, monsieur. Before they fall on us," Tonti called to them as he pulled a pistol from his belt.

"I will not give up so easily. The Natchez are the most civilized nation we've met on the lower river. I know I can convince them we had no part in their War Chief's death."

Burning Serpent walked down the slope, arousing the crowd's already high emotions. Natchez responded with shrill yells.

"Nika, tell the Great Sun we had nothing to do with the death of their War Chief. Wasn't he sick when we arrived? If I was so deathly ill wouldn't I have been incapable of casting any spells, if that's what they accuse me of?"

When La Salle's words reached the Great Sun, he ignored them. Warriors appeared with war clubs. La Salle approached Burning Serpent. "Explain to him, Nika."

"He doesn't want to understand," Tonti interrupted. "The War Chief leads men to war. And he's ready to prove he can handle the job."

La Salle anxiously watched Burning Serpent shout at his tribesmen. Warriors began to form a circle, cutting off an easy retreat. Nika pulled La Salle away. The explorer was reluctant. Tonti tried to join them but was blocked.

"Let's go while we still can."

"No, Nika. Tell them we didn't want their War chief to die. We want them to have a strong War Chief, because we want our enemies to be their enemies, so the French and Natchez can share the glory of warring on the Spaniards and English. Tell them."

"And what if they believe you?"

"Then all will be put right!"

"But the War Chief will still have died in bed. And if foreign devils don't get the blame, who will? Who had him in her charge? Who might have neglected him to cure the leader of the foreign devils?"

The words seared La Salle. He searched the sea of angry faces for Tattooed Orchid. Like the others she listened to Burning Serpent's speech, but feeling his eyes upon her, she looked over. Her expression was impenetrable. Pushing through the crowd, La Salle reached for her.

Tattooed Orchid stepped away from the man she had healed. La Salle grabbed her hand, and something in her manner told him that Nika's horrible verdict was true, that to save his fragile friendship with the Natchez he would have to doom her. And if that was what he chose, she would go to her death uncomplainingly, joining the War Chief's widow, taking the black pill and kneeling so a loved one could strangle her, as was the Natchez way for those who chose, or were chosen, to be sacrificed.

Tattooed Orchid studied the Frenchman, and knew the choice he faced. One way or another her time in his life had come to an end. She knew one or both of them might die soon, and that she had given him back his strength that he might bear this moment. Saddened but accepting of the events that had carried them all this far, Tattooed Orchid removed her hand from La Salle's grasp, and walked away. La Salle watched as she disappeared into the crowd.

Burning Serpent shoved La Salle, almost knocking him down. Tonti trained his pistol on the warrior. Pushing open a gap, Nika and La Salle escaped the circle.

"No guns, Tonti," La Salle cautioned. Then he addressed his frightened men. "If you must shoot, fire into the air."

La Salle blinked back hot tears. He clutched at his chest, instinctively trying to draw strength from his silver crucifix, but his cross was gone, given to the Tensas king. The men grouped together closely, ready to bolt.

"Steady," ordered Tonti.

La Salle looked to Nika, and knew he must quickly choose between saving Tattooed Orchid or, with no guarantee he could manage it, saving his allegiance with the Natchez. If he lost the Natchez now, it could maybe be put right later. Maybe. But the enmity of such a powerful tribe could condemn his future attempts to found a colony. They could block traffic up and down the river. Look how much ill the Seneca had done on the St. Lawrence. The Natchez might even prevent La Salle's return upriver to Quebec. Lying in wait, they might slaughter him and his men.

Against that risk, what was the life of one Indian woman? Had not hundreds, even thousands of Indian women and men, and French too, died in the building of the empire? Weren't there sure to be many thousands more deaths to come? What was Tattooed Orchid in the grand scheme, the mighty alliance of white and red, which La Salle had chosen to lead?

"To the boats," La Salle decided. "Give us an orderly retreat, Tonti." La Salle tried to put the consequences of his choice out of his mind. Tattooed Orchid had saved his life. If it was in his power, he must do the same for her.

They pushed through the mob crowding in around them. Burning Serpent saw their departure and yelled to the warriors, who answered with war cries. When young warriors took swings at the Europeans, Tonti shoved them back. La Salle bore himself like a deposed king past the angry crowd.

Through dark alleys of huts, the party made its way. Tonti instructed the men to take any torch they came across, knowing they would need them on the bluff. Turning a corner, they found their path blocked by an approaching group of Natchez.

"This is no place for a battle. We'll find another route." Tonti hastened his group back.

La Salle yanked a spare pistol from the soldier's belt. He

stepped forward, toward the wavering lights of the Natchez' nearing torches.

"Do you know the way to the trail, Tonti?"

Tonti looked around to fix his bearings. Nika emerged from the group. "I can find it."

"Take us there!"

As they moved down another alley hoots and war cries came louder.

"Keep going!"

The first of the party reached the steep trail down the bluff. Tonti shouted for those carrying torches to intersperse themselves evenly among the group. Soon the trail glowed like a loose string of bright beads on a necklace. Last to step onto the descending path, La Salle hesitated.

"I'll be back," he said to the dark woods. "I'll be back and once more the Natchez will embrace me."

When Burning Serpent emerged at the head of the path, La Salle lowered his torch to the grass. The dried brush crackled up brightly, silhouetting them both against the bluff. Burning Serpent's followers piled up behind him, their way blocked by spreading flames.

La Salle headed down the trail toward the disappearing flares of the expedition.

From the village, Tattooed Orchid saw the glow of the brush and heard the frustrated yells of Natchez warriors. She knew now she would not have to sacrifice herself at the War Chief's funeral. While she was not a coward, she was glad she would not have to leave this world. The strange Frenchman had given her a gift after all.

The canoes moved into the darkness toward the center of the river, past arrow shot. No one spoke. The sound of water against paddles meshed with the fading shouts of the Natchez. La Salle paused to bring cool water to his forehead and cheeks.

"It wasn't your fault," Tonti said as his canoe pulled alongside La Salle's.

"You travel this river but cannot control its current," Nika murmured. "You hunt the forest but you cannot tell the

leaves when to fall and when to sprout. You make allies or enemies of Indian tribes, but you will never control them."

There was a long moment as La Salle reflected on Nika's
words. Were they a challenge? Or a warning? The expedition
paddled into the night, heading south to claim Great River.

CHAPTER
NINETEEN

THE CANOE TRAILS DISSOLVED on Great River's brown expanse as the events of the Natchez village crowded La Salle's mind. Impressions left by Tattooed Orchid, Burning Serpent, and the majestic, inscrutable Great Sun would not be supplanted by the duties of his mission.

After their departure, when La Salle noticed the old Chickasaw was not among them, he had feared him left behind in the melee, but Nika had assured him the Chickasaw had intended to stay behind. Old age, he had told Nika, had sapped his desire to see new lands, but Nika knew he had decided to return to his own village with the trophies of his Natchez trade and many stories.

La Salle sketched a landform as the expedition passed. He hurried to finish as the bluff fell from sight, turning around in the canoe to add the last few lines. Soon bluffs gave way to flat, uncertain borders of land and water on both banks. Near where Great River made a broad turn east, a stream forked off to the south. La Salle sent men to investigate. It was not a tributary. The Fork, as he named it, flowed away from the main stream. La Salle guessed this was the beginning of a delta that would logically mark the mouth of such a broad river flowing through flat terrain. His chest swelled in anticipation of seeing the Spanish Sea.

Spring was upon them. La Salle suspected Great River was higher than its mean. Undeniably it was broad, as great as the St. Lawrence at least. He envisioned the forts the Frenchmen and Indians would build together. He had left Quebec believing those forts would civilize the natives. Now he knew the French had as much to learn from tribes like the Natchez. Would his countrymen take the time to learn it? Yes, he would see to it. Was he not La Salle, who had by now brought half a continent into the holy empire of King Louis? He would build a country that could be home to white man and red.

When he had rejoined the frightened group at Great River's edge he had momentarily regretted leaving behind in the Natchez town such a powerful adversary as Burning Serpent. But now, back on the river, the specter of conflict faded. Despite the warrior's inflamed words, La Salle felt certain of a future Natchez alliance. And if there were to be no such alliance, he still felt he had done the right thing in taking the blame for the War Chief's death.

The call of a hawk drew his attention. He watched it glide on updrafts for a long moment, until his focus returned to the river. Dipping a hand into the murky water, he brought it to his face, sniffed, then tasted it.

"How is its flavor, Monsieur La Salle?" called Tonti.

"Like eau-de-vie!"

Everyone laughed.

The party broke camp after an overnight stop. Woods runners exhibited their usual sluggish dawdling.

"Step lively. We launch in five minutes," Tonti encouraged. "Stow your bedrolls."

Alone among the men of the expedition, Nika realized the choice forced upon La Salle at the Natchez. When La Salle had called for the men to retreat, even under the threats of the angry warriors it had been a happy moment for Nika.

Since then, he'd felt closer to La Salle than he had for many months. He sensed that the spirits leading La Salle had let the explorer see a new vision. La Salle had not said as much, but Nika deduced it from his attitude. Nika felt his own journey had been worthwhile.

As they once more set out, La Salle studied the heavy sky. Low clouds billowed. Their flat undersides were yellow and gray. By afternoon, thunder pealed and rain fell, a brief intense shower that lasted no more than half an hour. Then the air was clear, refreshed by the anointment of warm rain.

As they paddled around a bend, Tonti pointed at something in the sky. The men's spirits brightened. La Salle looked, then nodded. A pair of sea gulls cawed as they chased each other across the warm blue. The whole party erupted into a spontaneous cheer.

La Salle recorded his astrolabe sightings and watched the men erect a roughhewn log cross. In the soggy ground it began to lean, but the men were too happy to care. Tonti carried the king's arms, a heavy lead plaque, to bury at its foot.

On La Salle's map, the river's course had been drawn in all the way to the Spanish Gulf. The arrival at his long-sought goal had been anticlimactic. The mighty river broke into a dozen smaller streams that formed its delta. The border land dribbled into mosquito-ridden marshes, neither truly land nor truly water. It had taken several expeditions until Saget found a major channel large enough for future ships to enter from the sea. Afterwards, they had had to travel back upstream for a day to find ground solid enough to plant the cross. Nowhere had La Salle seen a site like Quebec city, a natural bastion defending the first narrows, as if planned by God to monitor the entrance to a continent. But at least neither had he seen any sign of the Spanish.

La Salle sat upon his wooden chest and wiped clean each of his instruments. Nika approached and sat beside him.

Tonti leaned in. "A ration of brandy for the men?"

La Salle nodded. Tonti went to fetch the coveted cask saved for the occasion.

"What comes next, Nika? A colony? A city to be called New Paris?"

"I will have a house in your new city."

La Salle wondered what sort of place the settlement would be. Open enough so that the natives as well as woods runners could be merchants? He thought of Montreal, where the trading houses were willing to use the excuse of ancestry to squash potential competition. A sadness overtook La Salle.

"I will plant a cross and read a speech. We have five hundred leagues back to Quebec."

La Salle looked out over the river. A log floated on the current. It snagged. Dead, bare branches rose out of the water to twist against the blockage until it broke free to continue on downriver. La Salle wondered where the branch had come from. Had it once been part of a beaver dam, far to the north, that had fallen apart after Indians had decimated the beaver's habitat to feed the Frenchman's hunger for fur? Had it been uprooted when a buffalo rubbed against it to scratch himself? What would happen to all those buffalo once La Salle succeeded in building a trade in hides? Or had the branch been part of an Iroquois longhouse or Illinois wigwam or Tensas hut? A lodge vacated and gone to ruin when those who had dwelt in it had disappeared like the Mound Builders on the Oyo River or died from a war over hunting grounds to feed the fur trade?

"We're ready for the salute," shouted Tonti from where he tried to keep the exuberant men in line to fire a volley.

La Salle added his papers to the others atop his chest. A bright green lizard shot out from beneath them. He set down the astrolabe to weight the pile then walked to the cross.

"Steady arms. Ready. Fire," Tonti commanded. A roar of smoke echoed over the sparse hardwoods and damp prairies stretching to the gulf.

Father Zenoble started a hymn. Others joined in. La Salle stared out over the saw grass. When the hymn ended, he unrolled the proclamation. The men waited expectantly. La Salle looked at the lengthy speech, required to make legal his claim to the huge empire they had just traversed. He cleared his throat.

"In the name of the most high, mighty, invincible, and victorious Prince Louis the Great, by the grace of God, king of France and Navarre, Fourteenth of that name, this ninth day of April. . . . It is the ninth of April, is it not?"

Both Zenoble and Tonti nodded.

La Salle had been sure it was the ninth. He had written the date in his logbook just moments before. But some momentary flash of panic had worried him it was not.

"This ninth day of April, 1682, I, in virtue of the commission of His Majesty which I hold in my hand . . ."

La Salle looked at the paper. A court lawyer had framed this for him during the weeks he had waited for his audience with King Louis's minister, Colbert. He remembered the lawyer had smelled of street-bought perfume and rancid sweat, and had freely offered the opinion that the king would refuse La Salle's petition. Then he had charged La Salle for the supposedly useless document more than the ambitious explorer could afford. A gust carrying the salty pungency of the gulf brought La Salle back. He looked at the men.

"With this commission, which may be seen by all whom it may concern . . . ," he spoke with more confidence now, "I have taken, and do now take, in the name of His Majesty and his successors to the crown, possession of this country of Louisiana. . . ."

La Salle paused, realizing he had finally accomplished his dream. He had conquered Meche Sebe, Great River, the goal that had burned in his chest since he first heard of it while bartering for beaver pelts at La Chine so many years ago. It seemed so many lifetimes ago. He repeated the line, almost defiantly.

"I take possession of this country of Louisiana. . . ."

He examined the faces of the men. No one disputed him. He proclaimed the rest of the speech with vigor, his voice growing in power as he went on. The transformation was reflected in the contented faces of the expedition. Whether they fully understood the import of the proclamation or not, they all shared a moment of great accomplishment.

"The seas, harbors, ports, bays, adjacent straits; and all the nations, people, provinces, cities, towns, villages, mines, minerals, fisheries, streams, and rivers, from the mouth of the Great River to its source."

The men let out a cheer, flinging hats into the air.

EPILOGUE

WHILE RETURNING UPRIVER, at Fort Prudhomme, La Salle suffered a stroke, which would plague him the rest of his days. Nevertheless, within two years he had convinced King Louis to fully fund an expedition of four ships with cannon, and four hundred sailors and colonists to establish a stronghold in Louisiana. La Salle assembled Father Zenoble, Nika, Saget, and, against his better judgment, his brother, Jean, the Abbé Cavelier, to make the journey.

Meanwhile, Tonti traveled west from Quebec, intending to continue building their strength upriver on the Mississippi, and then sail down it to join La Salle's colony.

From France La Salle sailed to the Caribbean, losing one ship to Spanish pirates. From there they were to continue along the Gulf, locate the vast Mississippi delta, and ascend the channel La Salle had charted. In bitter contention with La Salle, the captain of the lead vessel refused to follow the Florida coast and instead sailed directly across the Gulf, a fatal mistake. The ships landed near Matagorda Bay in present-day Texas, where the spiteful captain abandoned his passengers and sailed back to France.

La Salle's colonists established a fort as far away from the cannibals occupying that region as they could manage. Ill after the long sea journey and discouraged by their distance from New France, many colonists died, among them Father Zenoble.

As the situation grew more desperate, La Salle, on foot, reconnoitered several times trying to find Great River and meet up with Tonti. On one such expedition, mutineers murdered Nika and Saget, who had gone to hunt. When La Salle went to look for his friends, he too was assassinated, killed by his own men. Jean was one of the few to survive his younger brother's failed attempt at a colony.

The frontier capital La Salle had tried to found would be attempted again by other men, first at Biloxi, then Mobile, and finally New Orleans.

A French post was eventually built among the Natchez, but after their War Chief led a massacre of its inhabitants, an armed French reprisal killed, scattered, or sold into slavery every last Natchez.

The empire La Salle had claimed would later be ceded to Spain, then one day reclaimed by France, and finally sold, thereby doubling the size of a young republic called the United States of America.